# BOYS OF BURLESQUE

## Burlesque River – Book Four

### Kitty Bardot

# PRAISE FOR BURLESQUE RIVER

## *Burlesque River*

*"This was one of the most beautiful love stories. Mike and Amanda have been friends and together since she was 11 years old. After high school they were set to marry, but Amanda's rough childhood compared to Mike's normal family life weighed to heavily on her and she never felt good enough for Mike. For 12 years the both floated along, never finding love or anything close to what they had. When Amanda's Burlesque troupe performs at Mike's bar completely by chance, the two are reunited and feelings come flooding back. Emotional struggles are hard enough, but Amanda has a secret that can tear them apart. Four steamy days together bring these two on quite the roller coaster and we get to go along for the ride. Beautiful, emotional, perfect."* ~MidnightMaiden

*"I haven't read many romance novels, but the few I have read lack the depth of emotion on display in Kitty Bardot's* Burlesque River. *Bardot tells the story of young lovers, Amanda and Mike, separated by life's unique cruelty, thrown back together 12 years later. Mistakes are made, arguments are had, and the lovers are forced to deal with the ramifications of their actions, some of which have left terrible scars. Also...in true romance novel style there is a lot of sex and a lot of different kinds of sex, always a good thing in a book like this. Most significantly though, there is a literary thrust (no pun intended) to it that elevates* Burlesque River *above similar novels. I, for one, can't wait for the sequel."* ~Kimberly

*"Even though it was an easy read, there was a great depth to the characters and story line. Not to mention this book is hot, hot, hot. I really enjoyed it, and can't wait for book number 2."* ~MrsBates2U

*"Romance is not my usual thing but I picked this up and ended up devouring it in two days. The love story is heartfelt, the sex is passionate, and the characters are all lovable and real. Definite recommend and I'm looking forward to the next book in the series!"*
~Joshua Kahn

# *Burlesque on Bourbon*

*"I devoured this book in one night as soon as the pre-order purchase went live. I am a fan of Kitty Bardot's real life connection in her books, its so easy to put yourself in the world and lives she creates. I connected so much with the character Bridgette, and I fell completely in love with Henri and his slow dripping southern drawl. I was completely hooked just a few pages in at "you have to be careful when dealing with papa legba cher"... 10/10 would recommend this book, I was sad when I flipped the last page. This Author is a rising star, and I am excited to read everything that will be coming next!"* ~NO.5

*"Burlesque on Bourbon is a sensually enticing tale that you will want to read nonstop from start to finish. The excitement, chemistry, and intensity explode off the pages and keep you enrapt in Brigette's adventure with Henri. The characters are authentic, realistic and perfectly matched. I highly recommend this tale."* ~Chef Rose

*"This is a sizzling romantic story between two people who have undeniable chemistry. They both also have a past that has left them with damages that are difficult to overcome. I really liked the book, I couldn't figure out how it would end. Kept me on the edge guessing."* ~Sandy L

*"From the beginning, the reader has the impression that Henri is very shallow. He is a known playboy picking up women and*

*discarding them just as quick. He comes from a different world than Bridgette tossing money around without a thought to how others see him. Even so, Bridgette sees there is more depth to Henri than a pretty face so she throws caution to the wind and takes a chance to get to know him better. The more Bridgette and Henri are together, readers can see Henri's mask slipping. It is difficult for Henri because he has never known a woman such as Bridgette. The more time they spend together and the more comfortable they are, secrets are bound to unravel in the most spectacular fashion. With Bardot at the wheel, her descriptions heighten the senses while the characters leap off the page wanting to tell their full, complete story."* ~Brenda

## *Burlesque Baby*

*"I loved this book and everything about it. The storyline was very well thought out, very well written too. The characters each had so much depth to them, I loved the dynamic between Olive and Vic. They are one scorching hot couple and you can feel the chemistry between them burning up the pages."* ~Book Reader

*"Olive has a fairy like spirit about her, she takes today in stride and does not count in tomorrow, it is not guaranteed. Vic is a bit more cautious about life always planning ahead. When these two crash into each other literally, its like their eyes have opened for the first time. But true to form Vic is cautious and Olive goes all in."* ~Vinessa Donatelli Wooten

*"This is a slow burn love story between Olive and Vic. She has taken on Burlesque and is finding her own way in life. Vic is never off her mind and their attraction is hard to deny. They have some things to get past on their path to happiness. She is perfect for him and his heart knows it. I enjoyed the story."* ~Samantha Davidson

*"A free-spirited loner by nature and circumstance, Olive joins a burlesque troupe and finds the family she's been missing for years. She also finds Vic, the one man she wants more than anything. Problem is, he's already taken, and Olive isn't the type to go after another woman's man. Vic tries to ignore his attraction to Olive, despite their instant connection, and to be a good man and do the right thing by his sorta, girlfriend, Emily, who likes to play mind games with his and everyone else's heads. Kitty Bardot takes you into the fascinating world of burlesque with characters you care about. I really enjoyed getting to revisit characters from her previous books, especially Mike and Amanda.."* ~MCB

www.BOROUGHSPUBLISHINGGROUP.com

BOYS OF BURLESQUE
Copyright © 2023 Kitty Bardot

ISBN: 978-1-957295-35-0

*This one's for the misfits who never knew where they belonged, the strange little kids who no one understood, and every lost boy looking for their Neverland.*
*Your tribe is out there and they are waiting for you.*

# ACKNOWLEDGMENTS

Special thanks to my family and friends for their continued support and encouragement. Also, to Michelle for her hours of editing, the emails, phone calls, and most importantly – guidance.

# BOYS OF BURLESQUE

# CHAPTER ONE
*Eli*

"Wake up." Eli feels a toe nudging his ribcage. Grumbling, he rolls away. The nudges grow in intensity, bordering on kicks, as Eric, Zach, or whatever his name is, becomes more agitated. His voice rises above gentle goading. "Come on, motherfucker, get up. My roommate will be back any minute. I don't want him finding you here in my fucking bed."

Eli stares at the tie-dyed tapestry hanging on the wall before him. A spiral of multi-colored Trip Bears march from the center out. He remembers, briefly, the fluttering scarfs and tapestries of the small tent villages that sprang up at his childhood home several times a year. Festival weekends began when the first tent went up. Delicious food, music, and dancing followed for days until the last tent was packed up and the sprawling fields were left empty. His drug-induced euphoria clings to the joyful memories of the parade of family, friends, and strangers he knew in his young life. He smiles at the marching bears. "Do you even know the Grateful Dead?" he asks, still basking in the rainbow joy of the tapestry and his lingering high.

"Fuck you, man. Get up and get out. You got what you wanted, now you have to leave." His new friend's voice quavers on the verge of tears.

Eli can feel the anxiety in the air. He smiles despite it, still wrapped up in the warmth of his last line. He throws the light blanket off, exposing his bare skin to cool air. The hairs on his body stand up as goosebumps spring up all over. The sensation isn't altogether a bad one.

His dick twitches with a weak attempt at arousal as he sits up and drops his feet to the plush rug. "Got any pills?" he asks, not recognizing his own voice heavy and coarse with sleep.

His nervous little closet twink stands with hands on his hips, fire in his eyes. Eli chuckles again at the fear and revulsion on the guy's face.

They are peers in age alone.

Where Eli spent years in and out of questionable foster homes across the Midwest, this guy was being doted on by his liberal, wealthy family in the Chicago suburbs. Instead of hitting the streets at eighteen with little to nothing in his pocket, he was sent to college with a substantial monthly stipend, allowing him to buy and sell drugs to anyone on campus who was looking.

"Get dressed. Get out," the guy spits.

"I don't know. I'm feeling pretty good right here. Maybe your roommate would like to join us for another round." Eli isn't proud of playing with the poor kid's emotions, but he's enjoying the hell out of it. "I mean, I don't even see my pants." He shrugs and reclines onto his elbows, challenging Eric Whatever with a grin.

"They're right here." Eric bends and picks up the pile of Eli's clothes, balling and throwing them at Eli's flaccid cock. A button snaps his balls with enough force to almost hurt. "Get dressed and get the fuck out. Now."

Eli huffs and shakes his underwear out of his pants. "Your mood certainly has changed." He recalls the moments that led them here. Eric was much friendlier at the bar, all smiles and laughter. He practically stripped Eli of his clothes upon entering the small dorm room, devouring him with kisses.

"So has yours," Eric sneers and looks from Eli to the clock on the wall. "You seriously have to get out of here. I'll give you pills. Shit, I'll give you money. Just get out and never come back."

"I don't want your money. I'm not a whore."

"Could've fooled me."

Eli's cheeks blaze with anger and embarrassment. The upper hand he felt he had was make-believe. This spoiled brat holds all the cards. Some of those cards Eli wants.

Eli dresses quickly, missing buttons on his shirt. "Look, I'm sorry. I'm leaving." He looks at the nervous kid, sees the shame written on his face, the tears threatening in his eyes. "Your roommate will never know I was here." They stand in awkward silence, communicating the reality of their own self-loathing.

"Here." Eric's face softens, and he turns to open his dresser drawer. The rattle of a pill bottle tickles Eli's mind. A smile twitches on his lips. "Don't come back. If you see me again, you don't know me."

Eli nods as three pills are dropped in his hand. Then he's in an empty hallway, the door closing and locking behind him.

Alone again.

***

*Chris*

"God, I hate that fucking smell," Tyler grumbles from the couch. Chris straightens his back and rubs his eyes. Rhinestones flash and twinkle, spread out on the table before him.

"I'm sorry, Ty. I try not to work on this stuff when you're home, but it's show week. You know how crazy it gets." Chris dabs the offensive-smelling glue on a black satin corset.

"Yeah, yeah. I know. It's show week." The sound of Tyler's voice is nothing short of mocking. His head of thinning hair bobs back and forth, reminding Chris of their age difference. It amazes him how much a person could change in five years.

He sighs, remembering the man Tyler used to be, and how he had swept Chris off his feet. It was his second year at the Art Institute of Chicago. He was out with friends, celebrating the end of finals week or maybe a birthday. They were all over-served and underaged. Someone's ID was spotted as a fake, and the whole group was thrown out.

As they sat on the curb, lamenting their woes, Tyler appeared like an angel in a beautifully tailored suit with a gleaming white smile and thick dark hair. He seemed too good to be true, escorting Chris and his friends to the many bars that'd turned a blind eye to underage college kids with fake IDs. Though Tyler was friendly with them, his gaze rarely left Chris. The next morning, Chris woke safely in his own bed with a waiting text message from Tyler inviting him to breakfast.

For months Tyler courted him. He showed up, unannounced, with gifts and trinkets from around the world. He would take Chris and his friends out to the finest restaurants and shows, always footing the bill, never batting an eye. Chris's friends were jealous, and he loved it. As the middle son with four brothers, Chris wasn't used to being spoiled. He was barely used to being seen. Then Tyler came along and saw only him.

By summer, Tyler convinced him to move to Rock Island, "Just until fall." By fall, he'd convinced Chris to never go back. Sure, Chris's mom was disappointed, but his dad didn't seem to mind. But then, his dad didn't seem too interested in anything he did after coming out. Though his friends and professors were sorry to see him go, there was no stopping him. All he needed was Tyler.

The months flew by. During the week, he played house, cooking his mom's best recipes and cleaning while Tyler worked. When Friday rolled around, they would be off on another adventure.

Then the adventures went from every other weekend to once a month or on long holidays. Chris hadn't minded though. He was really a homebody at heart, and he had Tyler. Fancy trips were the cherry on top of his kind and doting lover.

Eventually, the doting stopped. Kindness took a backseat. It'd been weeks since he and Tyler shared more than an awkward meal when Chris saw the ad in the paper looking for burlesque performers.

He hadn't realized how unhappy he was until he started to feel happy again. Joy had seeped slowly out of his life like the air through a pinhole in an inflatable mattress. At first, he'd been sleeping on a perfect fluffy cloud; four years later, he woke up on a cold, hard concrete floor with Tyler snoring beside him, completely oblivious.

Chris shakes his head and takes a deep breath, remembering all that Tyler's done for him over the years. All the love they shared. So what if things are a little stale? Isn't that how it goes for any long-term relationship?

"You know, I think you'd really enjoy a show if you came to see one," Chris offers as he places rhinestones on the glue dots with steady hands.

"I don't."

"Come on, baby." Chris pushes up from his seat, stretching his back before crawling over the arm of the couch. "You used to love going to shows. Remember how much fun we had?" He lays his head on Tyler's lap, blinking up at him.

"Yeah, that was then." Tyler glances down with a tight smile before looking back at the screen.

Chris's heart feels like lead in his chest. His throat closes around whatever words he would've spoken.

He blinks away his tears and sits up, watching Tyler watch TV and wondering where the last five years went.

# CHAPTER TWO
*Eli*

It's cold, much colder than it was when Eli walked to work that morning. His stained white t-shirt is still damp from the last four hours he spent in the dish room. "Fuck." His teeth chatter as he walks faster through a throng of people in costumes. Many are wearing far less than him. Despite the cold, they seem fine. But they aren't wet.

His day started off well enough: fully staffed kitchen, strong servers, and the owners, Pam and Bob, were gone for the weekend. There was no one to hover over his shoulder and question his every move. Despite the easy-going atmosphere The District Pub presents to the public, Pam and Bob are some of the most difficult people he's ever worked for. They have to have their hands in everything, and their mouths, which they run often. Besides them, however, it's a decent job. Easy menu, friendly co-workers, lots of hours available to work, and a quick walk from home. He could exist comfortably within a six-block radius. The District offers food, drinks, and nightlife.

Eli blows warm air into his hands as he surveys the area nightlife.

He turns down the alley toward his apartment and is met by another crowd of costumed revelers. They're shouting, laughing, and squealing as they stumble along. Drunken bodies cling to one another in cheap polyester. He sneers at the triviality of their Halloween revelry, remembering the Samhain bonfires from back home. The rich roasting meats, root vegetables, and sweetly spiced ciders. Horned men and women draped in layers of colorful robes and headdresses matching the autumn leaves dancing around enormous flames. His folks knew how to throw a party. Their feasts were known far and wide.

After his eighteenth birthday, he hitchhiked his way around the country for years, finding and reconnecting with people from his childhood. People from the before time, as he'd come to call it. Everyone he met, every smiling face that spoke of his parents, would talk about their parties, their love, and their family. How devastating the news had been. He felt like a vampire at times, wandering from home to home, sucking all he could from relative strangers. Draining their memories and moments before moving on.

He clings to those memories, to the better days. Nothing had been right since that moment so many years ago when his family was destroyed with one silent bullet, spattering blood, and his mother's wails.

The sound of her screams follows him down the alley, away from the happy partygoers, toward another sound. One even more familiar. One he hasn't heard for years. Her deep, rich laughter is unmistakable. As Eli comes out of the alley, he spies her standing in the alcove of the Speakeasy. The streetlight warms her face as she tosses her thick dark hair over her shoulder and huddles closer to a handsome man in full stage makeup. His laughter joins hers, and Eli is stuck, motionless, staring across the street at the only person in his world who knows his story.

The only one who lived it right along with him.

How long had it been? How many years? He'd traveled to California and back, then all the way up the East coast. How could they be living in the same city, on the same block, and not even know it?

"Olli?" Eli's voice cracks over dry lips. Her handsome friend looks his way and nudges her gently. She looks up; the street goes silent around them.

"Eli?" She steps away from the alcove. Her friend is watching with wide eyes. Eli moves to meet her. She runs to him, crushing him in her arms. "Oh my god, Eli. Is it really you?" He can feel her tears on his cheek. Or are they his? He wraps his arms around her slight waist and squeezes her back, overwhelmed by the torrent of emotions swirling in his chest and stomach.

"It is. How are you even here?" he asks, holding her, squeezing his eyes shut for fear that when he opens them, she'll be gone. Gone like she always is when he needs her most. A car horn blares, and she takes his hand, pulling him back to the alcove.

"I live here," she answers. "Come inside. You must be freezing." Olive holds tight to Eli's hand like she has a thousand times before, as though they haven't been separated by years of pain and loneliness. "Come on, Chris," she calls behind them. "You've got to meet my brother." She pushes through the door. "Vic, Bunny, everyone. Come and meet my brother."

The Speakeasy's house lights are an assault to his senses, especially paired with the small crowd gathering around them, all in different states of dress. Their painted faces are grinning, and his heart races. The excitement in every voice crowds together in one incoherent mess.

Eli struggles to focus on Olive. His heart pounds an anxious rhythm in his chest as his stomach rolls. He's taken back to the moments after the shooting, strange faces staring and talking at him. Strange people dragging him here and there. No one offering a moment of comfort.

Finding her face in the haze, he speaks barely above a whisper. "Olli, I can't. I can't do this." Before she can protest, he's out the door. The cold air hits his lungs, chilling his still-damp shirt. He runs as quickly as he can and ducks into an alley behind a parked service van. He hides there until their voices trail off in the opposite direction. *So many faces. So many people. That was too much. Too much.*

"Fuck," he breathes slowly. "What the fuck?" He slaps the heel of his palm against his head several times. The dull thuds and mild pain bring him back to reality. "Why did I run?" His tears run warm streams down his cheeks. Cold wind chills them. He moves quietly, sticking to the alleys until arriving safely at his building two blocks from the Speakeasy.

***

*Chris*

"Oh my god, Ty. It was the saddest, most confusing thing I've ever seen," Chris says over the ample breakfast he's laid out for them both. Sunday mornings are for big breakfasts.

"Hm." Tyler continues to look at his phone, shoveling food into his face.

"It was like Eli materialized out of thin air. Olive was so happy. Then, as quickly as he appeared, he was gone. We couldn't find him anywhere. Poor Olive. She was crushed." Chris dresses his pancakes while he talks.

"That's good." Tyler continues to read his news and eat his breakfast.

Chris's cheeks burn with irritation. He's no stranger to being ignored by the men in his life, but there was a time when Tyler would at least feign interest in their conversations. Looking back over the years, Chris now sees how one-sided those conversations were. "Are you even listening to me?"

"Hm?" Tyler looks up from his phone and blinks behind his thick-framed glasses. "Yeah." He gives a quick nod. "I've got to be honest with you, though: I could care less about Olive and her long-lost brother or any of the other burlesque people." With that, he's back to eating, reading, and ignoring.

Chris watches him from across the table, hurt and angry. He bites back words boiling in his belly. He struggles with the reality that someone he once loved more than anything in the world is now a stranger.

It seems the only thing they share anymore is an address.

He stands to clear his plate, barely touched, and starts cleaning up the kitchen without even a glance from Tyler. Loading the dishwasher with a heavy heart, Chris remembers better times. Times when they would leave the breakfast dishes on the table and snuggle the morning away. Then they would laugh and joke and clean up together, making plans for their evening.

Going back out to the table to gather condiments, he finds Tyler's empty plate. Tyler's taken his favorite place on the couch, ready to spend another morning ignoring him. Something burns and rolls in Chris's stomach. His throat tightens around the words he knows he should speak. He needs to say that he isn't happy. He needs to say something has to change. He needs to demand more from the man who once promised him the world.

Instead, as he stares at the crumbs, the ring of spilled coffee, and the soiled napkin lying beside the plate, Chris lets out a long trembling breath. "It's okay. I'll get the dishes." A tear of frustration escapes, and he brushes it away.

"Thanks, babe." Two words, once said with smiles and love, now hang in the air, withered and empty.

"Yeah." Chris hurries through his clean-up, fighting the lump in his throat, the tears in his eyes. Quickly, he wipes the table and heads to his room where he can lock the door and cry angry, heartbroken tears. Not over this one-sided conversation about his friends and their lives, but for all of the one-sided conversations he and Tyler have had.

For the lonely days and nights.

And for the fact that though he hasn't said the words out loud, he knows them to be true.

He and Tyler are over.

# CHAPTER THREE
*Eli*

Payday means shots at the bar. It means a bag of weed, some pills, maybe something stronger, if he can find it. It means Eli has a couple of days to completely forget he exists before the money runs out and he's left with the cold, hard reality that not only does he exist, but every terrible memory is real and fully his.

Not tonight though.

Tonight, he drinks away his dad falling dead at his feet, his mom's wailing cries as she ran to their sides. He drinks away the hands pulling him away from her, his sister gone.

He drinks away his dad's blood running down his cheek and drying there for hours as the men in black suits decided what to do with him.

He drinks away the weeks he didn't say one word in which he processed the death of his family and life as he knew it with no one to help.

He drinks away the years after struggling to stay afloat. He drinks until his mind is so thick with it that all the other memories don't have space. There is no room for the abuse from strangers, the dozens of foster homes, the camps meant to put him on a more righteous path.

Sometimes, they find their way in, all those memories. Before the alcohol takes his thoughts, before the weed takes his body, before he's able to numb it all.

Sitting under the neon lights as club music blares around him, the bass rumbling in his bones, he can all but feel the stinging hand on his cheek. The disgust and frustration on the face of his foster mother as he sang a verse from a song he'd always known. One he would sing along to with his family. He'd never known it was offensive or wrong.

His first foster family took him in with sad glances and looks of deep concern. They whispered things like, "How terrible," and "Poor boy," and "We'll set him right in no time." They talked while he sat silent. They talked as though he wasn't in the same room, hearing every word. They spoke of what monsters his parents were. How he'd never had a chance. Then, they offered him God.

They took him to church and prayed around him. Asked Jesus to guide him, to bring him back his voice. When he found it, he used it to ask questions, to try to understand what happened to his home, his sister, his family. He asked every question that came to his young mind about the new religion they were so proud to share. So much of it didn't make sense. The more he tried to understand it, the more irritated his foster parents became.

It wasn't long before he was moved from that home to another. The new family was less concerned with his religious upbringing and more concerned with the lack of media in his life.

There wasn't a single book in the whole house. Cable television and VCRs changed his world. He lost himself for hours watching movies, sitcoms, MTV, and PBS.

Late at night, he would sneak to the family room in the basement and watch infomercials until he fell asleep on the couch.

Cartoons blew his mind. That family, it seemed, really wanted to help. They saw his love for animation and bought him a sketchbook and some colored pencils. He filled up pages with memories and dreams. Some were beautiful, others dark.

When they asked to see what he was drawing, they changed their minds about him. "We can't have him around our kids," they said softly in the next room. "Look at what he's been drawing. We can't expose our babies to that."

He was sent off to another home, another family. He had no idea where his mom or sister had gone. He knew where his dad was and talked to him often. That disturbed the new family. It was back to church with him. Back to twice on Sunday and once on Wednesday. They were going to help him whether he liked it or not.

He didn't ask questions that time around. He sat quietly and took it all in. He listened and only spoke when spoken to. He learned the way they wanted him to behave and did all the things they expected. He was baptized and took the Lord Jesus Christ as his savior, whatever the hell that meant. It didn't matter what it meant. They were pleased with his progress, and he finally got to see his family— his real family.

His mom was a phantom of the woman she had been. Her once bright and glowing smile was heavy and sad. Her hair had gone fully gray. Her eyes were vacant. And Olive was a ghost as well. She barely looked at him.

As their mother held them both at the end of their thirty-minute visit, he noticed how weak her arms had become, how listless her energy. They sobbed together for all that was lost. She promised they'd be together again.

She lied. That was the only and last time he saw her. She died before their next visit. Olive disappeared.

He was left an orphan, alone to navigate the world.

"Fuck." Eli motions for another shot, shaking his head. The whiskey hits like it always does, warm and stinging its way through his chest, down to his belly. The familiar fuzz wraps around him. He orders another and swallows it down before any more memories can torment him.

It's late, and the club is full. People are dressed for the hunt. Men doused in cologne, women in heavy makeup and little dresses. They're drinking to forget. Some, like Eli, are trying to forget their lives. Others are there to forget their inhibitions. To drink until they are bold enough to do what they want to do. It seems they all are there to find someone to fuck. Eli is no different. After all, what more is there to do once the drugs and alcohol take over but give your body completely to a stranger to do with as they will?

The struggle is in the hunt itself. Women try to catch his eye. They smile and bat their false lashes. They brush past him at the bar, grazing his back with their breasts, leaving a trail of perfume for him to follow.

He's not interested.

He's looking for bold looks from men as angry as he is at the world. Men who want to fuck in a bathroom at the back of the bar and never see each other again.

Men who hate themselves too much to have a lover.

What he finds, instead, is a cautious glance from a beautiful face and an awkward smile. He sees a strawberry-blond with impeccable style, sipping wine and looking terribly out of place. A man like him who doesn't belong in a place like this. He belongs somewhere lovely. Somewhere where the clientele fully appreciates his beauty.

Somewhere that isn't predators and prey. A delicate beauty like him is sure to be prey in a place like this.

Through his whiskey cloud, Eli is determined to save this angel face from that plight.

***

*Chris*

"I'm not happy, Tyler. I feel invisible, more like a servant than a partner," Chris says clearly and confidently to his own reflection. It seems he's cried all the tears he can, wondering where his and Tyler's love went. He's been practicing what to say and how to say it for days. A person can be ignored for only so long before they disappear altogether. It feels like he already has in Tyler's world.

"I feel like I have to beg for your attention nowadays. And when I get it, it feels distant and broken. It doesn't feel like you're happy either. Are you? Happy?" He lets out a long sigh and pushes through the bathroom door.

Down the hall, he finds Tyler asleep on the couch. Chris sits down beside him, admiring his sleeping face. Tyler's still as attractive as when they first met. The gray at his temples makes his handsome face more distinguished. His thick-framed glasses sit, tilted awkwardly, on the bridge of his nose. Chris takes them off gently and sets them on the coffee table.

Tyler looks up, blinking the sleep away. "Hey," he says groggily.

"Hey. I think I'm going to go out tonight," Chris responds, unable to say the words he practiced so many times.

"Yeah?" Tyler sits up and shakes the cobwebs of dreams away. He looks Chris up and down before his gentle stare rests on Chris's face. "I knew this was coming."

Emotions catch in Chris's throat. His face burns. "What do you mean?"

"I knew once you started getting involved with the burlesque troupe, I wasn't going to be enough for you anymore. It was only a matter of time before you started looking for something better, more exciting." Tyler's voice is flat and calm with a hint of accusation.

Chris swallows the lump in his throat to speak. Anger bubbles gently to the surface, through the pain and sadness. Through the feelings of loss and disappointment. "This has nothing to do with burlesque." It's all he can manage as his cheeks burn with irritation.

"That's rich, Chris. What is it then?" Tyler's brows come together in mock confusion. "Is your life too easy? Are you bored? Are you done playing house now that you see something better on the horizon?"

Tyler's words sting like a slap across his face. Though he's not altogether wrong, Chris has to admit, but there is so much more to what he's feeling. "It's not like that," he defends. "There's more to it. We used to have so much fun. You used to make me feel special. Then one day it stopped. I started feeling more like a servant than a lover. You stopped *seeing* me. I stopped feeling like a priority." He sighs and looks away from Tyler's unyielding face. "All of my unravelling began long before I started doing burlesque. In fact…" He glances back to Tyler, still unmoved, and then goes on, "In fact, the whole reason I went to those auditions was because I was so lonely. I couldn't stand it."

"Is that so? I go to work and come home every day. I pay all the bills. I'm faithful. I'm generous. All I ask in return is that you take care of our home." Tyler's voice raises with each sentence.

"It's not *our* home," Chris shoots back with surprising control. "It's never been our home. You quarantine me to one room and spit daggers whenever my life slips out into any other space. You want me to be here, seen, but not heard.

"You want me to cook your meals and do your laundry. You want me to clean your toilet and wash your dishes. But when was the last time you held my hand and told me you loved me or appreciated me?

"This isn't about burlesque. This isn't about my new life or the friends I've made. It's about you not treating me the way you used to. It's about this"—Chris gestures between them—"not working anymore. I don't want to be the maid who you occasionally fuck. I want to feel loved and seen. One thing you're right about: my burlesque family makes me feel loved and seen. They make me feel like I'm worth more than what I'm experiencing right now."

Chris stands, positively vibrating with his newfound voice. "Look, Ty, I love you. I appreciate you and everything you've done for me over the years. But I can't keep living like this. I'm miserable, and something has to give. I'll stay home tonight if you want to talk this out."

Tyler offers a tight grin and blinks. "No. You're right. Go out, enjoy yourself. We can talk tomorrow. I'm over it for tonight." With that, he stands and leaves the room.

Chris slumps to the couch, trembling yet determined.

If Tyler had any interest in saving what they had, he would've stayed. He would've spoken up and said he was willing to do the work to make things right.

Instead, he walked away.

He left Chris alone.

Again.

***

It's been years since he went to a club like this one. In fact, as he stops to show his ID to the doorman, Chris realizes he's never been to a club such as this alone. He considers calling Olive or Bunny, but he knows that his night will end in one of their apartments, at the bottom of a bottle of wine with all his tears cried out in their arms.

That's not what he wants.

Tonight, he wants to be seen. He wants to feel alive, beautiful, and anonymous. He doesn't want to talk about years lost and loveless nights. He wants the excitement of meeting someone's gaze from across the bar and making conversation. He doesn't want to cheat, only to feel free. Then, he'll go home and cry a thousand more tears, sleep on the couch, and wait for Tyler to come home from work so they can really talk.

The flashing rainbow lights of the club pulse with the heavy bass from the dance floor. The room is full of people drinking, shouting, and grinding on one another. Bleary, drunken eyes look without seeing. Chris immediately regrets his choice to leave the house.

Spotting an empty seat at the bar, he takes it and waits for one of the harried bartenders to notice him. The music is oppressive as he takes his first sip of wine and considers leaving altogether. *Maybe Olive is still awake.*

As he moves to stand, he catches a look from a handsome man with dark hair and thick brows at the other end of the bar. His full lips seem meant to smile and laugh and kiss. Chris watches as the stranger brings a small glass of brown liquor to those delicious-looking lips and throws it back. The heavy shadow of a day-old beard frames his perfect smile as his gaze settles on Chris.

Chris's heart flutters with excitement as the stranger pays his tab, all while keeping his gaze on him. He disappears into the throng of people before materializing beside Chris. There's a vague familiarity about him. Something Chris can't quite place. Though he finds it comforting and utterly irresistible.

"You don't belong in a place like this," the stranger says with whiskey-born confidence.

Chris giggles behind his glass of wine. "Does that line really work?" he teases.

"It's not a line," the stranger says with a half smile and a subtle shake of his head. "This place is beneath you." He casts a glance up and down the bar, then back on Chris. "Shit, it's beneath me, and I'm pretty low."

"You look pretty high to me." Chris giggles again.

"Guilty." The stranger spreads his hands out before him to show he has nothing to hide. "For real, though, you've got more class in your little finger than this entire place."

"Please." Chris rolls his eyes, warmth flushing his cheeks. "But you aren't wrong. I regretted coming as soon as I walked through the door."

"That's what I thought." The guy smiles again, a charming smile of a man who doesn't know how attractive he is. "Are you here alone?"

Chris eyes him skeptically before answering. If he learned anything during his time in Chicago, it's that you never tell a stranger that you came alone. "No, I lost my friends out on the dance floor. Lord knows when I'll see them again." Chris shakes his head and lets out a little chuckle.

"It's easy to lose people here." The stranger shrugs. "Would you like another drink?" He nods to Chris's nearly empty glass.

"I can't let you buy me a drink. I don't even know your name." *This is what flirting feels like, and lord, I've missed it.*

"I'm Eli." He offers another bright smile. "How about that drink?"

"Wait. Eli?" Chris nearly drops his glass as the realization hits him. "I knew you looked familiar. You're Eli."

"Yeah. That's what I said." Eli raises his brow and pulls his lips in a confused grimace.

"I know your sister. She's been beside herself all week since you…" Chris stops short. Eli's pleasant demeanor evaporates. He steps back and looks Chris over.

"I…" Eli looks out over the dance floor. "Is she here with you?" he asks urgently.

"No." Chris shakes his head. "But she'll wish she was. I can't tell you how broken up she was last weekend."

"Yeah. Sorry about that. I was…" Eli looks away again. "We haven't seen each other for years. It was overwhelming."

"Can I call her to tell her I found you? She's not far from here. I bet she'd come down right away."

"I don't know." Eli looks at his feet, then back to Chris. "I didn't get your name?"

"I'm Chris. Your sister is my best friend."

"It's great to meet you, Chris. My sister's best friend." Eli chuckles. "I don't know if I'm in the right state of mind for a family reunion." A heavy sadness hangs between them. Eli looks like he's ready to run again. Chris knows he can't let him go.

"Hey, I get it." Chris shakes his head. "Instead of that drink, how about some fresh air?"

Eli smiles. "Deal. This place is kind of terrible." He looks around, then back at Chris with a grimace that turns into another sparkling smile.

# CHAPTER FOUR
*Eli*

"Tell me about yourself," Eli asks, feeling a warmth in his chest more intoxicating than the whiskey. Chris pulls himself up onto the ledge of a cement stage with ease. Eli notices the smooth movement of the muscles in his lean arms. He's stronger than he looks. Chris makes a face of mock disgust and brushes his hands on the legs of the light-washed jeans practically painted onto his well-shaped legs.

"What would you like to know?" Chris grins and pulls his feet up underneath him. There are people walking and talking loudly all around, enjoying the unseasonably warm night. Laughter and smoke hang in the air.

"How do you know my sister?" Eli pulls himself up and leans against a stone wall. Talking about Olive isn't his favorite topic at the moment, but it feels safe. Anything to keep this beautiful creature with him for as long as possible.

"We're on a burlesque troupe," Chris says with a large grin. His gray-blue eyes sparkle with joy. "We auditioned together over a year ago and became friends pretty much right from the start."

"So, you're a dancer?" Eli asks, not surprised. It explains the elegance with which he carries himself.

"You could say that. You could say that I'm a stripper too," Chris purrs and raises one eyebrow.

"But are you?"

"Well, yeah. I get paid to take off my clothes for an audience. I mean, we don't have a pole on stage, but I'd love to play with one if I got the chance."

"I imagine you get plenty of chances," Eli teases. The color rises to Chris's cheeks instantly.

"Oh god. I can't believe I said that." Chris covers his face and looks away with an awkward laugh. "You know what I mean."

"Yeah. Sorry about that. I've got the sense of humor of a fourteen-year-old boy."

"It's okay. I set it up for you."

"Do you have a day job? Or does burlesque pay the bills?"

A look of sadness crosses Chris's face. "No day job." He shrugs and looks away. "What about you? What do you do?" He looks back and offers a smile that doesn't reach his eyes.

"I'm a cook. Hence the sense of humor."

"I'm something of a cook myself," Chris says with a more genuine smile. "Where do you work?"

"District Pub. It's understaffed and the management is awful. But a guy's gotta eat."

"Oh. I love that place."

"Don't worry. It's clean. The staff we have is solid."

"I bet you've cooked my dinner before." Chris bats his lashes.

"I'm always there, so chances are pretty good. What's your favorite thing on the menu?"

"I almost always order the Cajun pasta. It's amazing."

"I could give you the recipe."

"Really?"

"Yeah, if you cook, it's easy. Or I could show you how to make it?" Eli tests the waters. He can't remember the last time he felt a genuine interest in someone. Aside from the instant physical attraction, there's something more here. He wants to know where Chris came from and where he's going. He wants to know about his dreams and desires.

Chris offers another sad smile. "That would be great. But…"

"But?"

"Sorry, Eli. I have a boyfriend." The pinched look on Chris's face isn't what Eli would expect from someone in love.

All the same, he speaks quickly to save face. "Oh. Yeah." Eli waves his hands in dismissal. "Of course you do. How could you not?" He shakes his head with a smile and wishes he was back at the bar. Despite the embarrassment of Chris's fast rejection, he stays. "I figured someday, in the future. I mean, if you're my sister's best friend, we'd probably find ourselves in a kitchen together. Then, I could show you how to make it. That's all." He shrugs and looks away.

A knowing smile grows on Chris's luscious lips. "That would make Olive so happy."

Eli bristles at the mention of Olive. Though he brought her up, it was only to mask his disappointment, not to make plans for a future dinner party. The desire to run begins to creep its way up his back again. But he's already told Chris where he works. Chris would tell Olive, and she would find him for sure. As he considers his means for escape, his emotions must read plainly on his face.

Chris says, "I can't say I can even begin to understand what happened between you two, but I do understand Olive. I know her heart, and she's one of the kindest, most genuine people I've ever met. I know she mourns the loss of your family and you, daily. She puts on a happy face and does the best with what she has. But I don't think she's ever truly happy. She's been a heartbroken mess all week." Chris levels his calm and understanding gaze on Eli.

"Yeah." Chris's words strike a chord deep inside Eli. It twangs, heavy and heart-wrenching. The whiskey buzz evaporates.

"I'm sorry. It's not any of my business." Chris straightens out his legs, dangling them off the wall. He looks like he's about to leave.

"No. I'm sorry." Eli swings his feet over the ledge as well, embarrassment warming his cheeks. "It's not a big deal. And you're right. I really do want to see Olive again. Last week was just…" He shakes his head. "It was overwhelming. I wasn't prepared for it. I'm really, actually truly embarrassed for running off like I did. Would it make more sense if I said I was stoned at the time?"

Chris cocks his brow with curiosity and pulls a half smile. "You two couldn't be more different." He chuckles and slides off the wall, landing gracefully.

"What's that supposed to mean?" Eli drops from the wall with a heavy thump. Standing closer to this gorgeous creature than he has all night, he realizes that he's looking up. Slightly.

Chris looks down at him with sparkling eyes. "She barely drinks and doesn't smoke. I honestly don't know if she's ever been high." He laughs. "While you seem to be perfectly at home with it."

"How about you?" Eli pulls a joint from behind his ear. "I was thinking about smoking this when I saw you inside."

"I'll smoke it if you got it," Chris says with a sexy grin.

Eli bites his tongue and swallows at least a dozen off-color responses. He lights up and inhales the sweet, skunky smoke. He walks away from the rowdy crowds to a less busy side street. Chris follows. "Here." He passes the joint.

Chris takes it in his hand. "This isn't some superweed, is it? I smoke, but I'm not trying to forget how to talk or piss my pants."

Eli grins. "You'll be fine." He watches as Chris holds the small joint to his lips. He admires the subtle movements of Chris's chin and throat as he inhales deeply, then as he tilts his head back and exhales. A sexy stream of smoke moves slowly from his mouth and nose.

"This isn't some superweed, is it?" Eli mocks as Chris takes another effortless hit and passes the joint back to him with a shy giggle.

"Whatever. I said I smoke. But some folks smoke to forget they exist. I can't handle that shit."

"I can't afford it." Eli chuckles and takes a hit. "Tell me something about yourself that doesn't involve my sister."

"I have four brothers, and I grew up on a hog farm."

"A hog farm? I don't believe it."

"What's not to believe?"

"You're so…" Eli takes another hit and hands the doobie back to Chris. "Refined."

Chris chokes on the smoke and his laughter. "Refined?" He doubles over cackling.

"What's so funny?"

"I suppose I put up a good front. I'll give you that." Chris hands off the joint.

"If this is a front, what are you really like?" Eli pulls another drag and offers it back to Chris.

"I'm good." Chris waves away the joint and straightens his already pristine outfit. "What am I really like? That's a good question. What are you really like?"

"You get what you see," Eli says with arms spread wide.

Chris looks him over with an appreciative smile. "Well, I'm a lazy slob who loves nothing more than drinking wine in my bathrobe all day and watching terrible reality TV. I cuss at the TV and eat my weight in junk food. And that's on Tuesday. Every three months or so, I crawl out of my hovel and pretend to be a glamorous burlesque dancer."

"What about tonight?" Eli asks softly.

"Tonight?" Chris's smile fades. "Tonight, I was lonely." He nods his head slowly and blinks his glistening eyes.

"How could anyone leave you lonely?" The words escape Eli's lips before he has the sense to stop them.

Chris looks at Eli with sad resignation. His bottom lip trembles, and he shrugs. They're standing alone on a quiet street. The noise of The District is far behind them. Tall buildings with darkened windows reach toward the starless sky.

Eli, in another moment of reckless emotion, opens his arms to Chris.

\*\*\*

*Chris*

Eli's arms are wide open. On his face is the expression of someone who understands. He might not understand exactly what Chris is going through, but he understands pain. Deep, unfettered pain. The kind that eats at a person's soul. Pain that pulls a man into himself for safety and solace. Pain Chris can't imagine. Yet, written on every angle of Eli's face is an offering of understanding without judgment.

Eli could've laughed off Chris's relationship issues as petty and superficial, considering what he's experienced in life. But what Chris sees inside those open arms is acceptance and compassion.

Chris steps forward. Eli closes him in his embrace.

The world falls away as the warmth of Eli's arms pulls him in.

Eli's lips brush Chris's neck, and sparks fly. Chris trembles, letting the electricity run through him. He holds tight to the body in his arms. He holds tight with a desperate need to be seen and known. Eli's broad chest is soft but strong, and his arms hold Chris in a steel-like grip. Chris crumbles into it, his dry sobs quaking between them.

Suddenly, Eli's hand is on his cheek, and his lips are on Chris's. He loses himself in the kiss. He sighs and moves his hands down Eli's back, then up his chest to his face. He revels in the soft stubble of Eli's beard and devours his mouth, hungry for everything he has to offer. His cock strains against his zipper while Eli's nudges his hip. Chris sighs and darts his tongue over Eli's soft, full lips. A sound comes from Eli's throat as he pulls him closer.

For the moment, Chris forgets everything that led him to where he stands. He forgets about Tyler, burlesque, leaving school, and his family. He forgets about every struggle and disappointment. All he knows are the lips against his and the arms around him.

But the joy is fleeting.

He sees Tyler with his big sleepy eyes watching him, judging him. He remembers all their best times, all of the passion and laughter they've shared over the years. Guilt shocks him like a thunderclap on a sunny day, and he pulls away from Eli's embrace.

"I'm sorry." Chris gasps. Eli looks up, eyes glazed with passion. "I shouldn't have done that."

Eli shakes his head, regaining his composure. "Yeah. No. You're right. I don't know what I was thinking. I'm sorry."

"No. You didn't do anything wrong. I did. You're fine. I'm the asshole." Chris lets out a nervous laugh and brushes his hair out of his face. "Look, I need to get out of here. I'm sorry. This isn't what I was trying to do tonight. I just wanted to go out and flirt a little. I didn't mean to lead you on."

"You didn't. It's okay. I shouldn't've kissed you. You told me upfront you were with someone." Eli steps back, giving Chris space.

They look at one another, each one stepping back, creating more space between them. The streetlights cast their orange glow over everything. If it weren't for the crushing guilt, Chris would feel empty from the absence of Eli's embrace. "You didn't do anything wrong. It was me," Eli offers.

"No, I did. I wanted you from the moment I saw you across the bar. I should've walked away a long time ago. I'm really sorry."

"I told you, there's nothing to apologize for."

Chris's racing heart slows. He focuses on Eli's face and sees genuine concern. He closes his eyes and takes a deep, steadying breath. "Thank you for being so understanding." He smiles. "Olive is going to be so happy to hear I ran into you." Darkness flits across Eli's face before he looks away. "What?" Chris asks.

"Could you not tell her you ran into me?" Eli's eyes dart uncomfortably from Chris to anywhere else.

"God, Eli, I don't know. That's going to be difficult."

"I know. I swear, I want to see her. And when I'm ready, I promise I'll find her. I know where to look. I just can't right now. I've got a lot I need to sort out."

Chris searches Eli's face, wondering what could be keeping him from wanting to be reunited with his sister. Then he remembers the open acceptance Eli offered him moments ago.

He swallows his better judgment and nods. "I won't tell her. You promise you'll come around though?"

Eli smiles with gratitude. "Yeah. I promise."

"She bartends at the Speakeasy and lives above it with Vic, the handsome-as-sin bar owner. You'll have no trouble finding her when you're ready."

"What about you?" Eli asks, raising both brows. "Will I be able to find you?"

"Yeah. When I'm ready." Chris feels a lump growing in his throat. Every fiber in his being wants to charge right back into Eli's arms. But Tyler is waiting at home. "Bye, Eli. It was great to meet you."

"You too, Chris. Are you okay to get home?"

"Yeah. I walked down from Broadway. It's not too far from here."

"Okay. Be safe." They stand a couple paces apart. Neither one moves. An awkward silence hangs between them. Chris takes in every line of Eli's face, from his dark stubble to his full lips.

"You too." Chris turns to walk away, feeling Eli's gaze on his back. He's tempted to look over his shoulder and steal another glimpse. If he did, what would stop him from running back into those warm, safe arms? What would stop him from seeking out those delicious lips?

Nothing.

So, he walks on under the glowing streetlamps, away from the business district with its tallish buildings and storefronts, all closed for the night. Away from the adventure Eli surely offered.

Chris crosses the wide streets. Traffic is slow at this time of night. The neighborhood welcomes him with its darkened brick-paved streets. Each Victorian-era house sits far from the curb, stretching two, sometimes three, stories high, many of them having been recently renovated to their former glory with fresh paint and new porches. In the spring and summer, families gather on the porches and in the yards. Kids ride their bikes over the broken sidewalks.

The large yards are full of flowers and shrubs that seem to have been planted when the houses were young.

Tyler and Chris used to walk together on mild evenings, admiring the lovely gardens and houses. It was a real slice of urban Americana.

Chris sighs as he approaches the large, three-story house where their apartment is. Their private porch on the top floor overlooks a well-maintained courtyard. In the beginning, it was magical. He remembers the good times as he climbs the stairs to the back door, then stops and looks out over the garden beds already put down for the season. He thinks of all the Sunday morning coffees they'd sipped on the deck, all the dreams they had once shared, and wonders if he and Tyler could ever be like that again.

Guilt surges in his gut as he sees Eli's smile instead of Tyler's bringing a steaming coffee mug to his lips. "Tyler deserves better than this," Chris scolds himself as he breathes in the sweet autumn air.

He flips on the light and remembers how his mom would always leave the light on when one of the family was out. "That way they can see their way back to you," she would say.

Chris always left the light on for Tyler. He wonders if the dark hallway is Tyler's way of saying he could care less if Chris found his way home.

He enters the kitchen to find a note on the counter, written in Tyler's straight, clear hand. It's an itemized bill for the apartment and utilities. Beneath the list of charges, it says:

*You're right, Chris. You can stay as long as you need to, but starting next month, I'll expect you to pay your share. I'd rather spare you the tears of talking this out. Let's just agree that this has run its course, and things are over between us romantically. You can keep the Nissan. It was a gift, after all.*

"What the fuck?" Chris breathes softly.

Anger and resentment bubble to the surface of his already-worn soul.

"He didn't even sign his name."

# CHAPTER FIVE
*Eli*

Eli curses as the sound of the printer screeches its demand on the other end of the line of white order tickets. He's in the middle of yet another understaffed lunch rush. He stares at tickets hanging before him demanding burgers and pastas. There's a server on the cold side struggling to make the salads and setup plates she serves every day. "Fuck, Alexis. C'mon. I need sets for these burgers before they die."

"I'm moving as fast as I can," she shouts over her shoulder.

The ticket printer goes off again.

"I swear, if Pam has to come back here and help us out, I'm going to ruin the rest of your week." Eli checks the temps on several burgers and chicken breasts before stirring sauces and then shakes three fryer baskets. He moves smoothly from one task to another.

"Fuck you."

"Just put the goddamn lettuce and tomato on the plates so I can move this food."

"You're lucky this is for my table."

"You're lucky you've got me today. Do you think Joe or Brian could handle this shit? Maybe I should call the dishwasher? Or the busboy? You want him touching your food?"

"Again, fuck you. Here are your plates." She shoves three plates, sloppily set, down the line. "I'm running these salads out, then I'll be back for those." She disappears through the swinging door, plastering on her server's grin.

"Eli. I need an ETA on table twelve," Pam shouts as she pushes through the swinging door. Her face appears on the other side of the window. The thick black eyeliner makes her already beady eyes seem smaller.

"Thirty seconds, Pam," Eli answers without checking the table's ticket. He's in his groove and can't be bothered with tracking down a specific table number. It'll be done when it's done. She knows that already. Her needless attempt to feel in control over her restaurant is infuriating.

"It's always thirty seconds with you. Do I need to put on an apron and come back there?" Her whiny voice doesn't have the authority she believes it does.

"You and I both know that won't help. Can you grab the setups for these next two tables, please?" He forces a smile and turns his focus back to the food. "Twelve is coming up," he says over his shoulder as he reads the incoming tickets.

A single order for Cajun pasta makes his heart skip a beat. *Is it him?* Chris has been on his mind since they met. Every order for Cajun pasta has him peeking out through the tiny window on the swinging door, hoping to catch a glimpse of him.

Another ticket spews from the tiny printer. Pam slides over two trays loaded with plates ready for food.

"I need the salads for one and six," she says with urgency.

"You're gonna have to get those too. Or send the servers back for them. I can't do it all."

"You're right. You're doing enough already," she says without a hint of derision. Eli stops and looks at her with shock. She's not one for giving compliments.

"What?" she asks. "You do a great job, Eli. We don't know what we would do without you."

"Huh, thanks." It's all he can say, unable to remember the last time he received anything resembling encouragement for a job well done.

"Really, Eli. Thank you." She offers a small smile and turns back to the cold table to make salads. Eli's cheeks warm with appreciation. He takes a brief moment to bask in the recognition before diving back into his work. The line is the only place where the world makes sense. He moves through the rest of the rush with ease, watching as he nears the single ticket for Cajun pasta.

"Hey, Alexis," he shouts through the window. She stops short with an angry glare. He's unfazed. She'll be his friend again after lunch is over.

"What?"

"Who's at one?"

"I don't know." She shrugs. "Some guy."

"Cajun pasta?" His heart skips a beat at the possibility. *Is it him?*

"Yeah."

"What's he look like?"

"I don't know. He's old, I guess. Kinda cute. Why?"

"Thought it might be someone." His heart sinks. At least he knows Chris has kept his promise. He hasn't told Olive where to find Eli. If she knew, she would've already hunted him down.

"Is it ready?"

"Thirty seconds," he responds quickly, turning his attention back to the line, but in the back of his mind, he wonders: *Will I ever see him again?* Does he have to go to Olive to make it happen? At this point, the idea of a family reunion is the last thing he wants. But if it means seeing Chris again, it would be worth it.

Maybe he should head over to the Speakeasy? Maybe she's working, and maybe he's there. It doesn't seem right to reconnect with Olive just to see Chris again. Besides, what would she think of Eli? He's done literally nothing with his life. He's a line cook who smokes and drinks his way through the hours between work and sleep. He has nothing to offer her. Nothing she could be proud of.

Chris said she barely drinks. She'll be so disappointed to see what Eli's done with his life. He's not ready to face that.

But, really, what has she done? She's a burlesque dancer. Not a typical profession, but if she was doing well, she wouldn't be a bartender too. The last time he saw her, she was a cocktail waitress at a crappy casino, living on a houseboat.

Sure, she's on land now, but how much has really changed? And why should that make a difference?

He wishes he knew more about her. He wishes they'd stayed together after they were taken away from their home. But no one wanted to take them both, and she was almost eighteen. Why didn't she come for him though? Why didn't she save him?

The printer sings its wretched song again and shakes him from his dark thoughts.

Pam pops her head in and shouts, "Got a ten top coming back," before disappearing again.

"Fuck." Eli watches as the long ticket prints and checks the clock on the wall.

Two hours before the night shift starts coming in. As he works, he thinks about what his life could've been if his parents were still alive. If the government and laws, which have changed immensely over the years, hadn't taken everything away from him and Olive.

He remembers how happy they all were and wonders if his parents had planned on introducing them to the family business or if they would have kept them in the dark forever.

That couldn't've been the plan. But were they going to teach them how to grow and distribute the drugs without ever telling them that they were illegal?

They'd always referred to the grow tents as medicine tents, and Eli had never asked otherwise. He trusted that his parents were good people who were producing medicine for the rest of the world.

He never thought they were doing a lot of somethings that were against the law. He didn't even know that law beyond the laws of nature existed.

And that was where they'd gone wrong. They raised their children for a world that never existed—or one that hadn't existed for centuries.

He and Olive never stood a chance.

Then again, while she might not have a "profession," she's made a life for herself with friends who seemed to love her like family, and a handsome live-in boyfriend.

Eli's an aimless drifter with a penchant for self-abasement, making him the perfect man for the job he's doing: nameless, faceless, and underpaid.

The printer screams again.

\*\*\*

*Chris*

"I can't stay there any longer." Chris is sitting inside the Speakeasy with Olive. Susan is onstage, practicing her routine for the next show. The rest of the troupe are holding their own conversations in hushed voices at tables away from the stage.

It's still early in the planning process for the next show, and Susan is walking through ideas. Everyone takes their turn doing it for several practices while the rest of the troupe politely ignores the awkward growing pains of any good routine.

"I told you, I talked with Vic. He's more than happy to have you stay with us. I know it's a tiny guest room. But we spend so much time down here, you'd feel like it was your place."

"I can't do that." Chris sighs and shakes his head.

"Why not?" Olive asks, her brow furrowed.

"Because the last thing I want to be surrounded by is someone's happily ever after."

Olive opens her mouth to speak, but Chris holds up his hand and goes on. "I don't want to hear it. I really appreciate the offer, but I don't know how I could possibly get along with you and Vic loving on each other and giggling around every corner. You're still in the honeymoon phase. You don't want a sad ghost of a man floating around your love nest, blubbering all day long."

"Give me a little more credit than that," Olive huffs with a smile playing on the corners of her mouth. Chris can see that she's only halfway committed to the conversation now that the idea of her and Vic's love nest is firmly planted in her mind. "It's not like we fuck all day long. You're thinking of Bunny and Mike."

"Yeah, I know, and they offered me a place to stay too. You bet your ass I said thanks but no thanks. Can you imagine what it would be like to live with them? They can barely make it three minutes without undressing each other with their eyes." Despite his sadness, he chuckles at the thought of how Bunny and Mike's love manifests all the time. Their story belongs in a novel. How they spent twelve years existing without each other is a marvel. They seem to need one another's touch more than air or water.

"I know what you mean. But Vic and I aren't like that," Olive says with a dreamy smile that states otherwise.

Chris rolls his eyes. "Please. You might not be as flagrant about it, but everyone knows. Besides, I'm sure I couldn't handle too many mornings seeing that man of yours walking through the place in his underwear. I've been practically celibate for months. You should've seen me the other night at the club." Chris realizes his slip-up instantly. He hasn't mentioned his night out with Eli to Olive for fear he wouldn't keep his word.

"What night?" Olive asks with a coy smile and a side glance.

"Oh, the other night." He makes his tone sound nonchalant as he waves a hand in the air. "I couldn't take the silence at home and went out to the bar. There was a cute boy there." He feels the color rise to his cheeks as he shakes his head. "If I hadn't had my wits about me, I probably would've gone home with him. He was so cute, and kind of a bad boy." Guilt rolls in his belly as he talks to Olive about her brother without giving anything away.

Her eyes and smile grow big with excitement. "Ooh, a boy. Tell me all about him. What's his name?"

"I didn't get it." Chris blushes furiously partly from the lie, but mostly from the memory of the way he felt in Eli's arms.

"How did you not tell me about this sooner?" Olive chides and crosses her arms over her chest in mock disdain.

"I don't know. I guess there really wasn't anything to tell. I mean, I didn't even get his name." He shrugs and looks away, remembering their whole exchange. "He was so cute though."

"You think you'll see him again?" Olive asks, dropping her fake disappointment.

"I think so. And I promise, you'll be the first to know when I do. But right now, I need to figure out what I'm going to do about my living situation. Tyler is being such a passive-aggressive dick about everything. My parents said I could come back home, but that is the last thing that I want to do with my life. They're too far away. I wouldn't be able to commute, and I do not want to leave the troupe. Literally, it's the only good thing in my world right now."

"We'll figure something out," Olive offers. "At least you've got a job."

"I do, and thank you for that. I know the Speakeasy wasn't really hiring, so I appreciate you getting Vic to give me a job."

"There was no getting him to do it. As soon as he heard you needed a job, he offered. He was also disappointed that the front apartment is currently occupied. He said he would've moved you in right away."

"You've got a good guy there." Chris sighs again.

"I do. I only wish we could help you more." She looks down at the carpet, then back at him with an excited grin. "You know, I haven't winterized the boat yet, and the weather is pretty mild right now. I know it's not a permanent fix, but you could stay as long as you need, rent-free."

"Really?" Chris feels a rush of relief followed by heavy guilt. Olive is such a good friend, and he is keeping a huge secret from her. She'd be crushed if she found out. But what choice does he have? Eli's whereabouts are his business. Maybe once Chris gets out of Tyler's place and settled into somewhere all his own, he can start working on bringing them—Olive and Eli—together. Then all the secret-keeping will be worth it. "That would be amazing. I don't know where I would put all my stuff. But that's something I can work out later. As long as I can get myself out of there, I can start to breathe again."

"You don't have to worry about that either. This place has a huge basement with nothing but cobwebs and some old props that haven't seen the light of day in who knows how long."

"Are you serious? You just made my month. You're the best friend a guy could have. Come here." He opens his arms and pulls her into a long, warm hug. In that moment, she feels like Eli. Her hair is the same color, her skin the same tone. He squeezes her tight and breathes deep his resolve to make it right with her.

He can't possibly keep this secret much longer.

He's going to see Eli sooner rather than later.

*****

It's late in the afternoon. The District Pub is all but empty. Three servers sit at a table near the bar, rolling silverware into cloth napkins. A stylish middle-aged woman sits at the bar, chatting with the bartender. Chris waits at the door to be noticed by one of them. The middle-aged woman looks over first and stands from her barstool, then walks over with a large, genuine smile.

"Hi there. Just one today?" She reaches for a menu and a roll of silverware.

"Yep." Chris nods and follows her to a seat by the window.

"Alexis will be right with you. Can I get you anything to drink?"

"Sure. Can I get a Moscato and some ice water, please?"

"Of course. We'll have that right out."

Moments later, a fierce-looking woman about his age approaches with his drinks. "Do you need a minute?" He hasn't touched his menu.

"No. I'll have the Cajun pasta."

"Good choice. Anything else?"

"Yeah, actually. Can you tell me if Eli is working today?"

His server takes the menu from the table and settles her weight on one foot, jutting out her hip. She eyes him with curiosity. "You're the one," she says slowly.

"What's that supposed to mean?"

"Nothing." She smiles and shakes her head. "For weeks, he's been asking every time someone comes in solo and orders the Cajun pasta." She looks him over with appreciation. "I get it. I'll see if he's available." She taps the menu on the table before sauntering away and pushing through the swinging door into the kitchen.

Chris unrolls the cloth napkin and lays it over his lap. He arranges his silverware on the table and takes a sip of wine. The sweet bubbles do nothing to calm his nerves. *Eli's been looking for me.*

He looks out the window absently, doing his best to ignore the feeling of Eli's co-workers' curious stares and their hushed voices and giggles. He feels like he's about to take the stage for the first time with his heart beating wildly and his palms sweaty.

He fidgets with his table setting, flipping through the drink menu, moving his silverware and glasses, smoothing his napkin. Music plays soft and low from overhead. He focuses on the lyrics of a song he's never heard and surely won't remember.

A woman walks along the sidewalk like someone out of a magazine. She seems to think her dark sunglasses hide the fact that she's watching herself in the large windows. Chris laughs to himself, admiring her impeccable style.

Then he hears the kitchen door swing and forces himself not to turn around. Instead, he watches the stranger as she saunters out of sight.

He can smell the food before it arrives at the table. His server smiles down at him as she presents the plate. "Eli said he'll be out in a bit. You need anything else?"

"No, I'm good." Chris shakes his head and looks at his plate. It smells amazing, but he's hardly hungry.

The idea of Eli being on the other side of the swinging door is too much. From the moment they met, the man has left an impression. Now that Chris is only moments away from seeing him again, he realizes just how deep that impression is.

He eats as he waits, imagining himself in the tiny kitchen of his new home and watching as Eli teaches him how to make the dish.

Chris pictures Eli's perfect lips grinning as he offers him a taste of the sauce. He remembers how soft Eli's almost-beard was to touch and realizes he doesn't know what color Eli's eyes are. He's been imagining them the same mossy green as Olive's, but it'd been too dark for him to be sure. And, he's been so focused on Eli's delicious lips and smile to the point of distraction.

"Hey." Chris jumps at the sound of Eli's greeting. He turns to see him approaching the table in a black chef coat and black-and-white-striped chef pants. His thick-framed glasses are similar to the ones Tyler wears but more stylish, and he has dime-sized shiny black gauges in both ears.

Chris assesses him unapologetically. Altogether it's a silly getup, but Eli wears it well. They share shy smiles and quiet giggles as they admire each other. "I was wondering if I would see you again." Eli motions for the seat across from Chris, who nods, and Eli sits. "How's it going?"

"It's pretty crazy, actually," Chris says, laying his fork on the table and wiping his mouth. Smiling behind his napkin, he notices Eli's eyes. They're like nothing he's seen before. One is a similar shade to Olive's, but slightly lighter, more blueish, and the other is split down the middle, green-blue on one side and deep brown on the other. There is nothing usual about Eli, nothing ordinary. Chris is thrilled at the prospect of the many surprises this man holds. He clears his throat and sips his wine. "I haven't told Olive about you."

Eli blinks his extraordinary eyes and gives a half smile. "I appreciate that. Though I can't tell you how many times I've thought how ridiculous I've been about it."

"You're not ridiculous," Chris assures. "I understand completely, but I've come to see you. Things have changed a lot since we met, and I don't know how much longer I can go keeping secrets from Olive. She's done so much for me in these last couple of weeks, I feel terribly guilty."

"I get it. To be one hundred percent honest, I've been tempted to go see her all week."

"Yeah?"

"Not for the right reasons though."

"How could there be a wrong reason for seeing your sister?"

Eli glances away, then back to Chris, his cheeks coloring slightly. "I wasn't thinking about seeing her."

"Oh." Chris feels his cheeks warming too. His heart flutters as he gets lost in Eli's beautiful eyes. "Well, I'm on my own now. Which is why I'm so indebted to Olive. She's helped me a lot. That's beside the point though. I was wondering if you wanted to get together after work?"

Eli's smile grows. "I'd like that. I'll be done here once night shift punches in, which is any minute. Let me go clean up. You'll hang around?"

"Yeah, sure."

Eli stands, smiles, and nods.

Chris smiles back. "See you soon, then."

# CHAPTER SIX
*Eli*

Chris is waiting for him outside, looking like a model. In his light denim jacket and matching jeans cuffed at the ankle, he exudes effortless style, casual comfort, and uncommon grace. His thick shock of strawberry-blond hair is intentionally tousled and a lovely contrast to the gray autumn sky. Eli takes a moment to appreciate Chris's supple dancer's build as he paces in the opposite direction.

Chris's face lights up as he turns to see Eli approaching. "Hello again." He waves with a sweet, wholesome grin.

"Hey." They're side by side, closer than they've been since the night they first met. The night Eli has been daydreaming about ever since. He feels almost guilty for the hot thoughts he's had in their time apart.

"How was your day?" Chris asks, seeming genuinely curious.

"Pretty good. Slow, actually. Do you mind if we swing by my place so I can change? I'm not far from here."

"Not at all. Full disclosure though: the more I know about you, the more I'm keeping from Olive, and the less comfortable I am with it."

Eli flinches at the sound of his sister's name. He knows he shouldn't feel the way he does. He knows she was a kid as well and suffered the same losses he did. But he also knows if he had a little brother lost to the system, when he turned eighteen, he would've done anything he could to get him back.

The feelings he has for her are complicated. On one hand, she's the only family he has, the only person who truly understands what their life was like and how it fell apart.

On the other, she abandoned him and never looked back. He suffered for years. His adolescence to young adulthood was one terrible experience after another. She could've protected him, and she didn't.

"I know" is all he can muster. He can't possibly explain to Chris the turmoil going on in his heart and mind.

"So does that mean you're ready to see her?" Chris asks hopefully.

"It means I'm ready to let things happen organically. I'm not going to seek her out any time soon. But I understand our reunion is inevitable, and next time, I won't run away." Eli shrugs, wishing Chris had come along without Olive in the picture.

"Well, I'm not going to run off and call her this instant, so don't worry about that. But I know I can't keep a secret to save my life, and the more I know, the more I'll have to offer. I would make a terrible spy." Chris laughs at himself.

Eli steals a glance his way. His pale cheeks are slightly pink from the cool breeze, accentuating the faint sprinkle of freckles, and not a trace of a beard or mustache.

"I'm not too good with secrets either," Eli offers as they cross the street heading to his building. The red and orange tiles and faded green awning of the closed restaurant welcome him home. His glimpse through the window finds the tables still set as if they are ready to open for dinner, but it's been years since a customer was welcomed for any meal. Eli's roommates claim it was the best Thai food that you could get outside of Chicago.

"This is it." Eli motions to the door leading to the apartment he shares with seven near strangers. Years ago, he answered an ad for a room when he first rolled into Rock Island. The apartment is quite large with high ceilings and an ample common room. The private rooms, however, are more like closets with barely enough room for a bed, let alone any personal items. He's always compared it to prison, lying in his small bed, thinking of how his mom wasted away in her cell. He shakes off the thought and turns to Chris. "You can come up if you want. It's not much." Eli shrugs again.

"Mine's not much either." Chris offers an encouraging smile as Eli opens the door and welcomes Chris to follow. The heavy scent of fried onions and ginger hangs in the air despite the time that has passed since the restaurant was open. The whole building smells of decades of stir-fries and curries.

"This is a bit of a drifter's place," Eli explains over his shoulder. "The rooms are rented out on a monthly basis, and people stay for a few weeks or, like me, years. I don't know any of my roommates very well. But they've never given me a reason not to trust them. A bunch of punk kids and wanderers, really."

"It sounds like fun," Chris says as they approach the door.

"It is what it is. Or what you make of it, I suppose." Eli turns to wait for Chris to meet him at the top of the stairway.

The man couldn't be more out of place. Like a member of the Hollywood elite finding himself on skid row. It's clear Chris has been kept and loved his whole life. The folks on the other side of the door have not.

"Gordo's probably in the main room. He's been here a lot longer than me. He's a good guy. Quiet, but friendly. He sleeps on a mat on the floor in the living room. Not sure why. I guess he wants to. If he's asleep, don't worry about it. You won't wake him. He keeps weird hours."

***

*Chris*

Chris tries to smile through his apprehension. What Eli is describing is literally the very thing his mother warned him about when he moved to Chicago years ago. She's told him to stay away from flophouses, whatever that meant. He's pretty sure he's about to find out. People sleeping on mats in living rooms while others moved about with their lives. Tiny rooms let by drifters. It seems like the perfect place to be raped and murdered and left for dead. But also, it sounds intriguing, exciting, and so different from anything he's ever seen or experienced that his heart beats to a new rhythm.

As the door opens, the sticky-sweet smell of unbathed bodies and trash wafts out. Stepping into the kitchen, he notices the sink, counters, and stovetop are loaded with empty bottles, takeout containers, and pizza boxes. A small table with no chairs holds more liquor bottles and overflowing ashtrays. Stale cigarette smoke hangs in the air. Chris does his best to hide his revulsion, but Eli sees it.

Eli looks around the kitchen, and his expression is filled with shame. "We used to have a really great lady staying here that cleaned up after everyone. She moved on, and no one took up the task. I tried to keep it up after she left. But a lot of these folks are animals. Harmless, yes. But still half-wild."

"Yeah. I get it. I have brothers," Chris jokes, pulling his arms in a little closer to his side and questioning his former excitement. True to Eli's word, Gordo is asleep on a mat in the corner, under a pile of dingy blankets and pillows. A cigarette burns in another overflowing ashtray on the floor beside him. The art hanging on every available space of the wall is an incredible mix of original paintings and thrift store finds. The overall aesthetic seems intentional, but from the looks of everything else he's seen, Chris is sure it's accidental. "The artwork in here is amazing," he offers as they pause under the open pocket doors.

"Yeah. Everyone who stays here leaves something for the wall. It's kinda cool to see how it's changed over the years."

"How long have you been here?"

"Longer than I want to admit." Eli's face grows dark.

"I'm sorry."

"Don't be. My space isn't so bad."

Chris follows Eli down a dimly lit hallway. Several doors with transom windows line either side. Each door has a number; most are covered with poetry, quotes, and doodles. Though some wear only the stains of the dirty hands that have used them throughout the years.

"Which one's yours?" Chris asks, noticing the sticky grip the floor has as he walks.

"Right here, near the bathroom." Eli nods toward the end of the hall. "And the fire escape."

Chris swallows the retch that bubbles up from his gut at the idea of what a communal bathroom in a place like this would look like. *How anyone can live like this?*

"It's not pretty," Eli says, acknowledging the look on Chris's face. And he thought he was doing so well to hide it. "I do what I can to make it tolerable, and believe it or not, I've seen worse."

"I believe it." Chris laughs an awkward laugh. "I mean, I've lived in a dorm. Without the CAs, it would've looked a lot like this. And honestly, this place has more style. And I was at an art school."

"Really? Chicago?" Eli asks as he unlocks his door.

"Yep. I went two years before I dropped out to move here with…" The thought of Tyler and everything Chris gave up to waste five years of his life playing housewife brings a burning anger to the surface he didn't expect to feel.

"With?" Eli pauses opening the door to look him over.

"It doesn't matter, does it? It didn't work out, and here I am."

Eli pushes the door open, stepping in ahead of him, and Chris follows. The room is small with a tiny wooden dresser, a twin-sized bed, and not much else. The walls are a deep, faded mauve. The bedding is worn but clean. Two thin pillows lie at the head of the bed. A few trinkets lie spread out on the dresser, and a chair in the corner holds a pile of folded laundry. The only window is the one above the door. Eli opens his top drawer and pulls out some fresh clothes. "You mind if I take a quick shower? I'll be done in five minutes. Then, we can get out of here."

"Go for it."

"I'll hurry," Eli assures and disappears through the door.

Chris lowers himself cautiously onto the small bed. Its springs squeak their disapproval. He wonders what he's gotten himself into and revels in the undeniable excitement churning in his belly.

Five minutes crawl by at an excruciating pace. He shifts, and the springs squeak again. *How many men have been here before me?* A pang of guilt shoots through his system. As much as he wants it not to matter, it does. After years in a monogamous relationship, he can't be naïve and trusting of every pretty face that comes his way. *Such a pretty face.*

As if on cue, Eli comes through the door, looking refreshed and a bit wet from the shower. The scent of soap follows him as he passes Chris, drying his short, thick hair roughly with a towel.

Eli's loose-fitting jeans hang lower than his plaid boxers. His bare chest and stomach are covered with dark hair. He runs the towel over them, then his shoulders, before hanging it on a hook by the door. Chris admires the definition of Eli's pecs and imagines resting his head on the cozy spot where Eli's chest meets his shoulder.

Eli catches his gaze and grins. "Eyes are up here." He points to his face.

Chris looks away quickly, blushing. "You're the one who came in here shirtless," he defends.

"Touché," Eli agrees with that same sparkling grin as he pulls a faded pink David Bowie t-shirt over his head before dragging on a heavy but worn black cardigan. "So where are we off to?"

\*\*\*

*Eli*

Eli isn't prepared for what he sees as they pull up to the marina. His parents' boat, the *S.S. Contingency*, floats near the dock filled with larger, nicer boats all wrapped in their shrink-wrapped winter tarps of blue. Dried and crinkling leaves swirl around their feet as they head to the boardwalk. To their right, the park is drab and empty, a perfect pairing for the feeling in Eli's gut. The last time he was on the boat was the last time he spoke to Olive. It hadn't ended well.

Once he had turned eighteen, he headed back to the farm. Over the years he'd convinced himself she would be there waiting for him, and she'd have figured things out and reclaimed their home. That the authorities were the reason she hadn't found him. But after one bus fare and several rides from kind strangers, he found a broken, empty house at the end of an overgrown lane. The windows were cracked or shattered, the porches rotting. It was a skeleton of what it had once been, devoid of life. Olive was nowhere to be found.

He must've followed her same train of thought: his next stop was the dock in Marquette where he found her living on the houseboat. They'd clung to one another like children with tears and laughter. The laughter didn't last. It wasn't long before Eli was back on the road, looking for something he would never find.

"Hey, I know it's not much. But at least I have a bathroom of my own," Chris jokes.

Eli shakes the memories away and focuses on him. "What?"

"I know I never would have thought I'd be living in a houseboat on the Mississippi. But Olive has it set up pretty cozy in there."

"I haven't seen it in years." Eli shakes his head with awe. "I guess I thought I wouldn't see it again."

"Oh my god, Eli. I didn't even think about what this place must mean to you. I'm so sorry. Do you want to go somewhere else?" Chris wrinkles his brow and grimaces.

"No. It's all right. I'm fine. In fact, I'm curious. It's been a long time since I've seen this old boat. Let alone been on it."

"Well, then. Let's go." Chris turns away.

The sour feeling in Eli's gut eases as he watches the subtle sway of Chris's hips.

Inside the little boat, it still smells like Olive and home. Eli is amazed at the visceral reaction he has to the scent. It's probably why he came back whenever he did, suffering through the awkward conversations and eventual arguments to revel in the sweet embrace of happier times.

"I'd say to make yourself at home, but it seems like you should be saying that to me."

"Not gonna lie, this is a trip." Eli stands in the kitchen, which hasn't changed since he was a boy. The cabinets his dad built still hang above the sink. The small table they'd carried together as a family sits where they secured it to the floor. The dishes they'd packed in from the house are still there. Building the boat is one of his earliest and best memories.

"You want a drink?" Chris asks, bringing him back to the present.

"Sure. What do you have?"

"Red or white?" Chris gestures to several bottles of cheap wine on the counter and opens the door of the small fridge to reveal more. "It's been a rough couple of weeks. The wine helps me sleep."

"I hear that. Let's go with red. I love a good dry red on a gray chilly day like today."

Chris grins. "Me too."

"Do you mind if I look around?" Eli asks, nostalgia pulling him deeper into the past.

"Not at all. I'm the guest here." Chris shrugs, popping the cork from the bottle and pulling some jelly jars from the cabinet.

Eli passes through the open doorway into the sleeping/living quarters of the boat. He sees the bed piled high with quilts made by his mother and the walls lined with his father's books. His heart aches more intensely than it has for years. He's frozen in place, surrounded by the life he'd begun to believe was a fairy tale that he'd written to cope with his terrible adolescence. Chris hands him a small glass filled with deep red wine. The oaky tang barely registers as he swallows a hearty drink, then another.

"Do you want to get out of here?" Chris leans in the doorway.

"No. I'm good." Eli swallows more of the wine, almost finishing the glass. Chris disappears briefly, then reappears with a bottle in hand. He fills Eli's near-empty cup. "It's weird," Eli says after another drink. "Being here without Olive. Like, she's always been here. So, I've never had this moment. I mean, I've been alone here. But never without her lingering presence or some fresh argument hanging in the air."

"I get it." Chris continues to lean in the doorway. "Would you like some time alone?"

Eli looks at him for what feels like the first time. He's taken off his jacket, revealing his lean, taut forearms. His button-down shirt is opened at the neck, revealing a sprinkle of fine, light hairs. He's watching Eli with compassion and understanding. "No, you're fine. I appreciate you being here. Sorry if I'm emotional."

"It's understandable. I'm sorry I didn't think of this being your home too."

Eli waves his hand in dismissal. "No apologies. This is weird. But everything about my life is. I'm not sure how I would process normal." Eli laughs and swallows more tangy wine. "Have you ever taken this out on the river?" The wine is doing its job, numbing things that are bigger than he wants to feel.

"No. Olive offered to take me out over the summer. But I wasn't really interested. I always hated fishing and boating when I was a kid. Preferred to stay home and make dinner with Mom."

"Your brothers would go though?"

"Well, yeah. I remember my littlest staying with us more often than the others. But he eventually chose the 'Bro Boat,' as they called it." Chris shakes his head. "I liked my afternoons with Mom though. They were quiet." He gives a small chuckle and a distant gaze.

"Hey," Eli calls him back. Chris looks up with a wistful smile. A smile Eli wants to keep on his face. "Tell me about them."

"My brothers?" Chris scrunches his nose.

"Your afternoons with your mom."

# CHAPTER SEVEN
*Chris*

"I can't believe we're on our second bottle already." Chris giggles as he uncorks another bottle of wine. His steps are uneasy from the wine as much as the rocking and swaying of the boat. Eli shakes his head as he's relaxing on a lounge chair, watching the sunset over the marina.

"It's going down easy." Eli holds his cup out for a refill. Chris fills it and settles into his own seat. They sit in comfortable silence, watching the golden-orange sunlight ripple on the river's surface. "I always took the sunset for granted back home," Eli says with a hint of awe. "I suppose people in the city see the same sunset, but it hits differently when the sky stretches out for miles. No buildings or power lines to break it up. Just the sun dipping lower by the moment, painting the sky, and eventually hitting the horizon behind the trees and distant hills." He's quiet again for a while, watching the sky, before he says, "Some of my best dreams are of those sunsets." He downs half his cup of wine, keeping his gaze trained on the sky.

"I remember the sunsets back home. I mean, a hog farm isn't all that picturesque, but we still have wide-open skies."

"We had some pigs." Eli looks to Chris. "Goats, chickens, ducks, and a donkey. God, I hated that donkey. It bit me once. Shit hurt so bad."

"You were bit by a donkey?" Chris cackles at the thought of the handsome, mysterious, sexy man beside him being bitten by a donkey.

"Don't laugh. It drew blood and everything. Fuck, I'm pretty sure I still have the scar." Eli sits up straight, pulling his sweater and t-shirt off of his shoulder. "See." He points to the spot where his shoulder meets his neck. A ring of fine silver scar tissue runs over the front and back.

"Jesus. I never thought of donkeys biting people. I knew they kicked. But that looks terrible."

"It was." Eli takes another long drink and laughs. "At the time for sure. I wanna say I was ten or so. I don't remember what I was doing. But I was fucking with him. Mom said I was lucky he didn't get me any worse. She was able to clean it up at home. Sometimes I wonder what would've happened if I had gone to the emergency room that day. They would've had so much explaining to do." He shakes his head and looks away, smoothing his shirt in place. "You know, I didn't even know what a television was until I was sent to my first foster home."

"I can't even imagine how that must have felt," Chris says, taking a small sip of wine and watching the sun slip out of sight.

"Most people can't." Eli shrugs and empties his glass, reaching for the bottle on the ground between them. "I know they thought they were protecting us. They really believed they were doing what was best. But how could my parents not have even considered the possibility of what happened? Like, they had no plan. Nowhere for us to go. No one that could take us. Did they really think that they were invincible? And what was their plan for the future? Did they think we were going to live there forever and never see what the rest of the world was like?" Eli's eyes are wide, his lips curled in a half-twisted smile. He shakes his head and laughs a dry laugh.

"I don't know." Chris bites back his response which would undoubtedly lead to mentioning a similar conversation he's had with Olive. He watches as Eli's expression relaxes, and Eli takes another swig of wine. Chris attempts to steer the conversation away from Eli's haunted past. "I was raised on television," he says with a shrug and another sip of wine.

"Me too, eventually," Eli responds, seeming grateful for the redirection. "Once I discovered it, I couldn't get enough. Shit, cartoons got me through most of what I'd had to live with. Such a wholesome way to disassociate."

"What was your favorite?"

"I loved it all. Started with a lot of kid's stuff like *Little Bear* and *Dragon Tales*. They were for babies, I know, but when I went into foster care, I was a bit of a baby, emotionally. And my first foster home had preschoolers with strict rules. Honestly, I'm surprised we got to watch any of it considering that Little Bear was naked the whole time." Eli laughs. Chris listens intently as he goes on. "It wasn't until I got into the second foster home that I discovered edgier stuff like *SpongeBob*, *Pokémon*, and the Cartoon Network. I'd watch for hours and try my best to replicate what I saw. That family wELias good to me. They gave me sketch pads and colored pencils and stuff. I loved drawing."

"Do you still draw?" Chris asks.

"Sometimes." Eli shrugs. "Not really."

"Me either."

"What do you draw?"

"Mostly design sketches. I used to make dresses for some queens in the area. Then I started doing burlesque and helping people with their costumes. Designing dresses took a back seat. My dream has always been to be a designer." Chris laughs at himself. "While you were watching *SpongeBob*, I was obsessed with *Project Runway*. Mom always made time to watch it with me on the weekends. It was really special."

"I imagine it was."

"She was so upset when I dropped out of school. She's never told me she's disappointed in me. But I know she is."

"How could she be?" Eli asks. He's leaned back in his chair, watching Chris with a drunken, dreamy smile.

"You're sweet," Chris answers, caught in Eli's powerful gaze.

"So are you." Eli blinks and shifts in his seat, setting his empty cup off to the side.

"It's getting chilly now that the sun's gone down." Chris gestures to the gray sky and its fading glow.

"Yeah. Should we open another bottle?" Eli asks.

"Maybe, inside?" They stand together and walk slowly to the door. Chris's stomach rolls with excitement. The hairs on the back of his neck stand on edge. He can feel the warmth of Eli's body as he follows him.

Inside, they stand face to face. An awkward smile plays on his lips as they inch closer together. There's no couch to sit on, no common room where they can pretend they don't share the same unspoken intentions until one of them breaks the barrier with an accidental graze or bump.

"You look cold," Eli says softly.

"I am." Chris is sure his cheeks are blazing from the cold air. Not to mention the nearness of Eli, who spreads his arms open wide.

Chris steps into them without a second thought. He feels the warmth of Eli's embrace instantly as they stand for a moment, unmoving and wrapped up in one another. Eli shifts and presses his soft, fuzzy cheek against Chris's, and he nuzzles into it. The clean musk of Eli's neck is more intoxicating than the two bottles of wine they've shared. Chris squeezes Eli's waist eagerly; Eli responds with his lips on Chris's neck. A charge runs from where lips meet skin, and Chris lets out a little whimper. Eli holds him tighter as his kisses trail up Chris's neck to his ear. He nibbles, tugging gently with his teeth. Another whimper escapes as Chris's cock springs to full attention. Eli presses his body into Chris's, overwhelming his half-drunk senses.

"Wait," he says and pulls away from Eli's kisses. "I don't have any protection."

"Me neither. Believe it or not, this wasn't my intention."

Chris chuckles and relaxes his forehead against Eli's. "In all honesty, I can't say it wasn't mine. I'm terribly unprepared. I've been with one man for a long time. I'm not so good with this sort of thing."

"It's all right," Eli coos in his ear. "We can still cuddle."

"Really?" Chris nearly squeals with excitement. "I have missed cuddling so much." Chris's heart soars. His skin sings.

"How long has it been?"

"I couldn't say. It's been pretty loveless for a while now."

"How anyone could live with you and not hold you every day is beyond me." Eli rocks him in his embrace. Chris settles into it.

Relief from months of longing to be touched and seen washes over him. All of the awkward physical exchanges fall away.

There's more passion in these few moments in Eli's arms than Chris found in years with Tyler.

\*\*\*

*Eli*

Chris takes his hand, leading him to the bedroom. His fingers are smooth yet strong. Eli delights in the sensation of being led by him anywhere, especially to bed. Eli notices the backs of Chris's ears are red and wonders if it's the cold air or the flush of excitement. He's not sure which is affecting him more.

Chris drops his hand and begins working at his own buttons. "You don't mind, do you?" He's almost bashful as he peels the shirt off of his lovely shoulders.

"How could I possibly mind?" Eli steadies his trembling voice. "You're beautiful."

Chris's cheeks color, and he looks away with a humble smile. "I don't know about all that." He dismisses Eli's compliment with an awkward head bob and rolls his twilight-colored eyes.

"You are." Eli slips out of his cardigan and tosses it on the chair behind him. He pulls his t-shirt over his head, and it gets caught on his glasses.

Chris chuckles. "So are you," he says as Eli pulls himself out of the tangle of shirt and glasses.

"Thanks." Eli's never been called beautiful. But somehow, under Chris's gentle, longing gaze, he believes it. It's his turn to blush.

"Come here." Chris extends his hand to Eli, who takes it. He's astounded again at the strength and the softness.

Then they're on the bed, nestled in a pile of pillows and blankets. Chris's skin smells clean with a hint of spice. Most of his torso is as smooth and strong as his hands, aside from the fine reddish-blond hairs sprinkled here and there. He's truly flawless.

Eli explores Chris's back, his shoulders, his arms, running his hands over the length of Chris's stomach again and again, relishing in every impeccable inch.

Chris's hands float over him. His strokes and sighs are almost more than Eli can handle. Their lips meet, soft at first, then eager. Chris clings to him, clutching his cheeks as their tongues dance over parted lips.

Eli strokes the length of Chris's back, delighting in his absolute perfection. He marvels at how cleverly Chris dresses down his Adonis build. He looks amazing in clothes. But nothing could've prepared Eli for how indescribably delicious the man in his arms is. *How anyone could let a man like Chris go?*

He pulls away from Chris's hungry kiss to admire him. The look on his face tells the story of a man nearly starved with desire.

Eli brings his finger to Chris's swollen lips to stop his desperate protest. Chris silently accepts their unspoken agreement and lies against the pile of pillows.

Eli places a chaste and gentle kiss on Chris's lips, then his chin. Working his way down his exposed neck, Eli drags his teeth over Chris's throat, then bites softly along his collar bones. He kisses his shoulders and chest before nibbling on the tiny pearls of his nipples.

Chris gasps and clutches the back of Eli's head. Eli trails his tongue along the bottom of each pec, then down the hard, smooth, rippling plane of his stomach.

A glance lets him see Chris's head thrown back in utter bliss. Eli runs one hand over the bulge straining against Chris's zipper. He tenses, then relaxes into Eli's gentle stroking.

Eli's mouth waters as he traces the length of Chris through his jeans, his hips rolling with each stroke. Eli slowly undoes Chris's button and zipper. Chris's eyes flash open, and his cheeks color even deeper.

Eli smiles in response, and Chris doesn't move to stop him.

His cock springs free from his boxers, beautiful and hard as stone, and Eli wraps his fingers around the smoothest skin he's ever felt. He brushes the tip against his lips. Chris whimpers and shucks off the rest of his pants.

Eli stops, stunned by the image of perfection. The soft curls that surround Chris's shaft are slightly darker and redder than the hair on his head. Eli's never seen a more eager erection or been more eager to taste one. His mouth waters.

As he sucks the tip into his mouth, Chris moans and bucks his hips. Eli works his tongue around the tip, tasting the clear and flavorless drip that he squeezes from the base. Longing for more, he pulls the entire length into his mouth until his nose is buried in the soft, silken hairs.

Eli's own cock jumps as he smells the sweet musk.

He works the length up and down with his mouth and his hands. Chris's moans and rolling hips are his guides. As he moves one hand to cup his lover's warm, fuzzy balls, he trails a finger down to where Chris's ass meets his taint. He knows he's found the sweet spot the moment Chris grips his head and bucks his hips wildly, filling Eli's mouth with his bittersweet cum.

Eli sucks harder, pulling the length of him back fully into his mouth. Chris writhes beneath him, panting wildly. Eli's cock screams for attention as Chris pulls away with a dreamy smile on his lips.

"Do I get to return the favor?" Chris breathes, barely a whisper as he blinks slowly and gives a sexy half smile. Eli imagines what his lover's lips would look like wrapped around Eli's cock and nearly loses his resolve.

Then, remembering the last man he was with, and every man before that—some with, some without protection—he knows he can't risk passing anything on to Chris. Plus, he can't remember the last time his dick worked as well as he'd like it to.

"You already have," Eli says as he pulls himself up alongside Chris, wrapping his arms around Chris's warm, silken torso. "I'd love to just hold you." He presses his lips to Chris's face and gives Chris a gentle squeeze.

Chris looks up, cocking his head to one side. Eli answers, "I haven't been monogamous or made the best choices."

"I understand." Chris nods his acceptance and snuggles into Eli's chest, pulling the blanket over them.

# CHAPTER EIGHT
*Chris*

"Jesus, Chris. That was fucking hot," Bunny exclaims. "You're always beautiful up there, but I can honestly say I've never seen you move like that. What's going on out there on the river?" she teases.

"What do you mean?" Chris asks, fanning himself under the stage lights. He knows exactly what she means, and guilt washes over him.

His last few nights have been filled with Eli's kisses and his embrace. He's never known the kind of attention Eli pays him. He was so young when he started dating Tyler. His lack of experience made him the perfect target for Tyler's narcissistic, one-sided love. Years of giving service blowjobs and passive bottoming left him wondering what all the fuss was about.

He always preferred cuddling to sex and attributed it to what he called his more feminine tendencies. Since meeting Bunny, Olive, and all the other women of Burlesque A La Mode, he's learned that feminine energy is not synonymous with low sex drive. He's found the opposite to be true. His friends are the most feminine and wildly sexual creatures he's ever known. They pour their sexuality into everything they do. These women have found lovers who encourage and celebrate them and their nature.

It seems Eli is doing the same for him. Though he's been guarded in taking his own pleasure, he's been more than generous in giving Chris the sexiest nights of his life. Chris's cock tingles at the thought of Eli's expert tongue and perfect lips doing their magic.

Until his first night with Eli, Chris believed himself to be an expert of fellatio. Now that he's experienced what Eli has to offer, he's not so sure. He's been taking notes in the afterglow, filing away all the tricks Eli's used for the future when he allows Chris to return the many favors he's shared.

"I know what's going on," Olive teases from beside Bunny. Chris's pleasant thoughts are replaced with the heavy weight of his guilt. He steps off the stage, avoiding Olive's conspiratorial grin. "It's him, isn't it?" she asks, raising her eyebrows and nodding her head. "It's the pretty bad boy from the other night."

Chris aches to tell his friends everything about his new affair. He longs to share his excitement. But he's promised to give Eli the time he needs. "What?" He feigns ignorance. "I don't know what you're talking about." He blushes despite his best efforts not to.

Eli *is* the pretty bad boy from the other night. He *is* the reason Chris is moving and feeling the way he does. Flashes of their moments together play out in his mind. Eli's proud grin looking up from yet another rolling orgasm he's given. His sleepy eyes, his soft lips, the smell of his skin.

"You can't hide it." Olive smiles.

"Shit, we can smell it on you." Bunny snorts.

"You're walking a bit taller," Susan offers her two cents. Chris looks around the room, thankful that no one else has taken an interest in his personal life.

"Well," Chris begins, unsure of how to get around this conversation without giving too much away. "You dirty birds might think it's all about sex and pretty boys. But I've got to say, whatever you're seeing, or smelling, in me is most likely the result of newfound freedom."

Olive, Bunny, and Susan exchange looks of disbelief. A grin creeps across Chris's face. "And maybe pretty boys thinking I'm sexy has something to do with it. I mean, I haven't paid much attention to other men for years. Now that I've started, they aren't disappointing me."

"Freedom is a powerful thing," Susan offers.

"That it is," Chris agrees as he snatches his shirt off of the stage floor and shakes it out.

"Whatever *it* is," Bunny says, tapping her pen on the tabletop, "I love it and can't wait to see more."

"Me too," Chris answers, buttoning his shirt and daydreaming about his evening plans. *Maybe tonight's the night.*

He knows Eli wanted to be tested before they became more intimate, and Eli's promised to do it sooner rather than later. But clinics and labs have their own schedules, and they don't take into account budding relationships longing for consummation.

"Are you going up next, Olive?" Bunny asks. Chris is thankful for the distraction. He's unsure of how much longer he can keep his secrets. He can feel Olive watching him and almost hear her thoughts. She knows something is going on.

"I don't have much, but sure." Olive takes the stage and starts talking through her routine with Bunny and Susan.

Chris takes his seat and watches their exchange. The New Year's Eve show is going to be their biggest yet. They're opening with aerialists, calling in all the best performers, and closing with a group routine countdown with full reveals, a balloon drop, and a champagne toast. It's going to be an amazing night. Also, an amazing amount of work. Chris believes in the troupe though. He believes in their ability to make anything happen, especially with Mike and Vic's help.

Both are men driven to give their lovers whatever they want. They've proven to be successful every time. As he thinks about the relationships that he's seen form and grow over the months, he realizes that Tyler was right. This group of people are the reason he grew discontent with his former relationship. They are why he realized he deserved more than what he was getting.

Seeing Mike and Vic here every week, Henri coming from New Orleans with Bridgette whenever she visits or performs, even the memory of Susan's dead husband, has set the bar so high. Their passion and devotion make a person long for the same. Even on their best days, Tyler had been reserved, giving the best gifts along with the smallest bits of love and warmth.

Chris had learned to live off of the crumbs. Seeing how fully the women in his world were loved allowed him to see he could, and should, expect more from his partner.

He knows it's early, possibly too soon. But Eli has what it takes. He loves with abandon. There's more passion in his fingertips than Tyler has in his entire being. Chris has learned more about his body and desire in their few nights together than in all the years he spent with Tyler.

The gratitude and joy he feels for having met Eli is overwhelming. If only he could get Eli to agree to see Olive again.

Eli texts him.

***Hey, I'm off early. Should I meet you at your place?***

Chris looks at Olive, half dancing, half walking across the stage. She sees that he's texting someone and cocks her head as if to ask who. He shrugs. The guilt of his secret weighs heavier by the moment. She smiles and shakes her head, then turns her focus back to her routine.

He wonders if, on some level, she knows what's really going on. Does she somewhere deep down know he's been sleeping with her estranged brother and keeping it from her?

Either way, *he* knows, and it's killing him. Something has to change and soon.

***I'm at practice now. Olive's here if you want to swing by...***

He types the words quickly, then rethinks them. Watching Olive dance and smile, he knows how happy she would be to have her brother back. Thinking of Eli's dark and broken past, his tortured memories, and the blame he places on Olive for it all, Chris knows Eli's answer without hitting send. He deletes it.

***Yes! I'll be home soonish.***

Sent. Despite the guilt he feels over the secret he's keeping, his heart flutters at the thought of spending another night in Eli's arms.

As he watches Olive dance across the stage, he promises to bring her up before Eli seduces all the thoughts out of his head.

*** 

*Eli*

Eli watches Chris suspended in ecstasy: his eyes are closed, and his head has fallen back against the mountain of pillows. A rush of pleasure runs through Eli's body. Of all the people he's been with, he's never known one who falls so fully into his own pleasure. Chris loses himself completely under Eli's touch, and it couldn't please him more. He leaves a trail of kisses up Chris's smooth stomach and chest, then pulls Chris's relaxed body into his embrace. He kisses the top of his head. "I'm off for the next couple days," he says as Chris snuggles into his chest.

"Me too. Should we do something?"

"I was hoping to." Absently, he strokes Chris's shoulder.

"Did you have something in mind?"

"I did. But before I ask, you have to promise to say no if you don't want to. I don't want to pressure you into anything too intense."

"Ooh. I'm intrigued." Chris sits up, leveling his curious gaze on him.

"How do you feel about psychedelics?" Eli makes a face between a grin and a flinch, not sure how Chris will react.

Chris leans against the wall and knits his brow in thought. He crosses his arms over his chest. "I'm not sure. I've never done them before." He looks down at his bare chest and arms, then back to Eli.

"I didn't think so. But I know you drink and smoke. I thought you might be interested in trying it. Maybe?" Eli holds his breath while Chris considers his response.

Shit. He regrets bringing it up. Regrets Chris slipping from his embrace to sit against the wall. He wants him back in his arms, resting against his chest.

"A guy I work with has some acid. I trust him. I know it's good stuff. And the weather is supposed to be awesome for the rest of the week. I thought maybe we could take some and go on a nature hike or something."

A wicked grin spreads across Chris's face. "That sounds like fun. I'll admit I've never thought of tripping before. But with you, I'd probably try anything." He bats his lashes with the suggestion.

Eli slips his arms around him and pulls him close again. "Be careful what you're saying. Don't make promises you can't keep."

"I mean it. You're the most mind-altering substance I've ever known. I feel like I'm under some kind of spell."

"You and me both. The question is, who's doing the casting?"

"I am clearly the innocent in this situation," Chris teases, offering Eli another wide-eyed stare.

"You aren't wrong. I feel like the devil himself with an angel like you in my arms."

"I'm no angel." Chris lays his head on Eli's chest and sighs. He takes his hand and laces their fingers together. After a comfortable silence, he speaks again. "Let's do it. Where should we go?"

Eli takes a deep, shuddering breath. Memories of rose-hued sunsets and fluttering golden leaves fill his mind's eye, along with a front porch piled high with the bounty of the final harvest, and with his family moving about their daily chores, all smiles and laughter.

As the images fade, the words slip out of him on a breath, almost involuntarily. "I wanna go home."

# CHAPTER NINE
*Chris*

"Are you sure this is safe?" Chris asks as he drives slowly down the dirt road. Tree limbs reach and dip, scratching the roof of his car. Late-morning sun filters through bare branches, casting playful shadows all around.

"I've never been hassled up here."

"Do you do this often?"

"I used to. I would hitch rides out this way and wander around the grounds. The doors of the house aren't even locked."

"Really? Did you ever think of staying?" Chris steals a glimpse at Eli, whose gaze is set on the narrow road.

"Yeah." Eli snorts a dry laugh. "It's great in the magical make-believe world I once lived in. But a foolish boy learns quickly he's not prepared to keep a homestead once the temperatures drop below freezing."

"So, you tried it?"

"I did. Back when I turned eighteen. This was where I came once I left foster care. I thought at first that Olive would be here waiting for me. When I found the whole place empty and rotting, I resolved to clean it up and make it my own again. With or without her. I didn't know anything about anything. Summer was all right. There were so many things left behind. Nothing of value really. Blankets, clothes, dishes, pieces of my life. So much of it was broken and torn. The government agents did a real number on the place, then left it to rot when they didn't find any money or drugs hidden away in the house. All the drugs were in the sheds. Who knows where the money was? As far as I know, they never found a penny."

"Oh my god, Eli. That's terrible."

"You're telling me." The trees seem to pull back from the road as it opens to a clearing. A once-adorable two-story farmhouse sits bathed in sunlight on the far end of an open field of tall golden grass. "I cleaned up quite a bit while I was here. Swept all the broken glass and debris. I slept in my parents' bed for weeks before I realized how completely futile it all was. That's when I went to find Olive."

"Are you sure this is such a good idea? I know I sound like a broken record. But this feels like maybe something you should do with Olive."

Eli shoots him a look that says exactly what he thinks about that idea. Then he forces a smile. Chris feels his heart rattle in his chest. He's never been so uncomfortable with Eli. Usually, Eli makes him feel safe and content. He's not himself. At least not the self that he's always let Chris see.

Chris brakes short. Eli rocks forward with a start.

"I don't like this. Not one bit. I think we should go somewhere else." He puts the car in park and turns to face Eli.

Eli's face softens. He turns in his seat and places a heavy hand on Chris's knee. "I'm sorry." He gives a gentle squeeze. "You aren't wrong. There's a lot that needs to happen between Olive and I if we're going to be in each other's lives. But it's not going to be easy. It's going to be a long process. And I'm going to fuck it up. I think that's why I'm so hesitant. I know I'm going to fuck up. I know I'm going to make it difficult for her and everyone involved. That includes you, and I don't want to make things difficult for you. I don't want to show you that side of me. The side Olive brings out."

"I don't understand. None of this was her fault. She suffered too. She's mourned the loss of your family every day of her life. Why can't you two work things out?" Chris's voice trembles on the verge of tears. The day is turning out to be a disaster, and it hasn't even begun. "I hate being stuck in the middle. I hate having you so close and not being able to tell her. Do you know what it's like to be happier than you've ever been in your life and not be able to share it with your closest friends?"

"You're happier than you've ever been?" Eli tilts his chin slightly; his eyes sparkle. A smile plays at the corner of his lips. "Really?"

"Yes, really. Being with you makes me the happiest man alive, and I can't share it with anyone. I hate it." The air in the car warms as the sun breaks over the top of the trees, shining its rays through the windows. Eli sits silent, looking at Chris as though he's seeing him for the first time. Chris's heart is racing as his stomach rolls.

"Because of me?" The disbelief is apparent on Eli's face.

"Yes, because of you."

"You make me happy too," Eli says with a shy smile. "Honestly, I have trouble believing I deserve to be this happy."

"That's silly. Everyone deserves to be happy."

"Yeah." Sadness replaces Eli's shy smile. He sits silent again. "We don't have to do this today. We can go back, order in, and spend the day in bed." His hand moves from Chris's knee, up his thigh, and back down. "And I promise I'll make some time for Olive soon. I forget how hard this must be for you. I know how much you love her."

"And I know how much she loves you."

"I know. I love her too. But it's complicated."

"I understand complicated."

"Let's go," Eli offers, pulling his hand away. Chris notices the cool absence of his touch like a blanket that was snatched off of him while sleeping. He reaches for Eli's hand and holds it in both hands.

"We came all this way. Let's at least walk around some. We'll hold off on the drugs." Chris chuckles and brings the back of Eli's hand to his lips, brushing it with a kiss.

"It is beautiful out here. And this is supposed to be fun."

"Well, let's have some fun, then." Chris shifts into drive and follows Eli's instructions, pulling behind the weathered barn and parking out of sight from anyone who might pull down the road.

***

*Eli*

"Are you sure?" Eli asks, holding the small tab of white on his fingertip. They'd been exploring the woods for over an hour, walking under the shimmering pink and golden canopy. The house and the car and all the bad feelings have evaporated with the unseasonably warm day.

"I am. How long will it last?"

"I'm only giving you half. But it could last for hours."

"Really?" Chris lets out a nervous chuckle. "Now I'm not so sure."

"We don't have to. It'll be dark before we come down."

"We have blankets, right? We can stay in the car if we need to. I've got nowhere to be tomorrow. Do you?"

"The only place I have to be is here with you."

A wicked grin spreads across Chris's face. It's beyond sexy. "Let's do it, then." Eli places the tab on his own tongue and pulls Chris against him, slipping his tongue and the tab into Chris's mouth. They kiss under the rippling leaves. Time stands still as their lips and tongues play, passing the small bitter paper back and forth as it dissolves.

"Your turn," Chris says as he pulls away with a giggle.

Eli places a whole tab and the other half of Chris's on his tongue and raises his brow in expectation.

"How long does it take?"

"About half an hour or so. Come on. I wanna show you something." They walk side by side, boots crunching over dry, crackling leaves and twigs. The paths from Eli's childhood have long since grown over, but the large rocks and twisted trees still serve as landmarks. The moss has grown thicker on the boulders, and the trees have grown taller, stretching through the dense canopy toward their own piece of sunny sky. The sweet and earthy scent of fallen leaves rises up around them. It's heavy and intoxicating.

Eli imagines the perfumed fingers of aroma from cartoons leading them deeper into the woods, away from society and its demands. Away from the real world and into the world of the Fae—a world he'd believed in much longer than he should have, only to find out that these things not only didn't exist but believing in them made him an object of ridicule, disdain, and, at times, fear.

He begins to hear their laughter again as he follows the path his feet still remember. Leaves of gold, brown, and burgundy flutter to the ground. Some spiral fast and sudden, others rock slowly, while others float and spin, caught on the drafts of wind that only they have found.

Birds sing and squirrels titter in the trees, unhappy about the unexpected visitors. Most likely, these woods haven't seen people since his last visit.

"What's that?" Chris calls from behind him. His words are watery and miles away. Eli turns to answer. Chris's golden-red hair glows like a halo. His eyes are wide, his lips parted with a smile of expectation. "Do you hear it?" he whispers, holding his hand up for quiet. It seems the animals understand: the woods go silent. Even the breeze shimmering in the leaves slows to a hush.

"Are you fucking magic or something?" Eli giggles and covers his mouth for quiet. "How did you do that?"

"How'd I do what?"

"You made the woods be still. How?"

"I don't know what you're talking about. I heard a rustle. Now it's gone."

"'Cause you stopped it all when you raised your hand. Are you the king of the Fae?" Eli steps closer to Chris, taking in every detail of his face. His smooth, freckled skin, his sparkling eyes, the black of his oversized pupils, and the rosy pink of his lips. Eli's overwhelmed as he brushes Chris's cheek. "Are you here to take me away?"

Chris cocks his head and wrinkles his brow. "I thought that was your job?" he teases.

"Can I kiss you?"

"Please do."

Eli places one hand on either side of Chris's face. His skin is impossibly soft. Pressing his lips to satiny bliss, Eli loses himself in the kiss of his fairy king. "You should have wings. Beautiful monarch wings that sparkle in the sun," Eli says against Chris's mouth as a giggle rises out of his belly.

He drinks more of Chris's kisses before taking his hand and leading him through the woods toward his original destination. Chris's laughter follows him as they crash through the undergrowth, clearing their own path.

Approaching their destination, Eli turns to see Chris watching the trees with a look of wonder. "We're almost there."

Chris blinks and looks at Eli as if for the first time. "I think I already am."

# CHAPTER TEN
*Chris*

"Come on, right through here." Eli's grin borders on manic as he looks over his shoulder while pushing aside the overgrown brush. The leaves shimmer and sparkle all around. Patches of sunlight dance at his feet. Chris catches the scent of Eli on the gentle breeze that pulls at his hair and clothes.

"What is it? Where are we?" Chris's voice sounds otherworldly, like it's coming from someplace outside of him.

"We're here. We made it through the wilds to the land of the Fairy King. I've brought you home, my liege, to sit on your throne." Eli's laughter ripples around him, then stops suddenly. He brings his finger to his lips and smiles behind it, nodding his head toward an orchard that has grown thick and wild over the years.

Among the trees laden with fruit stand two young doe. They've dropped their apples to watch the intruders. Their ears twitch. Their black eyes stare, unblinking. Chris stands behind Eli, in awe of the creatures. They must've been so engrossed in their feast they didn't hear Eli and Chris tromping through the woods. They're almost close enough to touch. He holds his breath for what seems like an eternity. Eli giggles softly. The doe take off in the opposite direction, white tails bobbing, and Chris lets out the breath he's been holding.

"Did you see that?" Eli asks.

"How could I miss them?"

"I wanted to make sure they were really there. You see a lot of crazy stuff in these woods. Especially tripping balls. What'd ya think?" Eli spins in place with his arms spread wide open. "This is where I should have grown up. With the trees, and the deer, and the apples, and the pears."

Chris shakes his head at the almost rhyme and walks toward the fruit trees. "This *is* magical."

"Isn't it? You want an apple?" Eli runs to the nearest tree and pulls a small pinkish fruit from a lower limb, and two more fall to the ground with solid plunks. He smiles like a little boy and grabs them off the ground. "Watch this." He starts juggling the apples, spinning in circles and throwing them higher and higher. He snatches one out of the air with his teeth, catches the other two in each hand, and gives a grand bow.

Joy bubbles around Chris. His laughter sings in the trees. "That's amazing. Where did you learn that?"

"This place used to be a circus from time to time. There were lots of people to teach me weird tricks." He hands an apple to Chris and walks between the trees. "This isn't what I wanted to show you though."

"Really? Because this is amazing."

"Just wait."

Chris holds the apple in his hand, marveling at the texture of the fruit. It's not smooth and waxy like one from the supermarket. Its thin skin is bumpy and several shades of yellow and pink. He lifts it to his nose and smells its sweetness. Then he notices the heavy scent of all the apples rotting on the ground under their feet. It's overwhelming and beautiful. His mouth waters, but he can't bring himself to take a bite. Suddenly the idea of chewing is the most foreign thing he can imagine. He follows Eli's squishing, crunching steps through the trees to the other side of the orchard.

"What do you think?" Eli says with more pride than he's ever shown.

Chris looks in the direction he's pointing and fails to see anything more than a large patch of brambles. "It's great." He feels the words drop from his lips, as heavy as the lie they are. His head feels larger than it should. Eli moves before him, slow and fast all at once. He's distorted one moment, then crystal clear the next. Hundreds of birds are perched in the trees, singing in unison. "I don't see it," he admits, stepping closer to Eli.

"Come down here on your knees." Eli drops to his knees in the sticky, mulchy dirt.

Chris settles down beside him, the smell of the rotten fruit even stronger. He looks again in the direction Eli is pointing. A fat ray of sun settles across an opening in the thicket. He begins to see the intentional shape of it and recognizes it for what it is. "Is this a fort?"

"It's better. It's a living fort."

"What does that mean?" Chris asks, settling onto his heels, searching Eli's face for answers.

"You use branches from a willow tree. Plant them in the ground and weave them together. Do it right and it grows and gets stronger every year. This one's been left alone for so long, it's not as nice as it could be. But it's still standing. Wanna go in?"

"I do." Chris drops to his hands and crawls toward the small doorway. Pausing before entering, he turns to see Eli watching him. "Are you coming with me? I feel like I might disappear if I go alone."

"Want me to go first?" Eli offers, crawling up beside him.

"Maybe." Chris settles back onto his heels. He brushes black dirt and bits of rotted fruit from his hands. Eli nods, then crawls through the darkened opening. Chris is back on his hands and knees, crawling over the loamy dirt like a child. He passes through the doorway and meets Eli in a surprisingly roomy space. Light filters down through the tightly woven walls. Eli is leaning back on his elbows, stretched to his full length with room to spare. It's warm and dry and smells of sunbaked hay. Chris sits with legs crossed beneath him. The sounds and smells from the orchard are muted. He hears his own breath, his pulse in his ears. "I feel strange."

Eli sits up quickly and takes his hand. "Good strange or bad strange?"

Chris looks down at his hand in Eli's. The warmth of his touch spreads from their hands, up his arms, and throughout his body. He wants to curl up in Eli's arms in the safety of their little grass hut. "Good strange. I think?" His heart and mind are racing. "But will you hold me just the same?"

Eli pulls him into his arms. Chris melts against him, burying his face in Eli's neck. He feels Eli's blood pulsing against his lips as Chris kisses and nuzzles him, wishing he could shrink small enough to climb in his pocket. "I want to be as close to you as I can get," he whispers against Eli's throat. The soft hairs of his beard feel like heaven against Chris's face. The musky sweet smell of Eli's skin is exactly what he needs. "I don't want to leave."

"We don't have to."

"I know. But I don't think that I ever want to leave. I don't know if I can. I think we might be stuck here forever." Chris clings to Eli's jacket and presses his face harder against Eli's skin. "I don't think I like this anymore. Everything is too much."

"Hey, it's okay," Eli coos in Chris's ear as he strokes his back. He kisses the top of his head and rocks him gently. "Nothing has changed since earlier today." He pushes the hair away from Chris's forehead. "The sun is still shining." He pauses. "The sky's still blue." Another pause. "The leaves are still falling." He sighs. "I'm still here with you."

Eli's simple rhyme tickles something deep within Chris. A half-hearted chuckle grows into wild rolling laughter. He pulls away from Eli's embrace and rocks on the edge of hysteria, rubbing his eyes and face with his hands. Once he's able to catch his breath, he asks, "What was that?" Then he levels his gaze on Eli, who's leaning back on his elbows again, grinning like the Cheshire Cat.

"What was what?"

"Your little poem there. What was it?"

"Magic words." Eli shrugs with a sad smile and lowers himself onto his back, resting his head on his hands. "Did they work?"

Chris settles himself alongside Eli, resting his head on his chest. "Yeah. I think they did."

"Good." Eli pulls him closer with one arm, then brushes Chris's shoulder absently with his thumb. "Olive and I used to make rhymes together. She was much better at it. Whenever I was angry or sad about something, she would come up with the silliest ones. Her magic words always worked. I used to lie in bed at night and try to remember them, but I never could. They were gone. Disappeared like everything else." His voice is soft and ragged, rumbling gently in his chest.

"I'm so sorry, babe. I can't even begin to imagine what that was like for you." Chris listens to the rhythmic beat of Eli's heart.

Eli sighs. "We built this fort together. Well, she really built it. I carried sticks and watched." He scoffs and shifts, squeezing Chris with one arm. "I fucking worshiped her. She was my best friend. Shit, my only friend. We did everything together. Then she was gone. Everything was gone." Eli's voice raises slightly with each word. "I was so alone. I was alone, and I was scared, and I was just a boy, and no one gave a fuck about me. Weird fucking little kid that scared the other kids with his stories and drawings. They sent me to so many places. Doctors and schools and churches. God, the fucking churches."

Chris can feel the tension in Eli's body. He hears Eli's heart race in his chest. The curious fear he felt earlier, before Eli's magic words, is replaced with real and visceral fear. The kind that has him wondering how he can get himself and his lover out of the terrible situation they put themselves in. How can he possibly calm Eli down when his own mind is slipping away?

"I love her so much. And I hate her. I hate her for leaving me. When they would send me to church, they would tell me to pray. So, I would. You know what I prayed for?" Eli sits up quickly; Chris does the same. They're sitting face to face in their small dome of shadow and light. Eli's eyes are wild, his lips pulled up in a grimace. "I prayed for her. I prayed that she would find me and bring me home." He shakes his head with a dry laugh, then looks around as though he's seeing everything for the first time. His irises are barely slivers around the black, watery depths of his pupils. "I'm sorry, Chris. I have to get out of here. I've got to go. Go somewhere. Anywhere but here."

"It's okay. We can go. I think I can drive. We can at least get out of the fort and get some fresh air." Whatever high Chris was feeling evaporates as he realizes what kind of shape Eli is in. He wonders how much of his half-dose he actually got from their kiss. He shakes the cobwebs from his head and moves to follow Eli out into the sun. Though he feels like he's moving through water, Chris clings to one thought as if it's a life raft.

*Keep Eli safe.*

\*\*\*

*Eli*

*Have to get away. Have to get away.* "I'm so sorry, Chris. It's not supposed to be like this. Are you okay? Do you need me? Do you need me to say magic words? Do you need me to say them for you?" Chris squints as he crawls out of the fort. Eli lowers himself to meet him. "I'll find them for you," Eli says. "I'll pluck them out of the sky. The words, the words. I need the words for you."

Chris stands and offers Eli his hand. As he moves to take it, Chris's fingers glow with a dozen tiny auras. His gaze moves from Chris's hand up to his face. He's beautiful and glowing in the light of the sun. The trees are singing. The wind is everywhere.

"I don't. I don't have them.", Eli spits as his heart breaks into a million pieces over his failure. Chris smiles a benevolent smile down at him. Eli snatches his hand quickly and kisses it over and over. He closes his eyes and dissolves into the kisses, melting.

"C'mon, Eli. Let's get out of here. Let's go home." Chris tugs at his hand.

"Yeah. Home. I need to get home." Eli pulls his hand free and charges into the brush. The careful steps and laughter from before are a distant memory as he runs, heart pounding, through the woods. He's barely aware of the branches slapping his face and shoulders or the thorns and sticks that drag and pull at his pant legs.

Home. He has to get home. There's someone chasing him, shouting his name. He pushes harder, faster. He'll be there soon. Tumbling lights and colors rush past as he hurries on. His body, his mind, his being—it all trails behind him like the tail of a comet. There's only one thing, one driving force.

To get home.

He's so close, he can smell it. He can feel it in his bones. Home is on the edge of the clearing. So close.

"Eli," Chris shouts behind him.

It doesn't matter. Nothing matters. Nothing but home.

Home.

The picture of joy.

Two stories painted sunflower yellow with red shutters, stained glass sparkling from within, a front porch filled with flowers where wind chimes sing in the breeze.

Bees and butterflies. Mom and Dad. Mom's smile. Dad's song. Eli's heart is full to bursting. He sees it all. He can smell the stain on the porch, the fresh-cut grass, the lemon balm, and basil. He can hear the fiddle, its strings singing their playful tune.

Then CRACK. Then silence.

The taste of blood.

It's not his own.

His mom wails, she screams. She holds him tight, brushing the sticky, wet hair from his face. Phantom hands pull him away.

He fights and screams and falls to his knees.

"Eli. Eli. It's me. It's Chris." The kindest face he's ever seen hovers above him. He blinks and shakes his head. The house stands behind Chris, decrepit and gray.

No fragrant blooms, no happy songs. Years of nature and neglect wearing away everything his parents built.

Dead vines cling to the walls.

Chris holds his shoulders firmly, his brow knit with concern.

Eli shakes his head and tries to focus on Chris's face.

"I can still taste his blood. His blood was on my tongue. It was on my face and in my hair. They didn't even let me clean myself. I sat for hours with his blood dried on my skin."

Eli closes his eyes and slumps, held up by Chris's strong grip on his shoulders.

"I don't want this," he mumbles as Chris's trusted hands become that of a stranger. He shrugs them off violently. "I don't want this," he screams.

Then he's on his feet and running again. Running away from the pain, from the memories. He hears his name in the distance but knows it's only the past screaming again.

Seeking safety, he pushes through the broken door of a medicine shed. The tables, once lined up neatly in double rows, are turned and broken. Clods of dirt and roots lie dead and dried.

Eli wanders down the row, looking for a safe place to hide. Light from the open door shines along the aisle. He's a child again, walking down the aisle of a church, pews on either side, strange faces nodding as he passes.

They're singing a sad hymnal about death and sin. The smile on the preacher is at least a mile wide. It looks as though he could swallow Eli whole.

Eli's heart races. He knows what he's supposed to do, what all the strange faces want from him. If he doesn't do what they want, they'll surely feed him to the preacher.

But none of it makes sense. How could he be a sinner when he doesn't know how to sin? How can he be bad when he's only ever been happy?

Was it his fault his parents were gone?

That Olive wasn't coming for him?

Was it his sin that made everything fall apart?

The preacher, in his suit and tie, places his hands on Eli and begins to pray loudly in a foreign tongue, like nothing he's ever heard before. As he prays, the song from the pews swells. The people sing loud and fast, clapping and howling.

"Save this boy. Save this boy," they shout in unison.

"Cleanse the evil from this boy's soul. Lord, bring this lost little lamb back into your flock. Help us guide him in your loving light. Save him from the fiery pits of hell and Satan's ways. He's but an innocent boy led astray by the evil of his parents."

The preacher prays. Eli struggles against his grip, but he's pulled firmly into his arms, then pinned to the ground, still struggling.

"Hey, hey. Eli." A calm voice breaks through, along with the light from the doorway. Eli stares in shock at the sunlit dirt. Strong arms hold him tightly against a solid chest. "Shh. It's okay. It's me. It's Chris." The gentle voice calls him back. "I've got you. You're safe."

Eli crumbles into the familiar embrace. He shudders and sobs heavily. "I'm sorry. I'm sorry," he whimpers and rolls into the warmth of Chris's chest.

"It's okay. It's okay." Chris's lips are against his ear as he gathers him closer, pulling him into his lap. Eli feels safe. He feels comfort. As Chris rocks him gently, a dam within him breaks. Tears flow like a river. His breath shudders in his chest. "You're okay," Chris half whispers. "You're okay."

"I don't want to be here anymore," Eli says weakly.

"Let's go, then." Chris's arms slip from his waist. A chill creeps around Eli in the absence of Chris's warm embrace.

Eli's face and neck are soaked with tears. Chris offers a hand and helps him to his feet. "Are you sure? Can you drive?" Eli sniffles, feeling more like a child than a man.

"Yeah. Are *you* sure?"

"I don't know. Maybe." Eli shrugs. The air shimmers around him. Chris's hand is like an anchor to reality. "I don't know what I want." The sun is sinking lower in the afternoon sky as they step out of the shed. "What time is it?" he asks, squinting and shivering, overwhelmed by everything.

Chris pulls his phone from his back pocket and glances at it. "It's past four."

"How is that even possible?"

"It'll be dark soon. What do you say?"

"Let's get out of here." Eli shudders, his mind still racing.

The air around him feels like it's pulling him back, like the ghosts of his parents are reaching for him, begging him to stay and put right what was destroyed. To fix what was broken.

As he takes one more look to the dilapidated house, he swears he sees young Olive peeking around the back of the house, beckoning him to another adventure.

*Fix what's broken.*

*Fix what's broken.*

The thought stays with him as they pull away from the house, down the dirt road, away from his past and on to his future.

# CHAPTER ELEVEN
*Chris*

"I'm sorry." Eli breaks the silence that's followed them since Chris led him shaking and disoriented to the car.

"It's okay." Chris waves away his apology, then returns his hand to the steering wheel. Luckily the sun is setting behind them. He's struggling to not watch it in the rearview mirror. The colors are so bright and fantastical. Though he managed to rein in his high to help Eli, there is still a watery, crystalline quality to the world. Now that they are safe and sound in his car, he's able to enjoy the beauty of it all. "Do you want to talk about it?"

"Not beyond apologizing. That was supposed to be fun. And it wasn't."

"Parts of it were." Chris shrugs.

"Yeah. Parts of it." Eli sighs and slumps low in his seat, his face turned toward the window.

The car grows eerily silent as Eli seems to fall into himself. The highway stretches before them, empty save for the shadows dancing with the setting sun. "You want to put on some music?" Chris hands Eli his phone. He looks grateful for the distraction. A mellow song with a classic sound fills the car. It's a song Chris has never heard, though it somehow feels familiar. "I like this." He begins rocking with the music, bobbing his head. A pleasant warmth creeps into the dark and worried corners of his mind.

"I thought you would." Eli taps his hand on his knee with the beat. "It's called 'California Sway' by Smooth Hound Smith. It makes me think of you."

Chris steals a quick glance Eli's way. He's more relaxed than he was even moments before, smiling even. It seems the drugs might be dissipating, and he's beginning to put some of the afternoon behind him. "Now I like it even more."

They move down the golden-lit highway, immersed completely in the music. Each song that plays after the first is a perfect blend of mellow, sexy, and fun.

Chris finds himself wondering if they'd had music back in the woods, would things have turned out differently? It could have been a different kind of day, perhaps mimicking the mood of the car. He has a hard time believing it was only an hour ago he was chasing Eli through the woods, screaming after him.

As the sun dips lower, it paints the sky with orange, pink, and purple. Chris catches himself staring into his rearview mirror instead of watching where he's going. "I need to pull over," he says abruptly.

Eli sits up quickly with a look of concern as Chris slows to a stop on the shoulder of the empty highway. "Are you okay?" he asks.

"Yeah. I need to watch the sunset though." Chris laughs at the absurdity of it. "I can't focus on driving while the sky looks like this." He gestures to the setting sun.

"All right." Eli opens his door and steps outside.

Chris follows, his heart again racing in his chest. They stand side by side, leaning against the trunk. The colors in the sky are indescribable, like the largest, most beautiful watercolor he's ever seen. The sun slips closer to the horizon, a perfect glowing orb of salmon-colored light. Chris wishes he could contain its beauty somehow. He wants to take it home and frame it on his wall, to never forget.

But sunsets are fleeting things, impossible to truly capture. Sure, he could take a picture, but it would never compare to the immensity of the sky and all its grandeur.

Eli leans his shoulder against Chris's. The sensation of their bodies touching is the most pleasant shock to his already overwhelmed system.

He searches for Eli's hand while his face is still turned to the setting sun. Their bare palms and fingers laced together send an erotic thrill through Chris.

Though the soft wind chills his face, the warmth from Eli's hand has him glowing from the inside. He turns toward him. Eli's huge pupils are staring with rapture at him instead of the setting sun.

"I need more of you," he barely whispers.

\*\*\*

The room smells clean despite the aged linens and worn carpet. Chris's eyes take a moment to adjust to the dim yellow light. The lady at the front desk insisted they take the double queen instead of the single king that was also available. Midwestern "nice" goes only far enough to welcome two gay men to the hotel, but not enough to accept they are indeed going to share a bed.

The walls and ceiling seem too close and confined compared to the wide-open sky and rustling trees where they spent their day. As Chris inspects the small but tidy room, he's almost forgotten what brought them here.

"Look what I stole for us," Eli whispers excitedly, dropping two oranges on the bed. The fruits' bright orange and yellow stand out starkly against the mossy-green duvet. The innocence of Eli's wicked glee over "stealing" fruit from the bowl in the lobby is undeniably cute. Chris takes a moment to fully appreciate Eli's childish grin before turning the deadbolt in the door.

"Those look amazing." Chris slips off his shoes and drops onto the bed. The fruit bounces beside him as Eli follows his lead.

"They are going to be." Eli plucks an orange up and rolls it in his palms. "Stolen fruit tastes the best."

92

Chris opens his mouth to tell Eli the fruit was there for the taking, then decides against it, picking up his own orange instead. The scent permeates the room as Eli bites into the thick peel. Chris's mouth waters instantly. He bites down on his own. The citrus oil spritzes his cheeks and nose. They sit cross-legged, facing one another, completely engrossed in their oranges, enveloped in the aroma and the sticky sweetness of the juice as it runs down their fingers. Chris pops one of the sparkling segments in his mouth and loses himself in the flavor. He's never chewed so slowly in his life. There's an ecstasy in eating he's never known. Before he's ready for more, the orange is gone. He's left with sticky, empty hands and the desire for another. Then he notices Eli with the same disappointment written on his face.

Chris crawls over the cast-off peels and presses his lips to Eli's. He smells like citrus, wind, and the woods. Eli's taken off guard at first, then brings his hands to Chris's cheeks, drinking his kisses. Chris vibrates with excitement and begins pulling at Eli's clothes. "I need you. I don't think I've ever needed anything this badly in all my life." Chris's voice feels detached again, coming from someplace other than his mouth.

Eli begins tearing at his own shirt. Once free, he goes to work undressing Chris. Bare-chested, they lie together on the pillows, tangled in each other's embrace. Their tongues dancing, lips sucking.

Their crushing need is all that exists as they cling to one another.

Boldly, Chris reaches for Eli's belt. Up to this point he's only received pleasure from Eli, who insisted on keeping his pants on. But this moment demands more. It demands every inch of their bodies to meet.

Eli's eyes snap open. He lays a hand over Chris's to stop him but begs with his gaze. He pleads without words. With a gentle nod, Eli releases his hand, telling him all he needs to know.

Eli is clean, and they are safe to do what they will. Chris wonders for the briefest of moments why he hadn't shared the news, but it's not the time to stop and ask why. Now is all about their skin and their bodies. It's about coming together and feeling everything.

Eli's pants are gone, and Chris slips out of his own. They are back in their embrace, lips dancing, hands exploring. Chris's cock strains against the taut fabric of his boxers. He presses against Eli, then slips his hand down over Eli's boxers and cups the heaviness of his thick, weighty cock. His taint twitches with excitement as he realizes how close he is to experiencing that thickness firsthand.

Eli lets out a low groan, and Chris's mouth waters. He tugs at Eli's boxers, revealing his cock in all its uncircumcised glory. "Oh my," Chris breathes.

Lowering his head, he breathes in Eli's earthy musk mingling with the lingering citrus from his hands. His own cock pulses as he wraps his hand around the full girth of Eli's. He pulls back the foreskin and nudges the glistening head with his nose.

He looks to Eli, whose eyes are closed, his head resting on the pillow as he strokes Chris's thigh. Eli grips Chris's ass as he pulls the plump, juicy head into his mouth and sucks. The taste of Eli's skin mixed with the orangey sweetness is overwhelming.

Chris pushes his ass into Eli's grip, then works his mouth around Eli's cock. He cups Eli's heavy, fuzzy balls in one hand and strokes his length with the other while licking and sucking at the head. The sound of Eli's moans is driving him to madness.

Eli pulls away suddenly. "Not yet." He sighs. "Come up here."

Chris turns his body and wriggles out of his boxers in one swift movement, coming face to face with Eli. He pulls Eli's mouth to his in a soft and searching kiss that seems to go on for an eternity as they sink into the pillows together.

Every inch of their nudity is pressed together in a glorious union. They seem to stretch on forever. Chris grinds against Eli, eager and unashamed. The heat of their cocks rocking and rubbing together is a delicious sensation.

Eli squeezes him hard against his chest as they grind their dicks together until a warm spurt wets them both. Eli slides his hand between them and begins stroking Chris, using his cum as lube. Chris shakes with an orgasm that matches the intensity of their day. His body shivers in Eli's embrace.

Eli presses his lips to Chris's forehead. "I'm sorry. It's been a while." He chuckles.

Chris takes a deep shuddering breath. "Don't be. We've got all night."

***

*Eli*

Standing at the window, Chris sleeping peacefully behind him, Eli watches the inky river rippling with the small city's orange and yellow lights. He leans on the sill, cold glass against his bare shoulder. He considers the day's events with embarrassment and shame. He planned to show Chris a magical time in the woods. Instead, he had a mental breakdown, forcing Chris to play nanny for Eli's broken inner child.

Chris stirs and sits up. He blinks his puffy eyes and scrunches his face in confusion. His thick shock of hair is perfectly mussed. Eli's stomach flips with a delicious excitement at the sight of him awake and bare-chested. "What's up?"

"Couldn't sleep."

"Come back to bed. It's cold without you."

Eli takes another moment to admire Chris's sleepy smile and silky skin bathed in the soft light from outside. He remembers the way those lips looked stretched around his cock and lets the curtain fall open. Then he's back under the covers, pulling Chris's warm body against his. Though the acid wore off hours ago, the feeling of Chris back in his arms has a narcotic effect of its own.

Their hands are hungry travelers as Eli and Chris explore every inch of each other. Eli marvels at the smoothness of Chris's body and the strength of his embrace. There's a purity in every kiss, a desire Eli has never known. He loses himself in a lush cloud of bliss as they tumble among soft blankets and filtered light.

"I want all of you," Chris whispers against his ear. He moves slowly, hovering, leaving a trail of kisses from Eli's ear, down his neck, and over his chest. He nips at one nipple, then the other, sucking and kissing each one. He nuzzles his face in the thick hair on Eli's chest and moves down his stomach, leaving kisses all the way down.

Eli lies there, stunned by the attention, savoring every sensation. Chris moans as he comes upon Eli's throbbing cock. He sucks the head into his mouth sloppily while stroking the base. He moves lower to suck his balls: first one, then the other, and trying for both. He moves lower still, pulling the loose skin of Eli's taint into his warm, wet mouth, all the while stroking Eli's cock.

Eli rocks with the rhythm of Chris's strokes, dangerously close to coming.

As Chris's tongue dips lower, a shock of pleasure runs the length of Eli's spine. Chris squeezes his cock, flicking his tongue over Eli's hole. With another moan, Chris lowers himself onto his stomach, pulls at Eli's hips, and buries his face in Eli's ass.

Chris groans and slurps hungrily, grinding his cock into the mattress. Eli can't recall a time he'd ever been so passionately devoured. The thrill of Chris's desire is almost more than he can bear. He tries to pull away, not wanting to come, but Chris holds tight, gripping Eli's hips with another moan that vibrates over his tongue, against Eli's ass.

Then he raises up and pulls Eli over his thighs, his cock nudging Eli's ass eagerly. "Can I fuck you?" Chris's voice is rough, hungry.

Eli's heart races, and his cock throbs in Chris's tight grip. He pushes himself against the stiffness of Chris's erection. Eli reaches for his wallet, fumbling in the dark for a condom. He sits up and rolls the slippery latex down Chris's eager cock, then Chris pushes him lightly back against the pillows.

He pulls Eli's thighs over his own and presses his swollen head gently against Eli's hole. Using one hand, he makes small circles around the rim with the slightest pressure. With his other, he strokes Eli's cock with featherlight caresses.

Eli melts into the sensation, giving himself completely to Chris.

He sighs and moves with the soft rhythm. Chris eases himself deeper still, and Eli pushes into it. He grinds, craving more of him. He shudders as Chris enters him completely.

Chris grips Eli's cock and grinds. Fully inside him, he bucks his hips, rocking Eli to the core. He pumps slowly, matching the same pace with his strokes of Eli's cock.

Pure pleasure courses through Eli's body as Chris quickens his thrusts. He grips Eli's hips and pulls him down almost roughly onto him, then pulls out slowly, only to spear him again with another rough thrust.

Eli's cock bounces freely, slapping his stomach as Chris holds his hips, moving his body up and down at his will. Then he's stroking the outer length of Eli's thighs with his hands, rolling his hips, slowing his thrusts.

A long, slow moan escapes Eli's throat. He vibrates with each pump from Chris's cock. As his moan grows louder, Chris holds tightly to his hips, digging his fingers in. He quickens his thrusts again, bouncing Eli's ass up and down his cock. Eli cries out, his own cock throbbing and pulsing with ecstasy. Chris grips him and strokes Eli until his cum spurts warm and wet over his stomach. On the next breath, Chris thrusts deeply, shaking and quivering with his own climax.

Moments later, they're tucked comfortably together under the blankets. Eli holds Chris to his chest, his messy hair tickling his nose. He breathes in the clean, warm scent of him as he squeezes him closer. Chris mumbles something incoherent and snuggles deep.

At that moment, Eli realizes he's never been happier than he is with Chris in his arms. He hasn't known a joy so pure in all of his adult life.

It's heartbreaking and thrilling all at once.

And so, he resolves to do whatever it takes to make Chris happy and keep him in his life.

# CHAPTER TWELVE
*Chris*

"I'm not sure how to say this." Chris shifts where he stands as he hands beer bottles to Olive.

Her big mossy eyes narrow. "What are you talking about?" She chuckles, taking the bottles and placing them in the open cooler.

"I've been keeping something from you. It's a big something, so I understand completely if you'll be angry. I would be angry too. In fact, I am angry. I'm so angry with myself I don't know what to do or say."

Olive slides the cooler door shut and turns to give Chris her full attention. She crosses her arms over her chest and leans against the glass. "What could be that big?"

Chris lets out a long sigh and leans against the counter, facing Olive. They aren't scheduled to open for over an hour. He wonders if it's enough time for her to wrap her mind around what he's about to say. If it's enough time for her to forgive him.

The backs of his ears are hot, and there's a lump in his throat that he can't swallow down. "First, you have to understand I didn't want to hurt you. The last thing I would ever want to do is hurt you." Chris shifts nervously from one foot to the other.

"Of course you wouldn't." Olive shakes her head, looking even more concerned. "But you are starting to scare me. What's going on?"

"I've been seeing Eli." The words tumble out of his mouth as if on their own. He feels his cheeks blaze, and he looks away from Olive, unable to make eye contact.

"What?" She sounds truly confused, at a loss for any words other than, "What do you mean?"

He steals a glance her way. She's shaking her head subtly, her brow knit with dismay.

"I've been dating him." He cringes as shock registers on her face. "I've been seeing him exclusively for weeks. We've spent almost every night together since it began."

"Why wouldn't you tell me?" Olive continues to shake her head, her shoulders slumping.

"He asked me not to." Chris looks at the ground.

"Why would he do that? Why would you?" Her voice rises, trembling slightly. She drops her hands to her sides and begins pacing.

"He's not in the best place, mentally. There's so much he has to work out. Stuff you have to work out together."

"How are we supposed to do that if he won't see me? If *you* keep us apart?" Her voice is bordering on shrill as she moves quickly from behind the bar.

Chris has never seen her so agitated. In fact, he's seen her dismiss verbal abuse with patience. He's watched her accept the loss of the man she loved with grace.

He's never known her to be anything but calm and understanding in even the worst situations. But as she's pacing the length of the empty Speakeasy, muttering under her breath, he sees a new side of her. One that's desperate and angry.

"Do you have any idea how long I've looked for him? How many hours of my life I've spent searching the internet? Obituaries? Inmate listings? Fruitless Google searches? I've cried myself to sleep more times than I haven't for losing him. And here you are, my *best friend*, fucking him every night in the home that I gave you."

She stands on the other side of the bar, her mouth set with anger, her eyes wet with tears. "How could you do this to me? I understand it from him. But you? You know how worried I've been since we saw him last. Since I saw him last." She spits out the last words and turns on her heel, stalking toward the office.

"Olive, wait," Chris calls after her.

She stops but doesn't turn back. Her hands are balled in fists, her head is down, shoulders up tightly.

"I'm so sorry." Chris moves from behind the bar, approaching her slowly. "He begged me not to tell you. He said he wasn't ready."

"You could've told me. At least so I wouldn't worry," she says softly, still looking away.

"Would that have been enough?" Chris asks timidly.

She lets out a long, slow breath and relaxes her shoulders, then turns to face him. Tears run down her cheeks. She presses her lips together and shakes her head before her sobs break loose.

"Why doesn't he want me?" She all but crumbles where she stands. Chris hurries to hold her up, hugging tightly, begging her forgiveness without words. "I miss him so much."

"He misses you too. He does want you. But he's..." Chris rocks her gently. "He's broken, Olive. And he's the only one who can pick up the pieces."

"I'm broken too," she whimpers into his chest. "We could pick up our pieces together. We could help each other."

Vic appears in the hallway, worry written over his handsome face. He charges toward them—Olive's golden knight there to protect her.

"Olive, what's wrong?"

She steps away from Chris and turns to Vic, who wraps her up in his strong arms. "It's Eli," she squeaks before another round of sobs breaks free.

Vic looks over her head at Chris, raising one eyebrow in a silent question.

"I've found him," Chris answers shamefully.

"What do you mean you found him? Is he okay?" Vic asks while stroking Olive's back as she sobs into his chest.

Chris nods, about to speak.

"He's fine. He doesn't want me," Olive breaks in, sounding more like a petulant child than the refined woman Chris has come to know and love.

Vic looks confused and beside himself with his inability to help.

"He does though, Olive," Chris tells her. "That's what I was trying to tell you. He's ready to see you."

Olive sniffles and stands with her face buried in Vic's chest for what feels like an eternity. Then she turns with a shy smile, wiping at the tears on her cheeks. "Really?" She sniffs again.

"Yeah, really." Chris nods.

"*Really,* really? When?" Olive's shy smile grows to her full megawatt grin.

"You tell me," Chris answers. "He's at work now, but he's off tomorrow all day."

"Tomorrow, then. Or tonight. When is he off? Where does he work? You have to tell me everything you know. Well maybe not *everything.*" She laughs her big, hearty laugh and hurries past Chris back to work, leaving them standing in her wake.

"I'll text him and see. I bet he'll want to wait until tomorrow. He's closing tonight." Chris sends a quick message.

"That's okay. We're closing too. He can come over after. We'll still be here."

Chris's phone pings almost immediately. "He said he'll call when he's off."

***

*Eli*

Eli stands on the corner down the street from the Speakeasy. After a relatively tame night at work, he took his time. A long shower, a couple of shots at the bar, and a slow walk led him here. As he nears the building, he considers his current circumstance.

He thinks of the happiness he feels with Chris. The warmth and safety he's known in his arms. He reminds himself of the promises he made since their day trip: to put serious effort into building a healthy relationship with Olive. He promised not only Chris but himself as well.

In the many hours he's spent with his thoughts, reflecting on all the demons that made themselves known during his trip back home, he realized that Olive is the missing link to his family and the happiness he once felt with them.

She's all that's left of the life he convinced himself was make-believe over all of his years of searching.

Eli moves slowly, searching for the right mindset for his reunion with his sister. Aside from their most recent meeting, they've all ended the same way. With tears and shouting, with Olive begging him to try harder, and him blaming every wrong thing that ever happened in his life on her.

The fallout occurred only three times over the years. But every time, it cut as deeply as the day he was taken from his family. The day she was nowhere to be found. Where was she that day? How had he never asked?

Their reunions always began with happy tears and hugs, followed by awkward conversation, leading to an eventual eruption from one or the other. They never made time for the real work that needed to be done. Always tiptoeing around the painful parts until something inane and unimportant sent one of them over the edge.

*It won't be that way this time*, Eli assures himself as he nears the alcove of the Speakeasy. Light shines through the glass door. A handsome, well-built man steps out. He moves with the slinking grace of a predator. Eli stops as the man's sharp gaze lands on him. He narrows his eyes and lets the door fall shut.

"Eli?" the man asks with an air of authority.

"That's me." Eli nods, feeling suddenly awkward and tempted to run.

"Good to meet you again," the handsome stranger says. "I'm Vic, Olive's man." His smile doesn't reach his eyes, and he stands still as a sentry with his arms crossed over his chest. "You aren't planning on running again, are you?" Vic asks. Though his posture and words are meant to intimidate, there's a tenderness that betrays him.

He's there to protect Olive. Eli's not surprised. He's not just some muscle-bound brute, he's got a big heart, and it's got Olive's name all over it. Eli relaxes and steps forward, surprising himself with his confidence.

"The only two people I love in this world are on the other side of that door. Why would I run?"

"That's good to hear, man." Vic relaxes and offers a true smile.

If there'd been any questions about why Olive was attracted to Vic, that smile answered them all. Eli smiles back and waits even more awkwardly to be welcomed in.

"You gonna stand out here in the cold all night?" Vic teases as he pushes the door open, inviting Eli into the warmth of the Speakeasy.

Olive is sitting beside Chris, fidgeting with her hands. She stands quickly upon seeing Eli. She's clearly nervous, afraid to charge and hug him as she had the last time they met. Vic closes the door behind them and steps around him. "You want a drink?" he asks as he steps behind the bar.

"Sure." Eli nods and steps toward his sister.

Chris stands and approaches him with a look of trepidation. "Hey, babe." He kisses Eli's cheek and whispers in his ear, "Do you want me to stay or go?"

"You can stay," Eli replies, approaching Olive.

She's smiling and shifting eagerly from one foot to the other, nearly dancing in place. "I'm so happy to see you," she says brightly through her tears.

"It's good to see you too," Eli offers, stepping within her reach.

Finished with being polite, she closes the distance between them, wrapping him in her arms. For the briefest moment he feels his mother's arms around him. He squeezes back with the desperation of all his lonely years. They cry together and seem to be mourning the loss of their family in a way they never have.

"I'm so sorry, Olli," he says into her soft, silky hair that smells like patchouli and flowers, just like their mom.

"I'm sorry too. I don't want to lose you again." She holds him tighter, her tears on his cheek.

"I'm not going anywhere this time. I promise." Memories flood Eli's mind as he holds on to his sister. Memories of happy times, of woodland adventures and magic words, of secret forts and swimming in the creek. Countless family dinners run by in a flash. He can all but taste them.

All the hours working in the gardens, tending the animals, bringing food to the table. In every moment, every memory, Olive was there by his side, teaching him everything she had already learned. Their parents are ghosts now, but she is here, standing before him. His only living family.

Olive gives him one more hearty squeeze before slipping out of his embrace. Eli steps back to admire her. She does the same with him.

"This isn't going to be easy," he says with complete confidence. "I know I'm going to fuck up."

"I'm sure I will too." She shakes her head and blinks back her lingering tears.

"But I won't run away this time."

"I won't let you."

"Neither will I," Chris speaks up from the periphery with an awkward laugh.

They turn to look at him as though they forgot he was there. Then Vic slides up, offering Eli a double shot of whiskey and Olive a glass of white wine.

"Whad'ya say we get out of here and leave them to it?" Vic asks Chris.

"I was thinking the same thing," Chris replies.

# CHAPTER THIRTEEN
*Eli*

"So, tell me about that." Olive nods toward the door. "How did that happen?" She sits back down at the table, her gaze never leaving his.

"What? Chris?" Eli asks, pleased with the easy direction of the conversation. He's sure he could talk about Chris for hours on end.

"Yeah. When did you meet?"

"It was after Halloween." He takes the seat across from Olive, remembering the night he first saw Chris. "He was alone at the bar, looking adorable and completely out of place. I was a couple shots in and feeling bold. He wanted to call you as soon as he realized who I was, but I wouldn't let him." Olive cringes. He goes on. "I owe it to you though. I don't think he would've been so comfortable or willing to talk with me without his connection to you. I mean, he was completely out of his element in that place. I know he wanted to be there. But I felt like I might've come on too strong and sent him running. He was still with Tyler then." Eli shrugs.

"So it was you?" Olive leans back in her chair. "You were the pretty bad boy from the bar?"

"Huh?" Eli's cheeks warm at the thought of being Chris's pretty bad boy.

"Oh, nothing." Olive shakes her head and takes a sip of her wine. "A while ago, we were chatting. I thought something was up when he gave me little to no details. As I'm sure you know, he's not one for leaving out details." Olive chuckles. "I should've known."

"You have to know, I'm the reason he didn't tell you," Eli says. "He talked about you every day. He begged and pleaded with me to come around. I kept refusing." Olive nods and sips her wine. "We didn't see each other again for a while."

"No?"

"Nope. I told him where I worked, but we didn't exchange numbers or anything. He told me he was in a relationship, so I stepped back and let him be." Eli sips his whiskey, thankful for the warmth spreading in his chest. "I looked for him every day though." He laughs at himself.

"Did you really?" Olive leans on the table, resting on her elbows.

"Have you seen him?" Eli asks with a grin.

"He is quite handsome. It's easy to forget. He's like a little brother to me." Olive shrugs absently. Then her eyes grow wide as she realizes what she's said, clearly mortified by the faux pas. "I mean, he's not a sexual creature to me. Like, there's no physical attraction there."

Eli holds up one hand and shakes his head, holding her eye contact. "It's okay. I know what you meant. Don't feel bad. I'm glad to know you've got him, and he has you. Plus, I'm fully aware of the role I played in our separation. I mean, I know I'm not easy to deal with. Fuck if I will ever understand what he sees in me."

They sit in silence, each one sipping instead of speaking.

"So, he showed up at my work one afternoon a couple of weeks later, and we went for a walk. You can imagine my surprise when he takes me back to his place and it's our place." Eli chuckles.

"Oh my god, Eli. That must've been so fucked up for you. I'm sorry."

"It wasn't that big of a deal, really. Weird? Yeah. Unexpected? For sure. But we connected that night and none of it mattered." Eli remembers their first embrace, the way Chris felt in his arms, the way he tasted. He blushes. "I would've followed him anywhere." He laughs again.

Olive gives a big warm smile. "Do you love him?"

Eli leans back in his seat, pausing while he asks himself the same question. "I don't know if I know what love is. But if it is, then I get why it makes people so crazy. I'd do anything for him."

"Is that why you're here?" Olive asks plainly without judgment or derision. She blinks and takes a long sip of wine.

"Partly." Eli shrugs and throws back the rest of his whiskey. "I know how happy this makes him. But I also know *I* need this. *We* need this." He drums his fingers on the table. "Did he tell you about our adventure?" he asks, raising an eyebrow.

Olive shakes her head. "No."

"I took him home to meet the folks." The joke slips out before he realizes how awful it sounds. Olive looks concerned, offended even.

"What?"

"Shit. My bad. That wasn't cool. I spend a lot of time in my own mind. I've been told I have a dark sense of humor." He lifts the empty glass to his lips, then lowers it. "I took him back to the farm. We went exploring in the woods, did some drugs, and had a great time. Until, that is, it wasn't great. I've never been back there with anyone, and I guess having a witness made it all the worse."

"Wait. You took him to the farm? To our house?"

"Yeah."

"Is that something you do often?" she asks, appearing shocked.

"Not all the time. I've been there a few times over the years. Usually to see if anything's changed. You've never gone?"

"Why would I? There's nothing there." She looks hurt and angry.

Eli feels the familiar pattern beginning. He takes a moment to consider his next words, something he's never done before with Olive. He takes in a big breath and rests his elbows on the table. "Mom and Dad are there, Olive. Our childhood is there. Every good thing I can remember happened in that house and on that land."

"The worst things happened there too." Her voice is barely a whisper.

"Yeah." Their joyful reunion has already run its course. Eli stares at his hands. He can feel Olive's gaze on him. Tears hover behind his eyes and tremble on his breath. He's full of accusations and anger, ready to start the fight. *Where was she that day?*

As if hearing his thoughts, she answers them. "I spent two nights in those woods." Her voice is thin. "I didn't know what to do. Mom told me to run. She told me to find you and run. But I ran first. By the time I saw you, it was too late. Everything had gone to shit. I didn't want them to take me. I was such a fucking coward. I should've gone to you, should've been there for you."

Eli watches as she stares into the past, unblinking.

"Everything happened so quickly. One moment I was rolling my eyes at some nonsense Mom was saying, the next I was running as fast as I could away from whatever she was so afraid of. If I'd known what was coming..." She drops her head. "Sometimes I think I imagined it. I hid in the bushes for hours, maybe, I don't know. I was in shock or something. I watched as everyone was taken away. Mom in handcuffs, you in the back of some stranger's car, and Dad in a body bag.

"They tore the house apart looking for me, for the drugs, the money, anything they could find. When a couple of them were instructed to search the woods for me, I ran again. I knew they couldn't find me in our woods.

"I went to the orchard and slept in our fort. Maybe I slept. I don't really know. I remember lying in the dirt and crying, jumping at every sound.

"I snuck back to the house the next morning, and they were still there. I think I was hoping I would come home and find it was all a nightmare. But it was as real as it could fucking be.

"You were gone. Mom and Dad were gone. Our home was destroyed, and they were still looking for me." She huffs, her gaze finally meeting Eli's as if she's suddenly remembered he's there.

"I hid again. Thought if I stayed hidden long enough, they would give up searching. Self-preservation, you know." She shrugs. "They found me the next day. I woke up to the sound of them crunching through the orchard. They wouldn't tell me where they took you or

Mom or why they were there. They shoved me in the back of one of their vans and took me to some government building. It wasn't long before I was dropped off at a stranger's house."

Eli listens to Olive's story, understanding why they always avoided sharing these memories with one another. As awful as Olive's experience must've been, it's got nothing on his. He wants to sympathize. He wants to offer support and understanding. But he can't fight the anger that boils in his chest as she talks.

"Have you ever tasted someone's blood?" he asks abruptly. Olive's eyes grow wide with shock. Eli goes on. "Did they make you sit in a room alone with your father's blood dried to your face and hair for hours? Did they tear you from your mother's side while you screamed for each other? You ran, Olive. You hid. But I couldn't.

"Fuck, I can't. I can't run from the taste of Dad's blood on my tongue, the smell of it drying on my skin. My clothes stained with my own piss. Do you have any idea what that was like? I would've given anything to be hiding in the woods with you. Anything."

Olive sits, blinking. Her jaw hangs slack.

"It was hours before someone had the decency to help wash me up." They sit silently again. Eli tries to rein in his anger, his need to show her the damage, the hurt he felt. But the words tumble out of him, unrelenting.

"Then there were the homes." He balls his fists. "God, the fucking homes. How many did you go to? Two? Four maybe?" Olive gives a little nod and looks at her hands lying flat on the table. "I lost count." His face is hot, his ears burning. The whiskey in his belly is fueling his fire.

"They were all going to save me one way or another. They all gave up. Every single one of them gave up. The whole time. Every fucking time they would pack me up and ship me out, I believed it would be back to you. Once they taught me about prayer, I prayed for you. But you never came. You hid, and you continued to hide. Where were you when you found out Mom died?" Eli pauses for her answer.

She shrugs. "I don't remember." She looks miserable as Eli pushes her to search her memory.

"I was in church. Well, leaving church, actually, when I had another episode," he spits out. "That's what they called it anyway. Imagine introducing concepts of eternal damnation, hell, and the fucking rapture to a child dealing with severe trauma and displacement. What the fuck was I supposed to do in those moments when it was all too much?"

Olive winces, pressing her lips together. Every word that falls from Eli's mouth seems to strike her physically.

"I lost my shit. That's what I did. I would scream and wail and thrash. I was so agitated once, I literally shit myself. Have you ever shit yourself in a room full of religious people? They started to fear me more than God. They feared me so much, they sent me away. Again. To another home. Another family who promised to help. Do you know what that meant? What they mean when they say they want to help? They mean they're going to change you. They're going to do everything in their power to make you fit into their world."

Eli watches as Olive squirms in her seat. He wants to stop, to relieve her of the discomfort. But he can't. The dam has broken, and the words are rushing out with all the power of a flood.

"Are you familiar with conversion therapy?" he snaps.

Olive's mouth drops open. She covers it quickly with one hand.

"Yep. Literally, the only *therapy* I've ever received was from Christians telling me my *proclivities* were against nature and God's will. They told me every thought and feeling I had in my mind and body was wrong. That the life I knew was wrong. That my parents were sinners now existing in eternal hellfire. They said the only way I could avoid my parents' fate was to acknowledge and accept an invisible magic man in the sky loved me and wanted me to rejoin his fucking flock.

"All of this before I had hair on my chest, before I'd ever even kissed a boy." His breath shudders in his chest as he stares at Olive.

"But please, tell me about your lonely life on the river in the boat lovingly built by our family." He spits out the final words with more venom than he intends. Olive trembles in her seat and doesn't respond. She covers her eyes with both hands and slumps, crying silent tears.

His rage simmers as he watches her whimper. He swirls the ice in his glass and sips at the melted cubes, wondering if Vic left the bottle out. He stands and heads behind the bar. Olive remains in her seat, hiding her face.

"I didn't know what to do." Her voice is barely audible from behind her hands. She lowers them slowly and looks his way. Her eyes are bloodshot, her cheeks stained with tears. "What was I supposed to do? I'm so sorry for you, for us. But what the fuck was I supposed to do, Eli? I was a fucking kid too. My life, every bit as sheltered as yours."

She gets up and crosses the room to stand across the bar from him. "We were both fucked from the beginning. Society fucked us. Our parents fucked us. What do you think their plans were for our future? You ever wonder about that?"

They stare at each other. Olive places her empty wine glass on the bar. Eli fills it with whiskey before filling his own. She looks at the glass, fingers tapping beside it, then throws back the double shot with a grimace. Eli does the same and refills both glasses.

"I should've been preparing for college, should've been worried about homework and prom dates and dumb high school shit."

"It's overrated." Eli takes a small sip of whiskey.

"I suppose you would know." She takes another sip and looks away, surveying the room. Eli follows her gaze over the empty tables and chairs to the darkened stage. "What do you think their plan was?"

"I don't know. I don't think they knew." He shrugs and stares at his half-empty glass of whiskey. "I traveled all over the country and met a lot of people. I didn't know what I was looking for. But I knew I wasn't finding it. All anyone ever talked about was how great our folks were. But…" Eli steps away from his drink and walks around the bar to stand next to Olive. "If they were so great, why didn't they have a plan for us? Why wasn't there a single person who could take us in? As much as I want to remember the happy times, as much as I've clung to them over the years, maybe it's finally time to accept they weren't all that good at being parents. At a lot of things."

Olive sighs and leans against the bar. "No, they were good. Uncommon? Sure. Half-wild? Yep. But definitely good.

"How many people have you met who grew up free, truly free? We danced and sang and painted and played. Sure, we were denied lots of stuff modern kids had. But I wouldn't trade the way we were raised for anything. I'm so sorry for everything that happened to you. I'm so sorry I didn't do more to save you, to bring you home to me. But please don't let what happened ruin what we had. Sure, our parents are to blame for not preparing us for life. For not having any back-up plans. But what was their crime? Not having the foresight to protect us from the feds? For living in a land of make-believe?"

"That and the large-scale manufacture and distribution of illegal narcotics." Eli rests his elbow on the bar and looks at his sister.

The wistful look on her face is replaced with shock, then a shimmer of humor. She presses her lips together, trying to hold back her laughter. It rumbles out of her, half acceptance, half dismay. Tears threaten to fall as the tension in the air evaporates. Eli joins her, appreciating the absurdity of it all. As their laughter fills the room, he relaxes, and it seems, so does his sister.

He finds they relax into each other's company, feeling a peace he hadn't known for years.

"We were born fucked, weren't we?" she asks after catching her breath.

"Sounds about right," Eli agrees.

# CHAPTER FOURTEEN
*Chris*

"I know that I promised not to make a big deal out of this. But I can't help myself. I've been wanting you to meet my friends for so long. And we're finally doing it. I'm ecstatic you're coming with me today." Chris steals a glance Eli's way, appreciating his holiday look. He's wearing a vintage paisley print shirt rolled up to his elbows, paired with a soft leather vest and bolo tie, all in chocolatey browns. He's topped it off with a burgundy stocking cap that works in a quirky way that only he could pull off. "You clean up nice."

Eli gives him a curious side-eye before looking down at his clothes. "Don't I always look this good?" He smiles. Chris is surprised how much he loves Eli's beard, which he started growing after they first met. Not only the look of it but the feel on his face when they snuggle and kiss.

"Of course you do. You usually have more of an 'I don't give a damn about style' sort of style, though, which is sexy as fuck. But I noticed you dress up for the occasion, and I kind of love it."

"I may've been raised half-wild in the woods, but we'd always dress up for holidays." Eli's eyes twinkle with playful light. "You look good too. You always do." He leans close to steal a kiss, leaving his hand on Chris's thigh.

There's something different about him since his night with Olive. Chris saw it in her too. They seem to walk taller and smile more easily. Though Eli hasn't said much about their conversation, he's said more than once how happy he is to have finally had it.

"I have to warn you before we get there: they can be a lot."

"You've seen where I live. I think I can handle a dinner party in an upper middle-class neighborhood."

"Lord only knows what kind of characters you've met in your adventures. Actually, they're more wholesome than you'd imagine, and behave like one big family. We look out for each other, and they're going to want to know everything they can about you. Add in that you're Olive's estranged brother, and they won't give you a minute of peace."

"Yeah, I figured as much." Eli squeezes Chris's leg again. "You might say I'm even looking forward to it. You've told me so much about them, I feel like I've already met them all."

"They're going to love you."

"I hope so."

They pull up in front of Susan's. Her double driveway is already full of cars. A beautiful wreath of dried flowers, leaves, and berries hangs on the door. Crossing the yard to the house, they can see through a large bay window that the party has already started.

Chris reaches for Eli's hand and pulls him back. "Thank you again for coming. It means a lot."

"Thank you," Eli says, leaning in for a quick kiss.

"For what?"

"For everything. For being you." Eli brushes Chris's lips with another kiss, and Chris kisses him back, soaking in the admiration, the warmth, and the happiness. For the briefest of moments, he considers taking Eli back home and saving him all for himself. *Would we really be missed from Susan's Friendsgiving?*

"Hey, you two. We were wondering if you'd gotten lost," Susan calls from the open door, smiling broadly. She's looking lovely as usual, with her own effortless style. Her lightweight floral kimono flows delightfully over her tunic, full skirts, and many necklaces. Chris watches as she gives Eli an appreciative scan. "You must be Eli," she says as they approach the door.

"That's me." Eli offers her one of his shy grins. Chris can see he's already won her over. "You're Susan? It's good to meet you."

"Good to meet you too. Now get in here. It's cold as fuck." Eli looks surprised, clearly not expecting someone who looks like Susan to talk like him. She chuckles. "Oh, stop. I've been cursing up a storm since before you were born. I just look good doing it."

"Yeah, there is more to Dame Monroe than meets the eye," Chris agrees, following Eli into the house.

The amazing smells drifting on the warm air are promises of what's to come.

The first time he visited, Chris learned that one doesn't bring a dish to Susan's dinner parties. She thanked him graciously for his Tupperware full of pasta salad, then placed it in the kitchen, never to join her spread. Later, he completely understood why.

Every dish she offered was beautiful, from the bowl or platter it was served on to the color and texture of the food itself. He could see she put hours into planning and executing culinary perfection. His pasta salad would have been like a dollar store brooch on one of his custom gowns. He did notice, though, that she not only served herself a large helping of his salad, she told everyone where to find it and how delicious it was.

Now, she leads them down the hallway decorated with beautiful things as the rise and fall of several conversations float from several rooms. Light jazz fills the air as they pass tapestries, vases, paintings, and masks from all around the world. Giant house plants thrive.

He always feels like entering Susan's house is akin to entering a temple of sorts. The goddess she worships is that of earthly delights.

As she floats around the corner, Eli reaches for his hand.

"You all right?" Chris asks, turning to see his brow strained with apprehension.

"A little nervous." Eli casts a look over the hall. "This *is* a lot."

Chris squeezes his hand. "Susan's one of the most down-to-earth people I know who happens to have exceptional taste."

"I feel like I'm gonna break something." Eli laughs.

"If you do, you can blame it on me." Chris leans in and plants a kiss on Eli's soft, scruffy cheek.

***

*Eli*

Introductions are a whirlwind, and Eli barely remembers which name goes with which face. Olive sits on one side of him and Chris on the other. The food and drinks are amazing, each dish a celebration of texture and flavor. He wonders if Susan would mind teaching him a trick or two in the kitchen.

Their conversations are easy, not as one-sided as he and Chris imagined they might be. There are enough people who have nothing to do with Chris and Olive and Burlesque A La Mode, so, much to his relief, he's able to blend in with the group.

Chris's hand rests on his knee under the table. Susan stands to start clearing empty plates. "Here." Eli stands. "Let me help."

"No, you're fine," Susan says. "I'm going to pile all of this on the counter and leave it for the morning. I'd hate for anyone to see the mess my kitchen is in."

Eli looks at the long table full of guests not offering to help. He looks at Olive and Chris, and they both shrug and shake their heads.

"She never lets anyone help," Olive says.

"I wouldn't be surprised to learn she's using witchcraft to make all of this happen," Chris says, gesturing to the table setting and empty plates.

"As long as you never see, you'll never know." Susan winks and chuckles before carrying a stack of plates through the kitchen door.

She returns shortly with two more open bottles of wine, placing one at each end of the table. She talks and jokes with her guests, glowing all the while. Though Eli knew he would like her the moment he saw her in the doorway, he hadn't figured on how much.

She reminds him of home in a way he may not have openly accepted before his talk with Olive.

Since the many days and conversations they've had on that first night of gut-wrenching truths and shattered dreams, they've both come to a level of acceptance that hadn't seemed possible when they were going it alone.

As Susan flutters around the table, clearing plates and replacing empty wine bottles with full ones, Eli takes in the scene. Chris, Olive, and Bunny talk excitedly about their upcoming show. Bunny's sitting across from Eli while leaning into her husband, Mike. He and Vic are chatting and joking.

Eli thinks of every dinner table he's shared over the years in pursuit of memories. He thinks of all the meals he's eaten hovering over a trash can in between a double shift. Then he remembers the many meals he shared with his family. Outside in the summer, around the small kitchen table in the winter—every one of them had been such a joy. They'd all worked together to provide for themselves, from planting to preserving, their hands involved in every step. There is something so reminiscent of his childhood in this meal, Eli almost believes that Susan has a magical garden somewhere, providing her with everything she needs.

He listens and admires the group around him.

Vic and Mike are so fucking handsome. Vic could be on the cover of *GQ*. Mike's a bit rougher around the edges, but his giant working-man hand resting on Bunny's shoulder is as sexy as they come.

From the way she looks at him like he's the king of the world, Eli has no doubt Mike knows how to use those large hands.

Then there's Bunny, Olive, and Susan. They're all beautiful. Not only physically attractive but for-real, drop-dead gorgeous. They're the types of women men clamor to be near. It's hard to believe there are so many stunners in one room. This is Rock Island, after all, not Hollywood.

Then there's Chris, the most beautiful among them all; the perfect blend of masculine and feminine, strength and beauty. Eli wonders how a trash goblin like himself found a seat at this table.

Chris smiles at him, offering to fill his empty glass, and Eli's inner storm settles.

Susan's supply of expensive wine seems to be endless, and her party guests are doing their best to consume it all.

Eli sips at the newly offered wine with relish. Though his funds don't allow for fine wine, his position at The Pub provides many opportunities to taste what he can't afford. Susan is serving sixty-dollar bottles like they came from the discount cart at the liquor store.

As he admires his surroundings, Eli realizes his host and the company he's keeping signify that he's shifted from simple survival to actually enjoying his life.

And he owes it all to Chris.

Overwhelmed, he excuses himself and heads to the restroom.

As he walks down the temple-like hallway toward an equally beautiful bathroom, he realizes good wine goes down differently than the cheap stuff. His buzz is light and airy, and he's warm and fuzzy inside, and feels like he could take on the world.

The man looking back at him in the mirror is unrecognizable. Maybe it's the grin, or maybe it's his posture or the clothes. Whatever it is, he looks happy. Truly happy.

Fear grips him suddenly as a tiny voice inside his head begins to whisper: *Don't get too comfortable. This won't last either. It will all disappear, just like it always does.*

A tremble begins where the joy had been. He splashes water on his face, breathes deep. *It doesn't have to end,* he tells himself. *But it will. Leave now. Before you get too comfortable.*

He fights the urge to run. To listen to that little voice. Watching water swirl down the drain, his heart races. The room contracts around him, then opens and spins. He turns off the water and stares at the droplets running down the sink.

"Stop," he breathes.

With a hand towel so soft it screams luxury, he dries his face, but the room is still spinning, and his heart is still beating like a hummingbird's wings.

"Eli," Chris calls from the hallway. "Eli?"

Chris is outside the door, laughter ringing in his voice. "Come out here and juggle for us. Bunny just had the best idea."

Eli listens as Chris's laughter trails away down the hall. With shuddering breaths, Eli takes one more look at the man in the mirror, does his best to hide the turmoil whirling inside, and returns to the dining room where he finds all eyes on him.

Bunny grins. "Chris was telling us you can juggle."

"I can." Eli looks nervously around the room, so many faces smiling up at him. It appears the wine has gone to everyone's heads.

"I want to see," Bunny says with the zeal of a child.

Without warning, she plucks a pomegranate from the centerpiece and chucks it his way. Despite his surprise, Eli snatches the flying fruit out of the air. Bunny squeals and claps her hands. "Thank you so much for catching that. I realized the moment it left my hand what a huge mistake it was. *I'm* the reason why we can't have nice things. I'm so sorry, Susan." She looks over with wide, earnest eyes.

"It's fine. We'll blame it on the wine," Susan says with an easy laugh as she fills her glass and passes the bottle. "How many can you do?" she asks, grabbing an orange from the same arrangement. She waits until he's ready and gently tosses it his way.

Eli's cheeks are burning as everyone watches. The little voice from the bathroom is quieted by the thrill of being the center of attention.

Having stuck to the shadows most of his life, it's a new sensation. Surprisingly pleasant. Eli reaches for his unfinished wine and downs it in one swallow, plucking two more oranges from the bowl. He steps back to clear the chandelier.

All conversation has stopped, and Eli can hear the music again.

He moves with the lively beat, juggling first three, then four fruits. He spins slowly, ever mindful of the space around him, and steals glances at Chris and the others.

Chris's face is alight with joy. Bunny is clapping, bouncing in her seat. Olive wears a wistful grin, blinking away happy tears. He moves faster as he grows more comfortable with his audience.

"I could use a drink," Eli says with a wink to Chris, who stands quickly and tips a wine glass to Eli's lips. He drinks long and slow while continuing to juggle. He gives a tiny nod toward Chris, who lowers the glass, then steps back.

Eli catches the last fruit as the song ends, and his small audience erupts with applause. The tiny thrill he feels from their attention grows into an all-encompassing delight.

"As bad as I feel about throwing that pomegranate, I'm so glad I did. That was amazing." Bunny giggles.

"Thanks." Eli blushes, still holding the fruits. Chris is beaming beside him.

"Would you want to do that for our New Year's Eve show?" Bunny asks excitedly.

"Really?" Eli asks, surprised. Bunny nods vigorously. "Sure." Eli shrugs and places the fruit back in the bowl, attempting to arrange them as well as Susan had and failing.

He takes his seat. Chris takes his beside him and leans close to whisper, "You're so cool."

Shivers run the length of Eli's spine as Chris's lips brush his ear.

# CHAPTER FIFTEEN

*Chris*

"You have to promise not to laugh," Chris says, feeling more bashful than he ever has at practice. Eli sits with him at a small table near the stage. The rest of the troupe is milling about in the club, working on costumes, eating snacks, chatting, and stretching. It's Eli's first time joining practice since Bunny invited him to perform in the New Year's Eve show.

"Why would I laugh?" Eli asks with a curious smile and a shake of his head.

"I don't know. I'm feeling self-conscious about you seeing me dance." Chris shifts uncomfortably in his seat, imagining what Eli will think when he sees him on stage.

"I've seen you do quite a bit more than dance." Eli chuckles and drums his fingers absently on the table.

"Yeah, I know. But this is different. Like, I'm still working out the kinks, and you're going to think my song is dumb."

"What's your song?"

"Ginuwine," Chris spits out quickly, his cheeks coloring instantly.

"Oh fuck. "Pony?"" Eli begins to chuckle, then covers his mouth and clears his throat.

"I knew you were going to laugh. You think it's corny."

"No. I think it's perfect. Are you doing a *Magic Mike* thing?"

"Sort of." Chris looks away, still embarrassed. Since Tyler refused to show Chris any support, he never had to worry about Tyler watching him perform.

Chris has always chosen songs for fun's sake. He never considered trying to impress his lover.

Burlesque has been a fun way to express himself and enjoy the company of his friends. Looking at the gentle humor on Eli's face and the glee he's attempting to hide, a new appreciation for Eli warms Chris's heart. His man is there because he wants to be with him. He's there to take part in something Chris loves. Chris shakes his head with a bold smile. "You know what? I'm going to prove to you it's a perfect song for dirty dancing."

"Oh, I don't doubt it. I bet you look sexy as fuck up there. But"—Eli pauses and looks away—"this is so embarrassing." Eli looks back at him with concern. "I already worked out my whole juggling bit, and you'll never guess the song I chose." A smile cracks his serious face.

"You are so full of shit." Chris rolls his eyes and laughs.

"You're right. I would never dance to 'Ginuwine.' I'm so above that." Eli turns his nose up in mock disgust, his playful smirk never leaving his face.

"You talk a lot of shit for a man who's never stripped in front of hundreds of people."

"Who says I haven't?"

Chris's jaw drops. He's suddenly aware of how little he knows about Eli's past, where he's been, and what he's done. "Oh my god, are you serious?"

Eli laughs. "Fuck no. No one is paying to see me take my clothes off."

"That's not true. I'd pay a pretty penny," Chris purrs, thinking about how delicious Eli looks lying back on a pile of pillows, sleepy and satisfied with his hair-covered chest, which happens to be the perfect pillow for Chris's head.

"Lucky you. It's yours for free." Eli wags his eyebrows. Chris basks in his playful, fun-loving nature. He remembers how oppressive and stuffy life with Tyler was, then shakes away the memory and leans across the table to plant a kiss on Eli's smiling face.

"Lucky indeed. Do you have an idea of what you want to do for the show?"

"I actually do." Eli sits up tall and leans back. "I was struck with inspiration at work the other day."

"Tell me." Chris bounces in his seat, surprising himself with his excitement.

"Okay. But you have to be honest and say if it's stupid. I've never done anything like this before, and I have no idea what I'm doing."

"Tell me. Tell me."

"Do you know the Dresden Dolls?"

"No."

"Okay." Eli pulls out his phone, and scrolls. "Here's the song." The sound of a music box plays for eight counts, then a woman sings the words 'Coin-operated boy…' The song goes on with humorous lyrics about the benefits of having a coin-operated boy, along with an almost childish drumbeat.

"I was thinking of painting my face like an old-time marionette, with pink circles on my cheeks and thick eyeliner and moving like a wind-up toy at first, then eventually starting to juggle, adding more balls for the peak of the song. Then dropping all of them here." Eli taps on his phone on his cue. "Then I scramble to pick them up and start juggling again through to the end, sort of struggling and failing a couple times, then getting my bearings until the end."

Chris watches Eli with wonder. "That sounds brilliant," he says dreamily.

"Really? You think so? You're not just saying that?" Eli shifts in his seat and smiles shyly.

"Yeah." Chris nods. "I really think so."

"I was thinking suspenders too," Eli says with an awkward grimace.

"Perfect. Bunny's going to love it. Do you want some stage time tonight?"

"I don't know." Eli shrugs. "Maybe later. I'm not sure if I'm ready to get up on stage yet."

"That's okay. I already told you I'm feeling a bit awkward to dance with you here, so I understand."

"Now, *that* is silly. You're a pro."

"I don't know about all that. I've been dancing in front of everyone here for only a few months."

"What about when you have an audience?"

"That's different. I want them to adore me and leave. I'm not going home with any of them. You could tease me mercilessly."

"I'll do that either way." Eli lowers his voice to a soft growl. "If you'd like me to."

Chris blushes instantly. "You know I would. But first we've got work to do. You wanna know about everyone you haven't met yet?"

"Sure."

"Okay. So over at that table are James and Marty. They are our emcees. Marty thinks he's the funny one, but really, it's James who carries the shows. They have a good dynamic. I think James could do a show without Marty, but not the other way around. They were the only two who auditioned. I can't help but think if there had been more competition, Marty wouldn't have made the cut. But then, Bunny welcomes everyone with open arms.

"He's harmless, I suppose. I adore James though. He's such a sweetheart." Eli nods, and Chris goes on. "You know Susan already, and as you'd expect, she's amazing on stage. Sitting with her is Julie. She's our stage manager, and she's so good at it. I don't think our shows would run as smoothly as they do without her.

"She's also our stage kitten, which means she picks up all the clothes we throw around during our performances. Except for that." Chris points to a strand of Mardi Gras beads hanging from a light on the ceiling and chuckles. "Bunny threw that months ago, and it's been dangling there ever since. I think Mike likes it up there."

"That's awesome. Who's that?" Eli nods toward the sound booth.

"Oh, that's Johnny Tuesday. He does lights and sound. I bet he's here to start working on cues and whatnot. Our New Year's Eve show is the biggest we've ever done. He's another one behind the scenes who makes the shows happen.

"Then, of course, there's Mike and Vic. They really are the best."

"I've got to be honest with you. This is surreal." Eli's voice shifts from playful to almost intense.

"What do you mean?" Chris tilts his head.

"I don't know. It doesn't even feel real. All these people, working together happily with no drama, supporting one another. And they're all so damn good looking. It's like I woke up in a movie or something."

"Oh, there's plenty of drama." Chris chuckles with relief. "So much drama sometimes. But the core group works together well. We share a common interest and really do love each other, for the most part. And as far as them being so pretty, I've no idea how that happened. It's the genetic lottery, I suppose, and they all won. You should see the folks from Chicago and New Orleans. Henri is like a damn Disney prince with his *savoir faire*. And I'd be lying if I didn't say I'm a little concerned about you meeting Calvin."

"Why's that?" Eli cocks his chin and raises one eyebrow.

"He's the most ethereal creature I've ever seen. He's Mr. 'Sorry I stole your man, but I was just standing here eating a burrito or whatever.'" Chris laughs, remembering how smitten he was with Calvin in the beginning. "He's also one of the kindest, most gentle souls. You'll understand when you meet him."

"I think I might be jealous already." Eli leans across the table, resting his hand on Chris's, and a tingle runs up his arm.

"Don't be. I'm yours." Chris raises Eli's hand to his lips and brushes the backs of his fingers with a kiss.

\*\*\*

*Eli*

"I'm yours." Chris's words circle in Eli's mind as the kiss lingers on his knuckles. *Has anyone ever been mine?* he wonders.

"Hey guys." Olive plops beside them with a big grin. "How's it going?"

Eli still isn't used to having her around. He's not used to having anyone around. Though Chris has been a welcome distraction from the ever-present loneliness, Olive and the rest of Burlesque A La Mode are far more demanding of his energy.

Having been on his own for such a long time, with so many people taking interest in what he's doing, it's an altogether new experience.

"It's going," Chris sings happily. "Eli was just telling me about his ideas for his juggling bit. It's going to be fantastic."

"I'm sure it is. You always loved to dance and sing. Do you remember the little plays we used to put on during our solstice celebrations?"

Olive's question hits him hard with nostalgia. To have someone who was there, who remembers, someone who lived it right along with him, seems unreal.

"I forgot all about those," he responds, looking beyond Olive and Chris, into the caves of his memory. He always remembered the parties and the people but completely forgot the skits and plays that he, Olive, and the other children would put on.

"You would demand to be the Fairy King every time, dragging the children away into the night." Olive laughs.

"It sounds sinister when you say it." Eli looks her way, then to Chris. "I wanted to keep them like lost boys, not eat them or swallow their souls or anything."

"I don't know, babe. It all sounds kinda dark. Even the lost boys part." Chris chuckles and pats Eli's hand. "But I'd let you take me away any night."

"Good to know, as there's always a place for you in my kingdom."

"All right, everyone," Bunny calls from the stage. "We've got three weeks before dress rehearsals, and Christmas in two weeks. I don't know what lunatic decided to put on the biggest show we've ever done during the holiday season, but Mike's going to have to buy her some wigs because she's pulling all her hair out." She giggles at herself and goes on discussing the logistics of certain routines and guest performers, all things that Eli has no point of reference for.

He watches her without listening, feeling the warmth of Chris's hand resting on his.

"... And I want everyone who hasn't had a chance yet to meet Eli. Chris's new beau, Olive's brother, and our new juggler," Bunny says. "Not that we had an old juggler, but I've always wanted one, and here he is. So, everyone, welcome Eli."

The group turns his way with smiles and words of welcome. Eli's ears burn with discomfort of being the center of attention—something he'll have to work on if he's really going to stand up in front of hundreds of people on New Year's Eve.

"Hi, everyone," he says as brightly as possible, despite the churning of nerves in his belly. Chris gives his hand a gentle squeeze.

"Okay, then. Let's get to it. Who's ready to hit the stage?" Bunny raises both hands and wiggles them.

The flurry of activity that follows is a thing of beauty. It's organized chaos, or wild coordination, or some other kind of lovely oxymoron that will eventually end in a theatrical production.

Eli's impressed with how well everyone works together, and when Chris takes the stage, he's left speechless. All he can think is how unbelievable it is that someone as sexy, confident, and downright perfect as Chris would even look his way, let alone welcome him into his life with open arms.

The group cheers wildly as the music fades, and Chris hurries to scoop up his discarded clothes. His endearing smile competes for attention with his sumptuous ass in tiny boxer briefs.

"He's pretty amazing, isn't he?" Olive says beside him.

"That he is," Eli responds, his eyes still on Chris. "I'll never think of 'Ginuwine' the same way again."

"That's the truth." Olive laughs with a little snort, then settles her gaze on Eli. "It's so great to have you here. I know I keep saying it, but I couldn't've dreamed in a million years that you would be joining this troupe and performing with me. I'm so happy." Tears wet the corners of her eyes. She wipes at them with the back of her hand and chuckles at herself. "Sorry. I still don't believe it sometimes."

Eli's heart swells with love for his big sister. Love that he hasn't allowed himself to feel for many years. "I'm happy too," he agrees as Chris saunters to them, cheeks red.

"So?" Chris asks, sliding into the seat beside him. "Be honest. But also, lie if you didn't like it."

"You were amazing." The word doesn't fully encompass all Eli wants to say, but it'll have to suffice. He's not sure a word exists that could describe how much he enjoyed watching Chris dance.

"Really? You think so?" Chris grins widely.

"I've never seen you so modest," Olive teases.

"Well, I actually care about his opinion," Chris shoots back. "Besides, I know you adore me." He laughs.

Eli watches the comfortable exchange between his lover and his sister. He imagines their friendship beginning the moment they met and wonders how Olive can be so open to forming relationships while he has been running from any real connection for as long as he can remember.

"It's true," she responds. "You've always been my favorite. You have competition now though." Olive nods toward Eli, and his heart warms at the thought. There was once a time when all they had was each other.

"I can't compete." Eli raises both hands. "He's my favorite too."

"Anybody else want stage time?" Bunny asks half-heartedly. Her gaze falls on the doorway filled by Mike's large frame.

"It's cold as fuck out there," Mike says, pulling his gloves off his giant hands. "Thought you might want a ride in a warm truck." He crosses the room to her with long, even strides, brushing the snow from his shoulders and opening his coat.

As if they are the only two in the room, Bunny bites her bottom lip and gives a smile full of secrets only Mike knows. She bounds to him and slides her arms into his open coat.

"You mind locking up, Olive?" Bunny asks, wrapped in Mike's arms.

"Not at all." Olive smiles and shakes her head.

"Awesome. Thank you. See everyone on Monday. Let's try to have all our costume pieces ready no later than Wednesday."

As suddenly as Mike arrived, he and Bunny disappear.

One by one the rest follow, leaving Eli, Chris, and Olive. They're sharing their second bottle of wine, passing it around the table without glasses, chatting about nothing in particular.

Olive stretches and yawns loudly. "I think I need to call it a night, guys," she says sleepily. "Are you good to drive?"

Chris nods and passes the bottle to Eli. "Yeah. I've been taking much smaller sips than you two."

Eli watches their exchange and smiles from behind the bottle as he takes another hearty swig of the oaky red wine.

Olive stands up and kisses Chris on the top of his head, something Eli remembers their mom doing to him and Olive every night at bedtime.

She moves to Eli, placing her hand on his shoulder and kissing the top of his head.

Maybe it's the wine, or maybe the moment. He reaches for her hand resting on his shoulder and holds it tight, unwilling to let go.

The warmth filling him up would've been foreign only two months ago. Before he found Chris, affection was not something he remembered or had emotional access to.

To feel warm and safe and loved was so far from his experience, he'd stopped longing for it. He'd given up on ever feeling it again.

But here, with Olive's hand on his shoulder and Chris's smile before him, Eli feels something he dare not name for fear that it'll disappear.

Tears form. He blinks them away and hides behind another swig from the bottle.

"Goodnight," Olive says, patting his shoulder and slipping from his grip. "Be safe. You'll lock up, right?" she asks Chris.

"Yep."

Eli watches as she slips away down the back hallway toward the exit. Chris turns to him. "You okay?" he asks softly, concern etched on his brow.

"Hmm?" Eli gives his head a shake and focuses on Chris. "Yeah. Actually, I am." He nods and smiles. "I'm more than okay." He stands to lean over Chris, planting a kiss on his delicious lips. "Now what do you say? Let's play with my balls." Chris pulls back with a look of surprise that melts into humor as Eli pulls a small sack of balls out of his bag.

"Jesus." Chris rolls his eyes and shakes his head with a smile. "Feeling bold now that everyone's gone?"

"I suppose I am." Eli moves to kiss him again. He takes his time, lingering over Chris's lips just to taste them again. "But I'm losing interest in these balls." He drops the bag on the table with a heavy thump.

"Whoa, boy," Chris teases, his lips trailing Eli's chin. "You probably should take this opportunity if you want to have some quiet time on stage. This show is coming like a freight train, and it's not going to get any easier."

"Gah," Eli huffs, resting his forehead on Chris's. "You're right." He takes a deep breath to focus his energy on the task before him. "I'll do it once. Then, home?" The word falls from his lips with ease but lands before him with a surprising weight.

He hasn't been to his place for more than a shower and a change of clothes in weeks. He's spent every night with Chris instead, wrapped up in their tiny love nest, rocking with the rippling water of the near-frozen river.

"Works for me," Chris says with a shrug and a smile.

*** 

Eli lies in the middle of the stage, out of breath and sweating. His first run-through was a disaster, the second and third as well. It took five for him to feel that he'd made any progress at all. Chris sits beside him, rolling three small rubber balls from one hand to the other. "That was fucking work," Eli says, watching the dust float through the stage lights. His song plays from his phone beside him.

"Yeah. It's a different game when you're on stage under the lights."

"No kidding."

"It's going to be amazing." Chris attempts to juggle the balls in his hand and fails.

"You really think so?" Eli sits upright and wipes at the sweat on his face. "It's not dumb?"

"No. It's great. I really can't believe you've never performed before."

"Not for a very long time. It feels good though. Like when I heard the song and the inspiration hit. It was a rush. All the details sort of flowed in and came together in my mind while I was making burgers and steaks."

"That's how it goes. Careful though. It consumes you." Chris laughs and tosses the balls one at a time to Eli, who catches them easily without looking away from Chris. His smile, his laugh, his voice. Everything about him makes Eli feel like he's floating. The energy Chris radiates is more intoxicating than any drug he's ever done.

"*You* consume me."

Chris's eyes flash. Blush colors his cheeks. He lowers his lids and crawls toward Eli, then settles beside him, inches from his face. "Should we get out of here?"

"Maybe?" Eli's cock quickens at the nearness of him. "Kiss me."

Chris's soft lips are against his in an instant, plump and slick.

He kisses hungrily, pulling Eli closer with his hands on his cheeks. He runs one hand over Eli's chest, down to his cock, and it twitches under his sweats. Chris kneads Eli's balls and squeezes his cock as he drinks his fill of kisses.

Chris pulls away from Eli's kiss, grins, and then stands with fluid grace to slip out of his shirt and pants. When he lowers himself to straddle Eli, Chris grinds with the beat, barely grazing Eli's cock with his ass.

Chris bites his bottom lip and moves lower, nestling Eli's cock between his firm ass cheeks. Chris's tiny boxer briefs barely contain his erection as it bounces with each thrust and roll of his hips. Eli aches against the pressure. Chris bends to kiss him, then sucks and nibbles at his lip as he continues to grind against Eli.

Eli's pulse rushes in his ears, and thrills run the length of his body. The ecstasy of Chris's body against him is nearly overwhelming. Chris's lips move to his neck, where he nips at his ears. He hovers over Eli's chest for a moment before moving lower still, tugging at his sweats. Chris sighs with fluttering lashes before taking Eli's cock in his mouth. First just the tip, then all that he can fit.

He runs his mouth over the side of Eli's shaft, maintaining eye contact the whole time, then flicks at the tip with his warm pink tongue. Eli lets his head fall back as Chris works his cock and balls. He laps at every inch of Eli with vigor, rolling his hips in time with his tongue and the music.

The warm stage lights dancing off Chris's bare shoulders and shining hair remind Eli that they're completely exposed. The large room is empty, and though it's late and cold outside, Olive or anyone with a key could walk in at any moment.

The possibility of being caught thrills and excites him, more than he would've guessed. A beautiful man sucking his dick in the middle of a fully lit stage is something he never imagined.

But as he watches Chris lick and suck and wag his ass, Eli imagines a silent audience caught up in awe by their lovemaking. All of them waiting on bated breath for his climax. As Chris swallows him nearly whole, Eli cums hard and fast, his body wracked with quivers as Chris seems to be sucking at his soul through his cock.

Bliss surges through him as Chris pulls away and settles on his heels with a satisfied grin. He wipes at his chin and swipes his mussed hair out of his eyes.

Eli barrels into him without warning to cover him with kisses. He moves over every delectable inch of skin, tasting sweat. He aches to give him the same feeling, to please him equally.

Chris laughs and rolls, wrapping his arms around him, his hard cock prodding Eli's belly.

"Stand up." Eli's voice sounds more desperate than he intended.

Chris stands quickly without a word of protest. Eli pulls at his boxer briefs, and Chris's dick bounces in Eli's face. He takes it in his mouth and sucks hungrily. Digging his fingers into Chris's hips, Eli pulls and sucks with all the intensity he feels for Chris.

Chris is rocking and cumming with a long, slow groan, clutching Eli's short hair at the roots. He lowers himself to his knees and rests his forehead against Eli's. They lean into one another, breathing in the moment.

Completely naked under the lights, on display for no one and everyone.

For years he was told his desires were sinful. That all of the things that made him who he was were nothing more than a phase to be grown out of, or a trauma to recover from. He'd been conditioned to think his love was wrong to give. Not only was it wrong, but eternal damnation awaited him unless he could change his ways.

Though he knew in his heart it was nonsense, it didn't stop his young, still-developing mind from thinking he was broken. He was wrong, and different, and needed to be fixed. But here with Chris, their love feels like heaven. It feels transcendent, like a beautiful thing that should be celebrated, not shunned or shamed.

"We should probably get out of here," Chris says softly, breathless.

"You mean we can't stay here like this forever?" Eli chuckles.

"Not unless the crowd gets comfortable with a lot of things real quick." Chris smirks. Eli pulls him into his arms, warm, silken skin against his. "Let's go home," Chris says into Eli's chest.

"All right, let's go home." Eli's heart nearly bursts with the thought.

# CHAPTER SIXTEEN
*Chris*

The road seems never-ending. The only thing keeping him from falling asleep at the wheel is the playlist Eli made for him. Chris's cheeks bloom with the memory of their love play on the Speakeasy stage. A cascade of memories fills his mind, all the way back to their first kiss in the alley while he was still with Tyler. Briefly, Chris wonders what Tyler is up to these days, then brushes the thought away. Tyler is no longer a part of his life, and Chris is so much better for it. Chris's family will be pleased. Though they were always too polite to say it, Chris knows they didn't care for Tyler. Early on, his dad mentioned that Tyler seemed a bit old for him, and that was the end of it. He never brought it up again. And he would never have to, because this year, despite the fact Chris is traveling alone, he's traveling away from a man who has made him happier than he's ever been.

As the gray road meets the gray sky and white lines dash beneath him, he imagines Eli in the passenger seat. He wonders what his family will think of Eli. *Mom will love him.* As he imagines his mom wrapping Eli in one of her best hugs, Chris wishes that he'd convinced Eli to come along. He'll fit right in with his brothers, and he's sure his dad will like him too.

One thing his dad appreciates is hard work, and Eli works almost as hard as he plays. A tremor of arousal passes through Chris as he recalls Eli's playfulness.

The family never needs to see that side. *That's just for me.*

Chris licks his lips and swears he can still taste Eli. Only a couple hours have passed since they kissed goodbye on the dock of the marina, with Eli agreeing to stay on the boat while Chris is gone. He feels better knowing Eli will be "home" while Chris is away. Six months ago, he never would've imagined he'd be making love to a sweet and passionate man every night, living on a houseboat. Caught up in his reverie, he almost misses his exit.

***

"Hey, Mom." Chris steps into the warm kitchen of his family's two-story farmhouse. His mom stands at the sink, her back to him. She turns with a bright smile on her round face.

"Hi, honey," she calls out, wiping her hands on a towel and dropping it on the counter. The scent of home surrounds him. Something delicious and meaty is roasting in the oven, a cake is on the counter, and potatoes are on the stove.

She crosses the kitchen and wraps him in her arms. Her fluffy red hair tickles his nose. She's been dying it for years to hide the gray, and that's a secret that Chris will take to his grave.

"Welcome home. Your dad and brothers are still out. Petey hasn't gotten his deer yet."

"Isn't the season about over?" Chris asks, remembering the one time he went hunting with them all and how he hated it. The smell of his dad field dressing a buck is a memory he can't erase, try as he might.

"Today's the last day. Otherwise, they'd be here to meet you."

"I hope Petey gets one," Chris says with a smile. The youngest of the brothers, it is Pete's first year joining the big deer hunt.

"Well, if he doesn't, he'll be all right. It's not like the family is going to starve or anything. Get in here and sit down," she says, pulling a chair out from the large table. "You want a beer, some coffee? I want to know all about what happened with Tyler and this new guy you've been seeing."

"I'll have a beer." Chris sets his bags on the floor beside the door and takes a seat. He hears the pop of two bottles being opened, then his mom is sitting across from him, her plump, ruddy cheeks radiant.

Chris takes the offered beer, thankful the guys are all gone. These moments were always his favorite ones growing up. Once his dad accepted Chris's distaste for all things hunting, he was free to spend the days with his mom.

Hunting season was the time for binge-watching reality TV in his pajamas while Mom flitted in and out of the room, asking for updates on who was doing what.

Now he has his own reality TV-esque tales to tell, and his mom loves every minute. She couldn't get enough of the Olive/Vic/Emily saga, and the series finale had not disappointed. "Are you ready?" he teases.

"Of course I am. Tell me everything."

"Well, there isn't much to really say about Tyler. I was miserable with him, and I didn't even realize it. He was so cold and unfeeling. It was like living with a robot. The more time I spent with the troupe and all their doting men, I started to ask myself if I was happy or if I was pretending to be happy because not being happy meant I had to do something to change it."

Chris takes a drink from the icy cold bottle and goes on. "I mean, I tried to talk to him. I tried to get him to show an interest in anything I was doing. But he didn't care. When I finally tried to have a real conversation about it, he shut down, and that was it."

Chris levels his gaze on his mom. "He left me an itemized bill for our new living arrangement and barely spoke another word to me." Chris's voice cracks, and tears threaten to spill. His throat tightens.

His mom's brow comes together with concern. She reaches across the table to pat his hand. He hadn't realized how badly he'd been hurt by Tyler. Telling his mom all the details of what happened opens the wounds that his time with Eli has kept him from feeling.

"He just threw me out like the trash, Mom." Chris shakes his head and presses his lips together tight. "I gave up so much for him, and I don't think he ever cared." He wipes at his eyes and sniffles, taking another swig from his beer.

"Oh, honey. I'm so sorry. I don't know if that man knew how to care." She squeezes his hand and shakes her head. "I know you probably don't want to hear it right now, but you're better off without him. I know you loved him, but he really was a boring man."

Chris huffs. "He was, and you're right. But you know what? I don't know if I ever really loved him. I loved the way he spoiled me and the way he looked at me in the beginning. I thought I loved him, but once all of that went away, I don't know why I stayed so long. I wasn't happy."

"Are you happy now?" She offers an expectant smile.

Chris imagines Eli sitting beside him at the table, charming his mom with his shy smile and off-color humor. Chris thinks of the passion in their first kiss and how each kiss feels like the first one. He longs for Eli's touch, his voice, his nearness. Chris's cheeks warm at the thought.

"I am." He nods and beams, feeling the joy reflecting on his mom's face. "I don't know if I've ever been this happy."

"I can't wait to meet him." As she looks out the darkening window, pride lights her face. "Look outside," she says with a nod. "Looks like Petey got a buck."

Two trucks are parked in the driveway. His dad and brothers spill out of the open doors. Petey, his cheeks red from the cold, is grinning from ear to ear as his dad and Josh open the bed, revealing a good-sized eight-pointer. They're all patting his shoulders and cheering, looking toward the window and waving at Chris and his mom.

"We'll probably have to stop calling him Petey now that he's a man," Chris jokes.

"Oh, he's going to be my Petey no matter how many bucks he shoots." She chuckles and stands up, ready to welcome the rest of her boys home.

Chris marvels at her in her oversized sweatshirt and jeans as she goes back to work. He wonders what she would've done with her life if she hadn't spent the majority of it feeding boys.

He compares her to Susan, who's so glamorous and refined. Then he thinks of Olive, Bunny, and the rest of the women he's met over the months that he's been dancing with Burlesque A La Mode. What if his mom had chosen to live for herself? Who would she have been?

Then he thinks of Eli and Olive, how they lost their mom and dad. Maybe it's because of the long drive or the raw nerves from finally seeing her after leaving Tyler. Whatever it is, he's overwhelmed with love and appreciation for his mom like never before. He crosses the room and wraps her in his arms, holding tight. She makes a curious little sound, then squeezes back. "Thank you," he says into her fluffy hair.

"For what?" She pats and rubs his back.

"Just thank you. I love you so much, Mom." He keeps hold of her 'til the door opens, and five rowdy men fill the kitchen with shouts of welcome home.

Hugs and beers are passed around. Even Petey's offered a Busch Light.

Chris is surrounded by love and laughter.

He's home, and the only thing missing is Eli by his side.

***

*Eli*

"Fuuuuuck." Eli groans as the ticket printer screeches again. "It's Christmas Eve. Don't these people have families to go to?" he shouts at no one in particular. His fellow cooks grumble in unison. They represent the B team, the guys scheduled when it's sure to be a slow night. Eli's there because he had nowhere better to be. Despite the invitations from Olive and her friends to join them at the Speakeasy for Christmas cocktails, he chose to work. Going anywhere wouldn't be much fun without Chris by his side. Though he's gotten used to the group and has come to enjoy their company, they lose a bit of their luster without Chris there to translate their many high-pitched conversations.

He wasn't prepared for this kind of traffic on Christmas Eve. But then, when were they prepared for any kind of traffic? If he isn't short-staffed, he is out of half of his menu items, struggling to fill orders with his minimal stock.

Then there is fucking Pam. Always flitting around with her nervous face, her beady eyes darting around while her gaudy costume jewelry dangles from her ears and neck. She lumbers back as if on cue. "Where's table ten? I need table ten."

"That ticket came in five minutes ago. It's four well-done steaks." Eli lets out a long, slow breath.

"That's impossible. They've been here for over an hour." She shakes her head and stares dumbly through the window.

"I don't know what to tell you, Pam. I got the ticket five minutes ago. The steaks are on, but I can't cook them any faster. You want me to send out some fries? I've got those."

She lets out an angry little huff. "No, I don't want you to send out fries," she mocks. "We lose enough money in this place. We don't need to be giving food away. Just get them done fast," she demands before whisking out the way she came in, leaving two full tickets worth of food dying in the window.

"Jesus Christ." Eli growls as three servers push through the door, clamoring for his attention. Each one is looking for him to fix their mistakes. His line is struggling to stay afloat. The whole damn restaurant is in the weeds.

"God damn it. Someone take the food out of the fucking window so I can put more in it. This shit is dying." The servers jump at the sound of his booming shouts, then scramble, snatching tickets and grabbing plates. The first two are gone in a flash.

"Eli?" the new girl, Sarah, asks, barely above a whisper. She's so small and can't be much older than eighteen. Eli wonders why she isn't home with family for the holiday. He takes a long, slow breath to calm himself. It's not her fault the whole place is fucked.

"What's up?"

"I'm so sorry. I forgot to put in a kid's chicken strip for table three, and everything else is up. They've already been waiting so long," she says with tears in her eyes.

He sighs and asks as gently as he can, "Just one?"

"Yeah, with fries." The grease-stained ticket shakes in her trembling hand.

"Give me two seconds," he says calmly as he plates the meal himself. "Fire another kids' strip," he shouts to his fry cook as he slides the basket through the window.

"Thank you so much." She breathes a sigh of relief and hurries through the door.

"Where are we on ten?" Pam pushes through the door, shouting as it swings behind her.

"It's still four well-done steaks," Eli says through his teeth.

"What about the kid's meal? They've got a grumpy, hungry toddler out there. I'll take his chicken strips."

"I don't have strips yet." He turns away to check the bubbling skillets behind him.

"What do you mean you don't have strips? They take only five minutes to cook."

"And the steaks take at least ten, so the chicken is cooking right now," he lies to protect Sarah. No reason she should feel the wrath of Pam, whose face is red.

Pam presses her lips into a thin line and blinks. "Well, I need them on the fly. Let me know as soon as they're up," she demands before pushing through the swinging door. The sound of broken glass crashes over the holiday music floating through the door. "You stupid girl," Pam shouts as she follows Sarah back through. "Why weren't you watching where you were going?" Pam half whines, half yells as she rushes for the broom and dustpan.

"I'm so sorry, Pam. I was in such a rush, I just pushed right through the door. I didn't see you there." Tears are running down Sarah's cheeks. Eli knows it was Pam who ran into her.

"I don't know why I ever hired you," Pam growls as she wipes at the wet spot on her shirt. "You're worthless. Can't even carry a tray of dirty dishes." She pushes through the swinging door as Sarah begins to sob.

Eli drops what he's doing, leaves the line, and offers her a clean handkerchief from his pocket. "Hey, it's okay. Shit happens. Especially in this place." She looks up at him with red eyes and nods her thanks before dabbing away the tears.

"What are you doing out here?" Pam shouts as she comes back through the door with a dustpan full of broken glass. "I need table ten, and I need it now," she demands, dumping the glass into the trashcan.

"Table ten can wait. I think this takes precedence," Eli says, gesturing toward the crying girl.

"Oh, please. She's just a spoiled little brat who doesn't know how to do her job."

"I don't know many spoiled brats that work on Christmas Eve," Eli says quickly.

"Get back there and cook those steaks or get the fuck out of my kitchen." Pam's words drip with venom as her upper lip quivers.

Their silent standoff goes on for what feels like an eternity. Eli's leaning against the drink station; Pam's standing, her pudgy hands gripping the broom handle as if it were a weapon she meant to swing.

"Take your little girlfriend too. I don't have time for a waitress who can't carry a fucking tray."

Eli tears his apron off and drops it on the counter. "Merry Christmas to you too, Pam." He pushes past her to the breakroom for his coat. Sarah follows on his heels.

Pam's standing at the window, attempting to gather the food for table ten. "I don't know why you care so much about her. I thought you were a queer," she says under her breath, just loud enough for Eli to hear.

He stops in his tracks. Rows of glistening carafes full of water sit on the drink station, waiting to go out to tables. "It doesn't take wanting to fuck someone to want to show human decency," he says without looking her way.

Then, in the sheer mania of the moment, he swipes at the carafes, sending most of them crashing to the ground. Shattering glass and the stifled laughter of the line crew are the only thing he hears as the door swings behind him and Sarah. Wide eyes follow them as they pass through the door of The District Pub for the last time.

His only regret is not seeing Pam's face when the glass hit the tiles.

# CHAPTER SEVENTEEN
*Chris*

"Wait." Chris cackles wildly. "What did you do?" He's sitting on the kitchen table in the houseboat, and Eli is standing before him with a wicked grin. Eli's just finished recounting his tale of his night before Christmas. "Oh my god, babe. I can't believe you did that. What did your boss do?"

"She's not my boss anymore. So…" Eli shrugs and straightens his glasses. He's looking positively delicious in his sweatpants, t-shirt, and cardigan. It's chilly on the boat, and Chris wants nothing more than to crawl under the blankets and make up for the last five nights without Eli.

"Do you have any idea how sexy you are right now?" Chris asks, reaching for Eli, who steps forward between his legs.

"If it's even half as sexy as you, we're both in trouble." Eli leans in with a kiss. "I missed you," he says, so close that each word is a kiss in itself.

"I missed you too." Chris scoots closer to the edge of the table, wrapping his legs and arms around Eli. A thrill runs the length of his body. "Will you come with me next time?" He runs a finger over Eli's soft beard.

Eli cocks his head with a little smirk. Then he brings his eyebrows together with a serious stare. "You really want me to come with you?"

"Why wouldn't I?" Chris kisses the wrinkle on his forehead.

"I don't know." Eli shrugs, shakes his head, and steps out of Chris's embrace, avoiding eye contact. "I guess I'm used to being someone's dirty little secret."

Chris reaches out to take both of Eli's hands in his. He tugs him closer. "Hey," he says softly. Eli looks at him, blinking his extraordinary two-toned eyes. "I don't know how anyone could keep you a secret. All I wanted to do, from the moment you held me in your arms and kissed me, was tell the world what I'd found. I wish you could see yourself the way I do." A chuckle escapes Eli's lips, and he looks away again, his cheeks coloring. "I mean it, Eli. You don't give yourself enough credit. To go through what you've gone through and still see beauty everywhere. To be this genuine and kind and playful despite it all." Chris pulls him closer and holds Eli's face in one hand so he can't look away.

Eli gives his head a tiny shake and closes his eyes. A small smile plays at the corners of his full lips. "You're describing yourself, you know?" He opens his eyes, holding Chris in his dazzling gaze. "You're the kind one, the beautiful one. I still don't know what I did to be so lucky to be with you."

Chris reaches up and slips Eli's glasses from his face for a better look at his incredible eyes. "You didn't do anything. You're you, and *you* make me happier than I've ever been. I can't wait for my family to meet you. They're going to fall in love with you, just like I have."

Eli cocks his head, a look of surprise on his face. Chris realizes what he's said with a jolt. Then he straightens his shoulders with resolve.

"That's right, Eli. I said it, and I meant it. I love you. I think I have since that first night when you held me so close."

Eli's lips are on his in an instant, his hands holding Chris's face as he all but devours him. He steps back into Chris's embrace fully.

"I love you too." Eli's voice sounds desperate between kisses. "I didn't know love like this was even possible. You make me feel like I've never felt before. Shit, Chris, you make me *feel*. I've been numb for so long." He continues with his crushing kisses, pressing his body against Chris. "So numb." More kisses. "Now look at me." His erection throbs against Chris, whose own cock responds. "I can't stop feeling. I want all of you all the time."

"I want you too," Chris says, gripping the soft, worn fabric of Eli's cardigan, then pushing it off his shoulders. As he peels off his own shirt, cool air hits his skin.

They rush from the kitchen to the unmade bed piled high with blankets and pillows. They dive in together, and Eli pulls the blankets up around their bare shoulders. He leaves kisses wherever he finds skin: Chris's shoulder, his neck, his chin, his cheek, his lips.

Eli moves over him, pulling the blankets over their heads. He smiles wildly and moves down Chris's torso with a barrage of kisses. The sweet musk of their arousal fills their little blanket fort. Words fall away. Touch is the only language they need.

Eli's love confession is a tactile thing as he kisses and hungrily licks Chris, who writhes beneath his hand and lips and tongue. He loses sense of time and reality, suspended in a dreamlike world of pleasure and joy. Eli's hands roam his body, creating warmth over every inch of him. He sighs and moans as Eli's soft beard tickles his skin.

Then Eli's above him, low light filtering through the blanket. There's an intensity in the look Eli gives him: his lips slack with desire, his breath almost ragged.

They exchange no words as the thick head of Eli's dick prods at his ass. A tremor of fear passes through Chris as he realizes the difference between Eli and Tyler. His face burns with excitement. A quick shuffle out of the blankets and Eli returns. Icy cold lube drips down Chris's ass crack, and Eli catches it, massaging it all over with gentle strokes. The snapping of stretching skin is all Chris can feel as Eli eases his weighty glans slowly into place. Fire runs the length of Chris's body, from his face to his ass. It's excruciating and beautiful all at once.

He whimpers and squirms. Eli pulls out with a pop. "I'm sorry," he says quickly, covering Chris's face with kisses. "I'm sorry. Are you okay?"

"I'm more than okay. Surprised is all." Chris returns his kisses. "Do it again."

Eli gives his most wicked grin. More cold lube and gentle massaging. He's there again, filling Chris up completely. There's nothing Chris can do but surrender to the aching fullness. He relaxes into Eli's careful thrusts, sliding a bit deeper with each one.

Pleasure blooms, and Chris forgets to breathe, suspended by the delicious torture.

Eli rises up, letting the blankets fall away. Cold air kisses every inch of Chris's burning skin, and he shivers. Eli's hand travels over Chris's chest and stomach, caressing him with reverence.

Then, chilly lube runs down his cock. Eli strokes it slowly with one hand, holding Chris's hip with the other. Eli rolls his hips, working his fat cock deeper still.

Chris calls out from pain and pleasure. Eli stops moving his hips but continues working Chris's cock. He's impaled, and every stroke of Eli's hand feels like a million tiny kisses of pleasure.

"Do you want me to stop?" Eli asks gently.

"No." The word is barely a breath. The heat spreading from Eli's cock is almost more than Chris can bear. But the idea of it being gone is the worst thing he can imagine.

Eli gives Chris's cock a tender squeeze, then continues moving his hips and stroking the length of his dick that's never been harder. He quickens his pace, moving faster but still carefully.

Chris watches Eli's face, lost in bliss. His eyes are closed, and his jaw, set only moments ago with determination and control, is now relaxed. His white teeth flash as he bites his bottom lip.

Then he's gripping both Chris's hip and cock. He squeezes as he pulses deep inside of Chris, sending a tremor so rich and sublime, Chris cums harder than he ever has. His cock twitches in Eli's hand as their bodies relax. When Eli slides out of him, he feels impossibly full and empty all at once. As Eli moves beside him and wraps his arms around Chris squeezing gently.

"You're amazing," Chris says, still out of breath.

"Says the most incredible creature I've ever seen." Eli's sleepy words are followed by a chuckle.

\*\*\*

*Eli*

"Good morning," Eli sings from the kitchen as he pours two cups of coffee and carries them to Chris in bed.

"Good morning." Chris sits up, his thick hair mussed beautifully, blankets falling around him. He yawns, and Eli takes in every lovely inch of his sleepy face before sitting beside him and offering the piping cup. "Thank you." Chris takes it and curls up against the pillows piled high in the corner, making room for Eli.

"What are your plans for today?"

"I don't have any, really. I'm off until Tuesday. Then it's practice every night until the show. How about you?" Chris asks, sipping at his mug.

"Well, I'm unemployed, so I've got nothing. I doubt I'll be able to find another job before New Year's. It's a slow week for restaurants. Everyone's broke and full of cheese." Eli leans against the wall and looks around the room. He takes in the bookshelves, loaded with old paperbacks. He remembers his dad on their lazy river days, laid back in the hammock, reading, and wonders what life would be like if his parents hadn't been stolen from him. "I always wonder what their plan was," he says absently.

"Whose plan?" Chris asks.

"My folks'. What were they going to do with us as we got older? I mean, Olive was almost eighteen when everything went down, and they had never talked about college. Never talked about her going anywhere or doing anything. At least not in front of me. What was their plan? Didn't they realize that children grow and become adults who live lives of their own? Were we supposed to stay there on the farm forever, always in the dark about what they were doing? Or were they raising us to take on the family business with no idea about the consequences involved in said business?"

"I'm sure they had a plan," Chris says. "They had to."

"Did they? I mean, I spent so many years of my life heartbroken and angry about what happened. I never thought to blame them for any of it. I've got to start being honest with myself though. They were as much at fault, maybe more so than the agents who gunned my dad down. They could've been teachers, or artists, or fucking line cooks. They could've sent us to school and taught us about the fucking world as it really was. Instead, they kept us like little pets, living in a make-believe world that didn't prepare us for life, and didn't fucking exist."

"Your world existed, Eli," Chris reassures. "I'm not sure what their plans were, but from everything you and Olive have told me, your parents were good people, and they loved you very much. Maybe they lacked some foresight. They were dreamers, idealists. They believed they were doing what was best for both of you. Don't let your anger sully your memories of them."

"I know that in my heart. I do. It's only, sometimes, when I'm really thinking about it, I get so angry. How could there have been no plan whatsoever?"

"They had to've had one." Chris pulls his feet under his body and sits up against the wall. "Think of the situation though. Once your dad was gone and your mom in prison, there was no privacy. Every meeting you had with your mom was observed. She couldn't have told you anything."

"I don't know." Eli shakes his head and continues to scan the books on the wraparound shelves. "I spent weeks in that house looking for anything the feds might've missed. But all that was left behind was a bunch of shattered dishes and torn furniture. All the closets had been turned out and floorboards were broken. They didn't find a thing, and neither did I. There had to have been someone else somewhere. Someone who no one knew about. Like a kingpin or something. Maybe they weren't making any money and someone else was paying them to live there and take care of the place, and that person abandoned the whole property after the bust."

"Maybe. It's hard to say what was going on then. It was so long ago." Chris looks concerned.

"Sorry. I've been thinking a lot these last few days. Especially after I walked out on work. You weren't here, so I spent a lot of time alone with my thoughts."

"I understand. I can't begin to imagine what you and Olive have been through over the years. But I like to think that what you had before as children was something very special. You can't let what's happened since then rob you of that." Chris takes another sip of his coffee before setting the cup down in the windowsill, then he scoots down in the pillows and opens his arms wide.

Eli abandons his own cup to the floor and moves into his lover's embrace. "I know. It can be so frustrating sometimes."

"You know what you should do when that happens?" Chris strokes Eli's shoulder as he talks.

Eli looks up, his cheek resting on Chris's chest. "What?"

"You should call Olive. She's the only person that really knows what you're feeling. You can be each other's strength." Chris continues to run his hand over Eli's shoulder.

Eli sighs heavily. "I know. You're right. But she and Vic have their thing, and they're so happy. I always feel like I bring the mood down when I call or show up."

"That can't be true. I've never seen Olive happier than when I see her with you."

"Really? Vic seems to make her happy." Eli chuckles, thinking of how happy Chris makes him. A warmth of appreciation grows in his chest, not only for Chris but for Vic as well. They were there for Olive after she spent a decade living alone. The whole damn group of Burlesque A La Mode was there for her when he couldn't be.

"You were the missing piece." Chris scoots further down and wraps Eli in his arms. "Come to think of it, you're my missing piece too. I don't think you fully appreciate how wonderful you are," Chris says softly before meeting Eli's lips with a deep kiss.

Desire simmers in his belly as Chris's hands run up and down his back. He shifts his weight, curling his body into Chris's embrace.

"You're mine too," Eli breathes between hungry kisses.

They slip together under the blankets, lips and hands filling the space between them, saying what words cannot.

# CHAPTER EIGHTEEN
*Chris*

As Bunny reaches for her phone on the vanity table, Chris commands around the pins between his teeth, "Stand still, Bunny." Eli is perched on the opposite vanity, watching the exchange with amusement. It's still early in the afternoon, and they're the only ones in the dressing room. They rushed over after a harried Bunny called with a show-day emergency.

"I'm sorry, Chris. I can't believe this happened," she laments. "I mean, I know I've done nothing but eat since Thanksgiving, but shit, I didn't think I was this fat."

"You're not fat, dear. You're full-bodied," Chris says, still biting the pins. He pulls the seam of a broken zipper into place and pins it carefully every half inch. "What I don't understand is how this happened so suddenly. I know you didn't dress for rehearsals, but it zipped up just fine two weeks ago."

"Yeah, but two weeks is a long time for..." Bunny stops mid-sentence and looks around the room nervously.

"For what?" Chris plucks the pins from his mouth and turns Bunny to face him. She looks at the ground, then over his shoulder to the door. "Bunny?" Chris asks, narrowing his eyes.

She looks up at him with a sparkling grin. "For a pregnant woman." She flutters her lashes and blushes fully. "I'm twelve weeks today. Mike knows, but we were waiting to tell everyone tonight. We're going to have a baby." Bunny's eyes glisten with joyful tears. She wipes them away quickly, sniffles, and covers her grin with both hands. "We wanted to wait until we were in the clear and figured tonight would be a good night to make our announcement. But I've been feeling extra bloated all day, and I was afraid my dress wouldn't fit, so I snuck over early to try it on. I guess I forced the zipper and it broke." She begins to sob. "Can you fix it?"

Chris pulls her into his arms. "Oh, honey. Of course I can." He holds her tight, looking over her shoulder to Eli. Speaking with his eyes, he tells Eli to scoot. Eli smiles brightly and disappears without a word. "Let's get you out of this," Chris coos softly as he steps away from their hug. "I can give you a little more space if I nudge the pins a bit. It won't be permanent, but it'll work for tonight."

"Thank you so much, Chris. I don't know what I'm doing these days. My mind is all over the place." She chuckles and slides the dress over her ample hips. "I'm such a hot mess."

Chris assesses her body with this new knowledge. "How did I miss this?" He gestures to the slight swell of her stomach. "Now that I know, it's undeniable."

"Are you serious? Do I really look that bad?"

"Oh, honey, no. You look incredible. You're always so sexy. But now you have that glow."

As the director, Bunny goes through many practices without working on her own routines. She does a lot of her individual practice alone. Chris realizes he's only seen her walk through her routine in sweats a time or two. He hasn't seen her naked since the last show, before she was pregnant.

She's always had the most amazing hips. But now, with her small pregnant swell, she's absolutely divine. "You are a fucking goddess, Bunny, and you know it. Do I need to get that man of yours back here to remind you of that?" he asks with complete certainty that Mike finds Bunny's pregnant body the most irresistible thing in the world.

"No." Bunny chuckles and drops her gaze to her belly. "He does that every chance he gets." She blushes again and places her hand instinctively on her stomach. "Are you sure you can fix it?" she asks almost shyly.

"Of course I can, and you will be amazing tonight," Chris assures as he sits down and pulls the shimmering gown onto his lap to secure the zipper for the evening.

"Thank you so much." Bunny pulls on her sweats and sits beside him as he works. "So, tell me about you and Eli. I've been so inside my head lately, I feel like I've missed all of it."

"He's so wonderful," Chris says, a pin hovering above the dress. "He's like no one I've ever met. The most unique and interesting person I could imagine. He's so sexy and humble and smart and creative. Like I couldn't imagine a more perfect man for me. He's everything I've ever wanted and didn't know it."

Chris laughs. It's his turn to blush with joy. "I just wish he knew how truly amazing he is." He shakes his head and goes back to pinning Bunny's zipper into place. "I swear, Bunny, he could be a cult leader. And I mean that in the best possible way. Girl, I would drink the Kool-Aid." Bunny smiles and shakes her head. "I mean it. He's so damn captivating. He can be talking about fucking potatoes and I'm hanging on every word. And don't get me started on the sex."

"But that's my favorite subject." Bunny laughs, leaning toward him and resting her chin on her hand.

"It's incredible. Like, I don't know what I was doing before I met him, but it wasn't the same thing." Chris laughs, his cheeks warm with the thought of everything he and Eli have done in their short time together.

"I know what you mean, and this makes me so happy." Bunny looks him over with a dreamy grin. "I never liked Tyler," she says offhandedly.

"I don't even know if I did really." Chris shakes his head, sadness rolling over him at the thought of all those lost years. Then he looks at Bunny's smiling face and remembers all that's happened in the months since he met her. The wasted years don't seem to matter as much in the light of all he's gained.

He smiles back with more gratitude than she could possibly know and holds the finished dress up. "Let's try this on."

***

*Eli*

Eli whisks through the curtain to find Mike cursing from the top of a ladder. He's balancing his large frame with surprising grace as he drills something into the ceiling. Eli watches from his dark corner, considering the information he is now privy to. Chris has told him Mike and Bunny's story, at least what he knows of it, and Eli can only imagine how happy Mike is to be expecting a child with Bunny.

As he watches Mike, Eli thinks of his own father. He wonders about his parents before they had Olive. What was their life like? Had they wanted children? Or were Olive and Eli accidents that they had to make the best of? Was that why they never thought ahead? They never planned on having them in the first place? No. Maybe Olive had been a surprise. But surely, a child seven years later was intended. If not, his arrival couldn't have changed their lives too much.

They'd been such loving people, so kind and compassionate in everything they taught Eli and Olive. How could they have been so dismissive of their wellbeing?

Mike curses again. Eli's startled from his thoughts and looks up with surprise.

"Can you hand me that?" Mike asks sharply, pointing to a screw on the stage floor.

"Oh, shit. Yeah." Eli hurries to pick up the screw. He drops it and has to chase it awkwardly as it rolls away. Once it stops, he plucks it up and hands it up to Mike. Though he's given Eli no reason to be wary, the man is intimidating, to say the least. He's huge and says less than anyone else in the group. And he looks angry or annoyed most of the time, like he has somewhere better to be. Then Bunny shows up, and all his gruff exterior melts, his eyes soften, and he smiles so brilliantly anyone would fall in love.

But Bunny is backstage, getting pinned back into her dress. She won't make an appearance for some time to soften his rough edges, and Mike seems extra pissed. He levels his angry stare at Eli, who wishes he could disappear back into the dressing room.

"Could you hold this damn ladder?"

"Sure." Eli gives a short nod and hurries to hold the ladder.

"I can't believe Amanda didn't tell me about this until today. I could've had this rigged up weeks ago," Mike grumbles around the screws between his teeth and continues to curse under his breath.

Eli assumes Mike isn't looking for a response, so he stays quiet and holds the ladder still as Mike works at attaching a heavy metal ring to the ceiling above the stage.

"I've got to get another one of these up and two pulley systems rigged before doors open in three hours," Mike says, lumbering down the ladder. "Do you have some time to spare? I could use another set of hands. Vic's on a balloon run with Olive. I'm sure they'll be getting lunch and making a dozen stops along the way, so they'll be a while."

"Yeah. Sure." Eli glows inside at the thought of his sister running errands with Vic. Her life has been almost as solitary and fucked up as his. It's good to know there is some normalcy for them now. He steps aside as Mike lifts the ladder and carries it to the opposite side of the stage. Eli holds it steady and watches as he climbs back up, tool belt jangling.

"It's amazing what these gals have gotten me into." Mike shakes his head as a grin plays at the corners of his lips. Mike's not fooling anyone with the grumbling and cursing. He loves every minute of what he's doing.

As Eli watches him work, he realizes the man is all growl and no bite. Gods help anyone who would do harm to Bunny. He imagines

Mike would set the world on fire for her if he had to. Lucky for the world she's only asking him to hang aerial silks at the last minute.

"All right." Mike descends the ladder. "Let's see how these silks hold up." He picks up a folded length of deep red fabric, then climbs back up the ladder with one hand. A few moments later, the fabric falls with a whisper from the ceiling. Eli watches as Mike descends the ladder and drags it away.

Mike pulls himself up into the dangling loop and swings like a kid at the park. "If it'll hold my fat ass, it'll hold them for sure." He nods toward the ceiling to where the aerial performers are staying for the evening, then he chuckles and hops down. "Let's get the other one up. The pulleys are going to be the hard part."

Eli holds the ladder and watches Mike as he moves with the confidence of a man who knows he can do anything. Before too long, the pulleys are up and attached to the silks. Mike's grinning over a job well done as he raises and lowers them with ease.

Vic and Olive walk through the front door, carrying two bulging black trash bags each. "Don't put that ladder away yet," Vic shouts. "We've got balloons. So many fucking balloons." He laughs and drops the bags on the ground before heading back out.

Olive drops her bags and hugs Eli without warning. "I'm so excited. I can't believe we're performing together." Her excitement is contagious.

He squeezes her back. "I'm excited too. Not sure what to expect. But I'm here for it."

"You're going to love it. I promise. It's incredible."

"I hope so." Eli chuckles as he follows her through the open door. The air outside is bitterly cold. Wind and snow flurries whip at his face.

He's handed two light but cumbersome bags from the back of a covered pickup truck. Gripping them tightly, he hurries back inside, the winter wind doing its best to steal the bags of balloons.

After seeing the state of the weather, he wonders if anyone is going to come to the show. It's a terrible night for anything. In fact, if he could, he'd be home, snuggled with Chris and a bottle of wine, listening to the wind blow while waiting for spring to make its presence known.

As they bring in the last of fourteen bags of balloons, Mike is back up the ladder with a bag in hand. Eli and Olive watch as he pours silver and gold balloons into an already-secured net. "I had this up weeks ago," Mike says with a look of satisfaction. "It's got its own set of pulleys, so right at midnight, John can pull a couple strings and release the balloons." Mike heads back up the ladder with another bag.

Vic and Eli start handing them up to him, making quick work of the project.

Several bartenders arrive, shaking snow out of their hair. They're decked out for a party, looking like they would all be at home on the stage themselves. As the final bag of balloons is loaded into the net and the ladder is carried down to the back hallway, the first excited audience member arrives, shivering from the cold but beaming with excitement. Eli and Olive hurry backstage to get ready for the show.

*** 

Eli watches from behind the curtain, excitement bubbling all around. The aerialists are magnificent, and Mike's rigging holds beautifully. Then, one after another, his newfound friends take to the stage, stripping and dancing. The sold-out crowd cheers, claps, whistles, and laughs—the weather didn't keep them away. In fact, he heard Bunny saying they had to turn folks away at the door who tried to get in last minute.

Eli's heart is in his throat as he watches Susan dance herself out of her costume. Chris comes up behind him and wraps his arms around Eli's waist. "Are you ready?" he asks, his lips on Eli's ear.

"As I'll ever be. I think." Eli laughs nervously and turns away from the curtain into Chris's embrace. "I feel like an idiot. Like, the costume made sense in my mind, but now that it's happening in real life, I feel dumb as hell."

"Oh, stop. Look at me." Chris releases him and steps back, spreading his arms wide. He looks phenomenal in his shimmering tuxedo and top hat. "Look at Bunny." He gestures to Bunny standing in front of the mirror, fluffing her hair in a sparkling gown. No one would ever guess it was safety pinned together.

"You both look incredible. I feel like an Oompa Loompa." Eli looks down at his short pants and suspenders. He remembers his red cheeks and heavy black eye liner. "Or a fucking gingerbread man." He laughs at the ridiculousness of it all. "What am I doing here?"

Chris smiles back at him. "I think you look cute. In fact..." He pulls Eli into his arms and brushes his lips with a soft kiss. "I can't wait for the balloon to drop so I can get you home and make love to your adorable ass."

"Well, in that case." Eli kisses him again, as deeply as their makeup will allow. "I better get out there and get this over with." Susan whisks through the curtains, cheers from the crowd following her. Eli hears James and Marty take the stage, filling time with their banter.

"You're going to be amazing. I bet you're their favorite," Chris says with a sparkle in his eyes.

"Impossible." Eli shakes his head, looking Chris over from head to toe. "They're gonna love you even more."

"Ladies and gentlemen, Mr. Eli Meeks." He hears Marty's introduction and waits for his music. Since his search for a stage name came up fruitless and his own name had a simple sound and a natural humor to it, he didn't see a need to change it.

He passes through the curtains as his music plays loud and fills the room. A light snicker rolls over the audience. He begins to play with them and the music, drawing laughter and gasps out of them with surprising ease. They respond to everything he does the exact way he wants them to. And by the end of it all, they're laughing, cheering, applauding, and he's hooked. The adrenaline rush is like nothing he's ever felt, and he wants more. He bows a second and a third time, then pushes through the curtain to be taken into Chris's arms and squeezed tightly.

"You were amazing," Chris whispers in his ear before kissing his lobe. "I love you."

"I love you too." Eli's heart is full to bursting.

He can't believe what he's gotten himself into.

# CHAPTER NINETEEN
*Chris*

The audience of hundreds of people cheer and laugh as Chris pulls Eli in for a New Year's Eve kiss. Champagne has never tasted as delicious as it does off of Eli's lips. "Happy New Year," Chris says against Eli's mouth. "I'm so happy to be spending it with you."

Eli pulls away, his full lips spread into that sweet and shy smile. "I can't believe I'm spending it here with you," he says close to Chris's ear, the warmth of his breath sending a tingle down Chris's spine. "I've got a surprise for us," he whispers. Goosebumps spring up over Chris's entire body at the thought of what his surprise could be.

Eli takes him by the hand and leads him into the dressing room. The lights are low. Eli drops Chris's hand and turns to face him, leaning against a vanity. He's still in his suspenders and shorts with his eyes and cheeks painted, which makes the small baggie of cocaine he slips from his pocket all the more shocking.

"What?" Chris asks with more than a little apprehension.

Eli wiggles the bag in the air with an excited grin. "I thought it might be fun for tonight. What do you think?" he asks, his words already slurred from champagne and whiskey.

Chris is worried and questions if he wants to take drugs with Eli again after what happened the last time.

"It's coke, right?" Chris asks, stalling to give himself time to work out if he's going to do this.

"Yeah." Eli nods. "What else would it be?"

"I don't know. I've never tried it." Chris smiles. "What's it like? Am I going to end up chasing you through the woods again?"

Anger shifts across Eli's face for a flash of a moment. He shakes his head and shrugs. "It's fun. Nothing like an acid trip. It makes you feel ten feet tall and ready to take on the world. But we don't have to if you don't want to. Sometimes, I forget how sheltered you are."

Chris stares at Eli. He looks a bit like a kid being told it's time to leave the playground, and even though Chris has serious trepidations, he doesn't want to disappoint Eli. "I'm in." He steps in to steal a kiss. "Where should we do it?"

"Here," Eli says, looking around and shrugging, this time with an air of playful humor.

"Why not?" Chris throws up his hands.

Eli turns to the vanity and spills some of the white powder onto the countertop, then slips his wallet from his back pocket. He pulls out his debit card and starts cutting through the pile. It's an act Chris has seen dozens of times on TV and in movies, but he's never seen it in real life.

"Don't we need a straw or something?" Chris crowds in close.

"Here." Eli pulls a rolled-up dollar bill from his front pocket with a wicked smile. He bends over the two thin lines on the countertop. One disappears quickly up his nose. He hands the makeshift straw over and sniffs deeply, pinching his nose.

"So, I just do it." Chris places the straw into his nostril and copies Eli's movement without snorting anything.

"Yep," Eli agrees and nods his head with another sniff.

"All right. Here goes nothing." Chris chuckles nervously as he bends to do his very first line of cocaine. His heart is racing, his blood rushing in his ears. He swallows hard and inhales. It burns for a moment, then trickles down his throat, bitter and dry, followed by more burning. It tastes like aspirin. "Fuck. That's awful. Why? Why would you want to do that?"

"Just wait," Eli says with a little laugh as he dabs at the remnants on the tabletop and licks his finger, wagging his eyebrows. "Kiss me," he insists and pulls Chris into his arms, laying a wet, sloppy kiss on his lips.

"Woo," Olive cheers from behind them. She's carrying a champagne flute in each hand. Vic's behind her with his arms around her waist. "Happy New Year," she calls. "I love champagne." She giggles.

Reluctantly, Chris pulls away from Eli's kiss and turns to Olive and Vic. Everything is sharp and gleaming. He can feel his heartbeat in his chest. Olive and Vic are beautiful. Eli's hand on his hip feels like heaven. "So do I," he cheers and crosses the small dressing room to Olive. "Let's go get more."

"Okay," she squeals. "But I don't have any more hands."

"It's okay. I'll get two. Then we'll have four, and we can share them with each other if we need to." Chris laughs and looks over Olive's shoulder to Eli, who's grinning after him. "Do you want more?"

"Sure," Eli says as he and Vic fall into step behind them.

The after-party is in full swing as Chris and the others make their way through the crowd. Small groups of people are chattering all around, smiling at the train of performers as they head to the bar where Bunny is sipping a soda water with lime. She locks eyes with Chris and grins behind her glass. Mike stands beside her, his arm resting casually on her shoulder. He's watching her with nothing less than absolute adoration. Chris smiles back, knowing what they are waiting to reveal.

Eli steps beside him as they approach the bar. Rows of plastic champagne flutes line the bar's counter. Chris places his empty to the side, grabs two full glasses, and hands one over to Eli. The bubbles tickle his nose as he downs his second glass and reaches for another. The energy in the room is positively vibrating all around.

Looking to Eli, he's overwhelmed with the desire to drag him off to a dark corner somewhere for secret kisses and whispers. Also, maybe another line of coke. Eli wasn't kidding: Chris does feel ten feet tall and ready to take on the world. The chatter falls away as the bass line from the speakers picks up. Chris dances in place, rolling his body, taking small steps. He sips lightly at the champagne and watches the revelry that surrounds him.

The conversations are joyful and excited. A group of audience members pull Eli away to fawn over him in his costume. He gives Chris an awkward smile before being surrounded by the chattering group.

Chris grins and shakes his head, turning to Olive. "This has been an amazing night. I don't know how it could get better," he says as she replaces his empty champagne flute with a full one.

"I know." Olive beams. "In a million years, I never would've guessed Eli would be here performing with us. It's a dream come true. And he seems so happy. Look at him." She nods in his direction.

Chris follows her gaze. Eli is charming the group of drunken ladies with his lovely smile. The fact that he's dressed like a ridiculous doll doesn't stop the looks of admiration and outright lust from some of them. One particularly bold woman slips one arm around his waist and whispers something in his ear. Eli's lined eyes flash with amusement. His adorable smile grows into a grin as his gaze finds Chris over the women's heads. He mouths the word "help" before turning his attention back to the ladies.

"He's a natural," Olive says with admiration. "You better go save him though." She giggles and turns back to Vic, whose arms have been waiting to hold her.

"You're right." Chris laughs and grabs two more full champagne flutes. He makes his way through Eli's groupies, stepping beside him. "Sorry, ladies. I need this one's help backstage." They let their disappointment be known with a series of groans and curses. It's amazing what a night of drinks and stripping will do to a person's inhibitions. These ladies seem to have none.

"Bring him back in one piece," one of them shouts from behind Chris and Eli as they walk toward the stage.

"Jesus," Eli breathes. "Those women were wild. Did you see that one? She slipped her hand down the back of my pants." He laughs as they push through the curtains to backstage.

"Are you serious?" Chris turns and looks at him with shock.

"Yeah." Eli nods and smiles, slipping the white baggie from his pocket. "Should've heard what she said to me." He pours the coke out on the table and cuts two lines without asking. He does his line and offers the rolled-up bill to Chris, whose heart is pounding at the thought.

*How did he know I wanted another?* "What did she say?" Chris asks as he takes the bill and snorts the bitter powder up with ease. He's amazed at how good it feels.

"She offered to suck my dick. Then, slipped her hand down the back of my pants and grabbed my ass. I didn't know what to say."

"You should have taken the offer. I always do," Chris says with a flippant shrug. Eli's jaw drops as an uncomfortable silence fills the air. Chris cackles, unable to hold a straight face.

"Oh my god. I thought you were serious for a minute there." Eli goes to work on cutting two more lines.

Chris reins in his laughter, straightening his face. "Who said I wasn't?" More awkward silence as Eli pauses before snorting the next line. He cocks his head and eyes Chris curiously. "Okay, you're right. I would never. Those old girls do get a bit wild after a couple of cocktails, though, don't they?"

Eli chuckles and nods in agreement before bringing the bill back to his nose and sniffing quickly. Chris takes the offered roll-up and does the same. The rush is indescribable. It's like there's a party in his body, and every cell is invited. He feels good, plain and simple, like sex and champagne. A bit gritty maybe. But despite the grit, it's an allover warmth and giddiness that he's loving every minute of.

"What should we do now?" Chris asks, not wanting the feeling to end.

"Whatever you want to do," Eli offers, his eyes sparkling with mischief.

"I want to kiss you." Chris steps forward, reaching for Eli's face with both hands. He pulls him into a sloppy kiss.

"Hey, you two." Bunny's voice breaks through the moment. "The crowd has thinned out quite a bit. We're about to make our announcement. I know you both know already, but it doesn't seem right to make it without you there."

"All right." Chris clears his throat, feeling like he's been caught in some sordid act by his mom. "We'll be out in a minute."

Bunny chuckles lightly. "Okay. We'll wait. Don't take too long. I think Mike is trying to get me out of here soon. Pretty sure he likes the weight I've put on." She pats her belly with a glowing grin and pushes through the curtains.

"Oh, my goodness. She almost caught us." Chris giggles and kisses Eli again. "This is so much fun. Let's get more champagne." He takes Eli's hand in his and leads him through the curtains.

***

*Eli*

Bright morning sun filters through the curtains and onto Eli's face. He rolls to his side, searching the mattress for Chris. It's empty. The sound of retching in the tiny bathroom jars him as he rubs the sleep from his eyes. He sits up. "Are you okay?" he calls and lowers his feet to the floor.

"I'm fine," Chris barely squeaks from the other side of the tiny bathroom door. Eli stands to cross the room. "Don't come in here," Chris says quickly, his voice louder than before. "It's bad."

"Can I get you anything?" Eli asks, crossing the room anyway to stand outside the door. The smell of Chris's sick permeates the air. It's heavy and sweet in the absolute worst way.

"I don't know. Maybe water. How are you?" Chris asks, his voice trembling and weak.

Eli does a quick assessment of his own well-being. His head is swimming. He's a bit achy. Other than that, he's fine. He's worked plenty of twelve-hour days in much worse shape. "I'm fine. Why don't you come out of there and get back into bed. I can get you a bucket or something."

"I need a shower," Chris whimpers. "My head hurts so bad."

Eli's heart breaks. He's never heard Chris so miserable.

Sure, they've had their fair share of hangovers since they've been together, but they've never been so bad that a hot cup of coffee and a greasy breakfast wouldn't fix it.

The shower starts, and Eli heads to the kitchen to start a pot of coffee and rummage through the cabinets for a bowl large enough to double as a barf bin. He searches the fridge for some juice and finds little more than some takeout boxes and a couple bottles of wine.

Knowing what Chris is going through, Eli considers hiding the bottles to spare him the inevitable turning of his stomach.

Chris shuffles through the door. His normally bright, fluffy hair is limp and wet on his forehead. His freckles are stark against his pallid skin. There is no bloom to his cheeks, no sparkle in his eyes. He looks as close to death as a man can look while still walking.

"Oh, babe," Eli cries out upon seeing him. "I'm so sorry."

"I did this to myself," Chris grumbles. "Look at you. You seem fine."

"I've been abusing myself for years. You're new to it. I should've watched what you were doing."

"I can take care of myself. You don't need to feel guilty."

"Well, I do. How can I help?"

Chris leans on the doorframe and winces, placing one hand against his forehead and squeezing his eyes shut. "Can you make the pounding go away?"

"Sorry. The only thing you can do is sleep it off. Why don't I tuck you in and head out for a while? I can bring back some juice and Gatorade and stuff."

"I don't know if I will be able to fall asleep. I was already lying in bed for what felt like hours, trying not to throw up."

"We didn't get in until well after four this morning. You fell right out. It's only nine now. You couldn't have gotten much sleep. I bet you'll be able to sleep now. I'll hang around if you want me to," Eli offers, feeling terribly guilty for Chris's current state.

"I don't remember anything after Bunny and Mike made their announcement." Chris whines as he slinks back to the bed and wraps himself in as many blankets as he can. His teeth are chattering.

"You had a blast," Eli assures him, taking a towel from the hook on the bathroom door and crossing to the bed. "Let me dry your hair better. You're going to freeze with it this wet."

Chris scoots up in his spot and bends his neck. Eli roughs his sopping hair until it springs up, damp but lively.

"Here, put this on," Eli says. He grabs one of his stocking caps from their pile of coats and clothes in the chair. "It'll keep your head warm."

Chris pulls the hat over his hair and looks up, his bloodshot eyes glistening with unshed tears. "Thank you." He pouts and pulls the blankets around his shoulders, shivering as he lays his head on the pillows. "I'm pretty sure I'm dying," he says flatly from under the pile of blankets.

"I won't let you die." Eli chuckles to himself, wishing that he could magically take the pain away. "Do you want me to hang out a while?" Chris doesn't respond with words. He merely slips one hand from out of the covers, reaching for Eli. Eli slips under the covers to wrap Chris in his arms. "I'll wait 'til you're sleeping," he says softly. Chris snuggles against him, relaxing into his embrace.

"Thank you," Chris barely whispers. Before too long his breaths grow heavy with sleep, and Eli nods off himself, more hungover than he let on.

He wakes from a heavy sleep to the sound of shuffling around the room. Shaking lost dreams from his mind, Eli sits up against the wall. Chris is wearing his sweatpants and two sweaters. He still has the stocking cap on and has added two scarfs and a couple pairs of wooly socks to his look.

"It's so cold in here," Chris says through pale lips, pulled tight in discomfort. "I'm miserable." Chris slumps down onto the foot of the bed. Eli moves quickly to pull him close, the cold air a shock as his warm blankets fall away.

"I'm sorry, babe." Eli pulls him close with one arm. Chris leans into it. "I never should've bought the coke."

"No. I'm a big boy. I should've known when to stop. Besides, I'm pretty sure it's the champagne and cocktails more than the cocaine. I didn't eat anything yesterday."

"That would explain it." Eli squeezes his shoulder. "Are you hungry now?"

"I don't know if I should eat, but I want to."

"There isn't much here. Do you feel up to going out? I could run to the store and cook for you. Or we could get to the Pancake House. I'm pretty sure they're still open."

"That sounds nice. Maybe we could get Olive and Vic to meet us. They're just across the street. Maybe I could get them to let me use their shower. The trickle of almost warm water was hardly what I needed. Have you seen their shower? It's glorious."

"I have. And I bet they would. Why don't you pack a bag, and I'll go start the car and give them a call?"

\*\*\*

"Oh, Chris. Poor baby. Look at you," Olive calls from a booth near the door. The Pancake House is always busy, but it's packed during late-morning on New Year's Day.

Folks waiting for tables line the front counter, looking jealous as Eli and Chris walk past to their table. "How are you even up and walking?" she asks as she stands to wrap him in a hug. Eli watches as she holds Chris tight and sways slightly. It's the way their mom would hug: with every ounce of her being. His heart warms with the memory and the knowledge that those motherly hugs are no longer a thing of distant memory and dreams.

Olive looks over Chris's sagging shoulders, offering Eli a look of understanding. She steps aside to allow Chris access to the booth. He slides in and rests his head on his arms.

"I don't know if this was such a good idea," he mumbles from the safety of his head rest.

"Do you want to go next door and lie down? We can order you something and bring it up?" Olive asks, shooting Eli a look of concern.

"No, I'm fine. If the room would just stop spinning."

"Oh, honey," Olive sings and drapes an arm over his shoulder.

"He's looking much better than he was. If you can believe it." Eli slides into the empty side of the booth. "Is Vic coming?"

"Yeah. He's across the street doing some cleanup. We left the Speakeasy pretty wrecked last night." Olive chuckles and waves for the waitress. They order coffee, water, and juice for four. "When you called, I came over to get us a seat. We're lucky we got in. Look at this place."

"Maybe I should apply here. Diner hours are great. No late nights."

"I've always heard the chef here refuses to hire any help. They say he does it all on his own and sleeps in the basement. I don't know how much of it is true." Olive shrugs and looks over at Chris, then back to Eli. "What did you do to him?" she teases.

"I did it to myself," Chris says, sitting up. His eyes are still bloodshot, his skin still abnormally pale. "Now, if you'll excuse me, I need to get to the restroom. Immediately."

Olive slides out quickly, making room for him to pass. "Should we follow him?" She looks down at Eli, her brow knit with concern.

"He hasn't accepted any of my help all morning. I think he'd prefer privacy," Eli says. "Honestly, I think he'd prefer a nice hot shower and a real bed. That shit on the houseboat is fun in the summer on a perfect day, but if I know Chris, I imagine he could use some luxury therapy."

"You're right. There are few things worse than being hungover on a houseboat that rocks every time you move. Should we order to go, then?"

"Let's wait and see how he feels when he comes back."

Their coffee arrives, and Eli and Olive settle into a comfortable conversation that would've been impossible a few months ago.

"I'm really happy you're here, Eli," she says, stirring cream into her coffee. They share a quiet moment, exchanging smiles and unspoken words of love and acceptance.

"I'm happy too, Olive. For the first time in a very long time, I can honestly say that I am happy."

Chris stalks up to the booth, a hot red blush across his ashen cheeks. Anger and discomfort flash in his eyes. "We need to go," he demands, pulling his coat on and wiping tears from his eyes. "Now."

He looks from Eli to Olive and turns to the door.

They can see him crossing the street before they have their coats on.

# CHAPTER TWENTY
*Chris*

"Fuck." Chris sighs and washes his bile down the sink. The smell of coffee and pancakes was too much for his angry stomach. Luckily, he's had barely more than a sip of water all day. He splashes water on his face and steadies himself. His reflection stares back at him, a stranger. He's always been pale, but it's usually a lively, fresh-faced pale, youthful and healthy. Except now he's as pale as death—even his freckles seem to have faded somehow. The only real color he sees is in the pink of his bloodshot eyes and the dark rings under them.

His hair sticks out from under Eli's stocking cap in all directions. He looks like he belongs in Eli's apartment, crawling out from under a pile of dingy blankets and pillows. No, that's not right. It's honestly offensive to Gordo.

Chris looks like the walking dead. *What does it matter?* he asks himself. He'll be back home in Eli's arms in no time. After a solid meal and a good long sleep, he'll be back to his old self again. Drying his face with a paper towel, he turns to leave the cramped bathroom. The door swings open. He's standing face to face with Tyler.

"Jesus," Tyler breathes, making no attempt to hide his disgust. He even covers his nose and recoils slightly. "What the fuck, Chris?" He looks beautiful even with the disdain. The silver hair at his temples, his thick-framed glasses, the strong line of his jaw. He's put together, as always, but he looks like he's lost weight. As Chris drinks him in, he wants to cry. He's been painting his memories of

Tyler with all the anger and loneliness he felt at the end. He's forgotten what an attractive man Tyler is.

"New Year's Eve." Chris shrugs and feels his stomach turn. He might throw up again. The room shifts and spins slightly. His cheeks blaze with embarrassment.

"I can see things are going well." Tyler sneers down at him and steps aside, allowing a man to walk past him to the stall. He's as young and pretty as Chris was five years ago when he first met Tyler. The young man carries himself with pride. He's dressed impeccably and holding his chin high, his shoulders straight. Clearly, the guy feels like Tyler's queen, spoiled and loved. Chris remembers that feeling. He remembers how much he loved his friends' envy and the looks of strangers on the street. How he loved being kept. It came at a cost, though, far greater than the reward.

"I could say the same for you," Chris spits back, cocking his head in the direction of the stall. "You keep getting older. But they stay the same age." The rage and embarrassment rolling and burning in Chris's belly threatens to burst forth in another torrent of retching and bile.

For a moment he considers letting it loose onto Tyler's designer shoes. Instead, he gives a curt nod. "Now, if you'll excuse me." Chris pushes past, not giving Tyler an opportunity for a comeback. Then he rushes through the bustling dining room to the booth where Eli and Olive sit, sharing comfortable conversation—a moment that would've made his heart sing any other day.

Not today. He's horrified Tyler saw him here and at his absolute lowest point. "We need to go." He grabs his coat and throws it on quickly. "Now." On that, he turns and heads out into the cold winter morning. He crosses the slushy street to the Speakeasy, anger and shame coursing through him.

Pushing through the door, he runs right into Vic. "I'm sorry," Chris says through frustrated tears.

"Hey. What's up? Is everything okay? Where's Olive?" Vic asks, his voice rising slightly with fear as he realizes that Chris is alone.

"She's fine. Everyone is fine. I'm a fucking mess." Chris hates the sound of his own voice as he pushes past Vic, headed toward the bathroom. "I'm gonna throw up again."

"Chris," Eli calls from the doorway as the bathroom door swings shut behind him. Chris turns the lock and leans against the door, looking at himself in the mirror. He looks like hell, like absolute shit. Like a fucking junkie. There's no color in his lips, and the dark rings around his bloodshot eyes are heavy. The frizzy shock of red that sticks out of Eli's cap looks dry and brittle. There's a knock at the door.

"I'm fine. Go away, please," Chris says, knowing it's Eli on the other side of the door.

"What happened over there?" Through the door, Chris can hear the concern in Eli's voice.

"It's nothing. I just need a moment, please." He squeezes back tears and wipes at his face with bare hands. The room isn't spinning, but it shifts too much with every movement he makes. His head is heavy and somehow floating at the same time. Random memories of the night before sift through his hazy mind. Every glass of champagne, every line of coke, every cocktail. Then, several attempts at making love with two semi-flaccid cocks until one or both of them fell asleep. All to wake up to this. This awful looking creature in the mirror.

*Tyler must be so full of himself now.* The image of Tyler smirking down at him in the bathroom while he let his new little boy toy pass sparks the fires of rage and embarrassment again. *Why did he have to be there? Why today? But what day would I have picked to run into him? When have I not been hungover in the last few weeks?*

Looking back over the time since he left Tyler, Chris realizes he's barely been sober since he met Eli. They've shared more bottles of wine than he can count. How many new drugs has he tried in the last two months?

*Here comes that low moment of every hangover where I tell myself I'm never drinking again.*

Chris stares into his reflection. He's angry, broken, tired, and sick. Not to mention ashamed and embarrassed.

"Something has to change," he says to the reflection he barely recognizes.

***

*Eli*

Eli sits alone at a table, waiting. Olive and Vic have headed upstairs to order takeout, leaving an open invitation for him and Chris to join them. The air has the stale, familiar smell of lingering perfume and body odor. Spilled drinks never quite get cleaned from the carpet, and decades of cigarette smoke are embedded in the wall, despite the fact that there hasn't been a cigarette lit inside the building for years. It's how bars smell when they're empty.

It takes people and good times to make the smell go away, a magic he's never quite understood. *How do so many bodies in a room make it smell better?* He ponders this and many more random thoughts as he waits for Chris to exit the bathroom, concerned about whatever happened in the bathroom across the street.

"Hey," Chris says softly as he slips through the door, looking faded and worn.

"Hey. Are you okay?" Eli stands to wrap him in his arms. Chris holds up a hand to stop him.

"No. Please."

The hurt of Chris's rejection crushes him in a way he didn't think possible. He slouches in on himself and steps back.

"I'm sorry, Eli. I'm so sick and embarrassed. I can't even talk about it right now. I feel terrible and disgusting. I don't want to be touched or touch anyone. I want to curl up in a ball and cry. Or die, maybe. I don't know." Chris shrugs and leans against the wall.

Eli settles onto the tabletop, sliding his hands in his pockets, attempting to look casual as his heart crumbles. "What happened over there?" he asks softly.

Chris sighs and brings one hand to his head, covering his eyes. "I ran into Tyler." His words are barely a breath. "He was so smug." Chris drops his hand to rest across his waist and looks at Eli. "He was with someone."

Chris's words cut through Eli's mask of calm. Knowing it was Tyler who'd caused yet more pain for Chris makes Eli's blood boil. He's never been a jealous man. Hell, he's never had anyone to be jealous of or about. But the idea of Tyler being able to torment Chris in any way makes him feel things he's never felt before. Things he would rather not feel at all.

"What does it matter if he was with someone?" Eli snaps, surprising himself with the acrid tone of his voice.

Chris brings both hands to his face and rubs his temples, closing his eyes. "It doesn't." He shakes his head slightly. "It really doesn't. But the man, the boy, he was with was young and pretty and put together. He reminded me of me five years ago. And there I was," he scoffs and continues to rub his face in frustration, "looking like the absolute pile of trash I am right now."

"You're not a pile of trash," Eli says defensively, wishing he could take Chris in his arms.

"I beg to differ. You might be used to this." Chris gestures to himself and then to Eli. "To hangovers and self-loathing. But I'm not. I'm used to feeling vibrant and alive and proud. Look at me. Do I look proud? Do I look vibrant?"

Eli has never heard Chris speak with such anger and disgust. He feels about two inches tall, knowing Chris is blaming him for everything. For the drugs and the drinking, and for the embarrassing exchange with Tyler. He doesn't answer. He only stands, staring at his feet and the worn carpet beneath them.

"Do I?" Chris insists.

"You look hungover," Eli answers flatly, still looking at his feet. "I'm sorry for that. I never should've brought the coke."

"You seem fine. I never should've done it." Chris stands, his arms tucked around his waist, his voice absent of the love Eli has come to expect from him.

"Well, you know. Self-loathing and all. I'm used to it." Their gazes meet for the first time since Chris came out of the bathroom. His cold and distant expression warms a bit.

"That's not what I meant," Chris responds with little conviction.

"I know what you meant," Eli says calmly. They stand in silence for what feels like eternity. "Look. I'm going to take off. I've got my keys to my apartment. I'll hang out there. You should stay here with Olive and Vic. Get a good shower, sleep in a big bed. Rest. Hit me up later, if you want. I'll be around." Eli places the keys to Chris's car on the table beside him and heads to the door, hopeful that Chris will call his name.

He doesn't.

***

It's cold and bright in that sad gray way that only January can be. Eli walks along the sidewalk, feeling the old familiar loneliness and pain creep back into his heart. With every step he feels a wall going up between him and Chris, where each word Chris has spoken and not spoken is another heavy brick. Chris is shutting him out, pushing him away. And he should. Eli has never been any good for anyone. He's been fooling himself the entire time he's been with Chris, wasting both of their time, pretending he could be happy.

Cars move slowly down the slushy street. People mill in and out of the Pancake House. Eli wonders if one of them is Tyler. He wonders what the man looks like. For a moment he's tempted to go back inside, to see if he can't pick Tyler out of the room.

As he considers crossing the street, a handsome older man with oversized glasses and a fine black peacoat holds the door open for a lovely young man. They make an attractive pair, and Eli's sure it's Tyler and his new boy.

Eli watches them from where he stands. Tyler is the type of guy who Eli was always looking for in the bars and clubs. Except they usually went home to their wife and kids, not their pretty little boyfriends. Or maybe they did. Eli didn't know. He'd never cared to ask.

Watching as Tyler opens the car door for his friend, Eli understands what Chris was feeling. He imagines the life Tyler gave Chris, safe and luxurious. Chris surely had everything he ever wanted or needed with Tyler.

What did Eli have to offer him? He didn't even have a job, and he crashed on a houseboat that really didn't belong to either of them every night. No wonder Chris was throwing up those walls.

*Maybe, probably,* he thinks as he begins up the stairs to his apartment. *It's time for me to move on.*

# CHAPTER TWENTY-ONE
*Chris*

*This is heavenly.* Chris wakes in a soft, cozy bed. Heavy drapes are pulled tight over the large windows of the guest room, blocking the daylight well enough he has no idea if it's early or late. The pillows are full and soft, and the thick blankets smell freshly laundered.

As he rolls deeper into the pillows to drift back to sleep, memories of the last two days assault him. The show was great, and the after-party was a blast. The morning after, on the other hand… "Oh no." He remembers Tyler and his new boy briefly. Then, his exchange with Eli. He looked so hurt when he left the Speakeasy, telling Chris to call if he wanted. *If* he wanted.

The word cuts through Chris's heart like a hot knife through butter. What did he mean, *if?* Of course Chris wants to call him. In fact, only moments ago, he searched the empty side of the bed before he even realized where he was.

He paws at the bedside table for his phone. There isn't a single alert. No missed messages or phone calls. *Where is he?*

Chris throws off the blankets and rushes down the hall toward the kitchen. Vic and Olive are seated on barstools, sipping coffee and talking quietly. The warm earthy smell permeates the air.

"'Morning." Olive smiles over her cup.

"Good morning, Sleeping Beauty," Vic teases.

"What time is it?" Chris asks, helping himself to a mug from the cabinet and pouring himself a cup.

"Almost noon," Vic answers.

"Where's Eli?" Chris asks, taking his first sip of coffee, hoping Eli showed up at some point in the evening to sleep beside him and woke early.

"I was wondering the same thing," Olive says, placing her cup on the counter.

"He didn't come back last night?" Chris feels his stomach churn like he's hungover.

"Nope." Olive shakes her head. "He didn't answer any of my texts either. What happened yesterday?"

"Oh, shit." Chris looks from Olive to Vic. "He didn't message me at all." The coffee in his cup loses its luster as his mind begins to race. *Where could he be?*

"What happened yesterday?" Olive demands. "You came up here alone, barely said two words, took a shower, and went to bed for like twenty hours."

"Jesus. Really? I'm sorry. Yesterday is a blur. It was awful."

Olive purses her lips and tilts her head but says nothing.

Chris looks from her to Vic, then back. He sighs and stares into his cup. "I ran into Tyler at the restaurant. I was so embarrassed. I sort of lashed out at Eli, blamed him for all of it. He was eerily calm when he left."

"What do you mean?"

"You know how he does and says weird stuff when he's upset and gets all erratic?"

Olive and Vic nod in unison. Vic, a bit more exuberantly than necessary.

Chris ignores Vic's unspoken insult. "Well, he wasn't erratic at all. He was cool and calm. Just placed my keys on the table and told me to call him *if* I wanted." Chris's voice cracks at the end. He takes a sip from his mug to hide his trembling lip. "I guess I wasn't thinking too clearly. I wanted to take a real shower and sleep in a real bed and forget all about running into Tyler. I was being so selfish. I pushed Eli away, but I assumed he would be here when I woke up."

"Shit, Chris. We've got to find him."

"I'm sure he went home." Chris shrugs.

"'Home' home? To the boat?"

"No, to his place, down the street."

"Have you tried calling him?"

"No. When I saw that he hadn't messaged me, I thought he'd be out here. I honestly didn't realize how long I'd been sleeping."

"I'm sure he's fine," Vic says as he crosses the kitchen and leaves his mug in the sink.

"Me too," Chris agrees. Though he isn't sure. He's completely unsure of Eli's wellbeing. He sends a quick text and settles in the seat Vic left open. Olive pats his knee and offers a reassuring smile.

"I bet he's out job hunting." Her tone isn't convincing. Chris feels a heaviness in his chest. Eli almost always responds immediately to messages. The minutes pass as he sits quietly, watching his phone. Olive watches with him.

"He'll be okay. Eli's nothing if not resilient. I'm sure he's just sleeping off a hangover," Vic says, crossing to the doorway. "But let me know if you want to go looking for him."

"Thanks," Chris says. "I'm sure you're probably right. I think I'm going to head back to the boat though. Maybe he's there."

"I bet he is," Olive says with that same tone that says uncertainty.

"You don't really think he's there, do you?" Chris stands to place his cup in the sink. Olive looks at him with a pained expression.

"He could be anywhere," she says flatly. "This is part of his pattern. He disappears when he feels hurt or overwhelmed. I really hope we hear from him soon."

"Well, I'm not going to sit around and wait for him to get back to me. I'll swing by his apartment on my way back to the boat."

"I'll try to get a hold of him too. Maybe Vic is right, and he's just sleeping off a hangover."

"I honestly don't think he gets them. Not like a regular person. All he ever needs is a cup of coffee. But I hope you're right. I feel so bad for how cold I was to him." Chris slumps against the counter.

"Don't feel bad. You were in terrible shape yesterday. You were definitely not yourself," Olive says.

"I was myself enough to not talk to Eli like that. You and I both know how sensitive he is. I was hurt and angry and wanted someone else to be hurt and angry too."

"Do you want me to come with?" Olive asks, standing to join him.

"No. I've only got the two places to check. I'm going to keep my fingers crossed he's in one of them. I'll let you know as soon as I hear from him."

"I'll do the same." Olive offers a hopeful smile.

"Thanks." Chris gathers up his things, feeling defeated and disappointed in himself. He leaves Olive with a quick hug and more promises to call.

Outside offers no hope with its cold air and gray sky. People are moving about, slow and disinterested in the world around them as they shake off the haze of the holiday season. Cars creep by slowly, throwing slush in their wake. Chris watches his breath puff through the air and buries his hands in his pockets. A glance at his reflection shows him wearing the same clothes he had on yesterday and the same stocking cap pulled down to his ears.

Eli's cap.

Chris's face looks different though. Despite the pinched look of concern, he has color in his cheeks again, and his eyes are bright and clear. He could be anyone walking down the street on a cold winter's day.

He wishes that he'd had the same anonymity when he saw Tyler. If only he could've walked on past without engaging. He could've pretended not to see him, but that hadn't been the case. He practically ran right into him while the smell of his sick still hung in the air.

He remembers the look of disgust on Tyler's face, and anger swells in him. Not at Tyler, but at himself. At how he treated Eli in response to running into Tyler and the assumptions Chris made.

It isn't Eli's fault that Tyler is a pretentious douche bag who loves nothing more than to groom young men to be his little toys, spoiling them with the finer things until he grows tired and weary. *He'll leave his new boy as easily as he did me once things grow stale. Why do I even care what he does with that boy? I care about Eli. I need to make this right.*

Chris straightens his shoulders and pushes the buzzer on the door. After what feels like an eternity, Gordo pulls the door open barely enough to peek his head out. "'Sup?" he asks with the casual air that only a man who sleeps on the floor of a community room could possess.

"Is Eli around?"

"Eli?" Gordo seems to go blank for a moment, like a slow computer loading too much data. "Nope." He shakes his head with a casual shrug, then begins to close the door.

"Wait." Chris reaches for the door in desperation. "Has he been home recently?"

"He packed up his shit last night." Gordo moves to shut the door, then stops, narrowing his eyes at Chris. "You should see what he left behind though." He smiles and holds the door open wide, motioning for Chris to follow.

***

*Eli*

He almost forgot his entire life fit into his faded old backpack. His brief time with Chris, Olive, and all of Burlesque A La Mode made him almost believe life is more than sadness and searching for something that he will never find. He almost believed he'd found the something he's been searching for. He believed Chris was what he needed after all the years he's spent wandering and lost.

But no.

Chris was like everything else in this world: a temporary distraction from the heart-sinking pain of existence. Like a potent drug or a stiff drink, the euphoria always passes.

And Eli is left feeling empty and alone again.

*Olive will be okay*, he thinks as he stuffs socks and boxers into the bag and zips the top. Though this reunion has been their best yet, they never last long either.

She'll get over it, she always does. Besides, Eli is more than any one person wants to deal with. He's too much. Even for her. She'll be happier without him.

He'll send a postcard or something, once he settles somewhere. He examines the few trinkets he's held onto over the years. They sit in a line on top of his dresser, reflected in the smoke-stained mirror on the wall. There's one of his dad's many pocketknives—a small, red Swiss Army number, nearly rusted shut from years of lying in the busted garden shed, exposed to the elements. Around that is a chunky necklace made of colorful wooden beads. He remembers the day he and Olive made the necklace for their mom, and how Olive had held the string and allowed him to drop the fat beads onto it one at a time. Mom wore it most days. Lucky for him it wasn't valuable enough to warrant a second look from the feds. He found it lying in a mess of broken boards and tattered linens on his first visit home.

Beside those, he'd arranged several rocks that he collected from back home. They vary in size and color, though each one is smooth and rounded from being handled by his nervous hands so often over the years.

He scoops up everything unceremoniously and drops them into the small pouch on the front of his bag. His candles and incense burner can stay for whatever lost and sorry fool ends up renting this room.

"Hey, man," Gordo calls from the living room. He's moved from his mattress on the floor to the couch. Hunched over a bong on the cluttered coffee table, he takes a long pull and leans back. Blowing a large cloud of skunky, sweet smoke toward the ceiling, he levels his gaze on Eli. "You out of here for good?"

Eli leans his shoulder against the doorframe. He looks over the common room and remembers all the nights he's spent drinking and partying there. Gordo rarely leaves his space, but he's always a gracious host. It's rumored by the younger folks on the floor that he's a vampire. Another rumor is that he's secretly a millionaire who owns the entire building.

Eli knows the truth, though: Gordo is the nephew of the man who owns the building. He's allowed to stay there rent-free in exchange for "keeping the place up." He keeps his space neat enough by piling the trash in the kitchen.

"Yep," Eli answers.

"Well, shit, dude. Hang out and smoke with me. Once more, for old time's sake." Gordo slides to one side of the couch, making room for Eli to join him. "This is some good shit," he says before taking another long pull from the bong.

Eli swings his bag off of his shoulders and sits beside Gordo, taking the offered bong and lighter. He lights the freshly packed bowl and inhales deeply. He coughs unexpectedly and passes the bong back, remembering the first night he met Chris and sharing a joint with him. How he'd hit it like an old pro.

The thought of Chris makes Eli's chest hurt. He never should've gotten so comfortable. Never should've let him get so close or mean so much.

"You finally making it official?" Gordo asks, sliding the bong back his way.

"Hm?" Eli takes another hit, eager to be as far from sober as possible.

"You and the boyfriend. You finally moving in with him?"

Holding the bong resting on his knee, Eli looks at Gordo. Eli's known the man for years but never considered him a friend. At least not one for confiding in. "Nope," he says flatly. "I'm moving on. Been here too long. It's time to see what else the world has to offer."

"Really?" Gordo raises an eyebrow and takes the bong back, then taps out the spent bowl and refills it. "I thought you guys were good together," he says with a shrug before taking another hit.

"He was good for me. I didn't return the favor," Eli says, his heart feeling like stone in his chest.

"These things happen." Gordo nods through a cloud of smoke, looking like the sage caterpillar from Wonderland. "*C'est la vie.*"

"'Tis better to have loved and lost, or some shit like that," Eli responds, waving away all the emotions welling in his throat. He settles into his high, leaning back into the sagging, yet comfortable, couch.

They sit quietly. Music plays softly from somewhere. Eli's gaze floats around the room, admiring the haphazard curation of art on the walls. He's never considered this place home.

Sitting on the couch, stoned out of his mind, he realizes he's lived here longer than anywhere else after his parents' place. This apartment has been more home than any other. This, and the houseboat.

It didn't matter that the boat had been his father's or that Eli helped build it with his tiny hands so many years before. It wasn't the quilts, books, furniture, or dishes that had all been brought on the boat by his parents, by him and Olive.

No. It was Chris.

Chris made it feel like home.

Chris made every place feel like home.

But how did Eli repay it? By filling him with drugs and alcohol to the point of sickness and shame. He is ruining Chris's life. That's why he has to leave. He has to get as far away from Chris as possible.

"Hey," Gordo shouts.

Eli jumps. "Jesus. What?"

"You've got to leave something." Gordo sits up, turning to Eli.

"I don't have anything." Eli gestures to the backpack holding all his earthly possessions.

"It's tradition." Gordo stands, the belt of his bathrobe knocking an empty beer can from the table. Turning slowly, he assesses the walls. "Here." He steps toward the wall and removes a framed picture of a middle-aged woman and her cat. It looks to be from the early eighties. "We can find another place for this one." He lays the frame on the end table and plucks a handful of permanent markers from its drawer. "I trust you." He drops the markers into Eli's lap. "Make your mark."

The frame took up a much larger space than it needed. In removing it, Gordo has cleared a sizable space for Eli to draw on. Eli stares, his stoned mind dull. The song, *J't'emmène au vent* by Louise Attaque plays. Its lyrics pull at his already raw and broken heart. He used his phone to translate the song the first time he heard it.

*I'll take you to the wind, I take you over people, I want you to remember, our love is eternal.*

The song plays on, its upbeat rhythm a stark contrast to the lyrics. He rises slowly, moving through the pleasant haze.

He slides the markers into the pocket of his jeans and pops the lid off the black one with his teeth. Gordo stands beside him, having produced a handle of whiskey from somewhere. He takes a swig and hands it to Eli, who drinks deeply. The amber liquid slides down his throat, warming his belly.

Staring at the blank wall before him, he sees only one thing: Chris. His smiling eyes and tousled hair. Memories of traipsing through the woods with him. How Eli believed him to be the king of the Fae, and how he would've followed Chris into the deepest dark of the earth.

Music plays on, and Gordo stands beside him, offering swigs from the bottle every few moments. Eli drinks his fill and then some, focused on the image that blooms from the marker in his hand.

Autumn leaves surround a throne of branches and stone. Chris is sitting upon the throne, shining with life and love. Monarch butterfly wings open behind him, and there's a golden crown on his head.

"Fuck yeah, man. I dig it." Gordo laughs and takes another pull from the bottle. Eli takes the offered bottle with a hearty swallow. The room spins.

He's back on the couch. People come and go throughout the night, laughing, drinking, and offering a variety of drugs. Eli recognizes only a handful of their visitors. He spends most of the night staring at the wall.

Then he's outside, walking or trudging down the sidewalk. Confused and focused at the same time. He has one single task in mind: he can't leave without saying goodbye. The air is frigid; the wind is blowing and cutting through his light coat. He pushes through it with one sole purpose. *Get to Chris. Kiss his face. Say goodbye.*

It's late. It's cold. The streets are empty. No one around to hassle him. No one who cares. He continues on, leaning into the wind. The marina isn't too far. He'll be in Chris's arms soon. *One last embrace.*

He pushes through the door, breaking the lock.

The boat is empty.

Chris is gone.

Eli falls onto the bed, his chest heavy with the weight of Chris's absence. *How could he be gone? Where could he be?*

It's cold on the boat, cold and dark.

Eli pulls a blanket over his shoulders and shivers.

Tears wet the mattress beneath him.

Then there's nothing.

# CHAPTER TWENTY-TWO
*Chris*

Chris stands in the messy living room. The sickly, sweet smell of dirty dishes, cigarettes, weed, and old liquor fills the air. There's weight to it, one that won't be easily swept away. On the wall before him is the most curious drawing: a cartoon version of himself, seated upon a throne of wood and rocks, leaves fluttering all around. He has the wings of a monarch butterfly and a crown of autumn leaves. His chest aches at the sight. Eli had only talked about his art; he'd never been willing to share it. His talent is undeniable. Chris feels tears wet his eyes. "Where did he go?" he asks Gordo, who's sitting on the couch, bong in hand.

"Not sure." Gordo shrugs and lights the bowl. "He left sometime last night." With the bubbling of the bong, the conversation is over.

"Okay. Well, thanks." Chris looks around the room for any clue that might lead him to Eli's whereabouts. Nothing.

Gordo nods and turns his attention to the documentary playing on his laptop screen. Chris waits awkwardly for a moment, then sees himself out. Down the curry-scented stairway, he hopes upon hope that Eli found his way home.

At the marina, Chris hurries down the dock. His heart races as he spots the door hanging open on the houseboat. Feet pounding over the bouncing boards, he all but leaps onto the boat. It bobs under his weight, chilly water sloshing underneath. There's no sound of the generator running.

He rushes through the door, imagining the worst. Inside, it's slightly warmer. He finds Eli lying face down in their bed, one blanket pulled haphazardly over his shoulder.

"Eli," Chris calls, voice trembling. Eli doesn't move, and a lump forms in Chris's throat. His mouth goes dry. "Eli?" he asks again, kneeling beside Eli's unconscious form.

Laying a hand on Eli's shoulder, he gives a gentle shake. Nothing.

"Oh my god." Chris squeaks, tears forming in the corners of his eyes.

He pushes Eli, forcing him to roll over. Eli's face is caked with dried vomit that smells of whiskey and bile. His skin is cold to the touch.

"Oh my god, oh my god, oh my god." Chris shudders and sobs. "Eli," he shouts, shaking him roughly. Using a blanket, he wipes Eli's face clean and begins slapping his cheek, gently at first, then with more force.

He lowers his ear to Eli's chest and can't hear a heartbeat. "Fuck."

He dials 911.

"Nine one one. What's your emergency?" a female emergency operator answers.

"I need help!" Chris shouts into his phone.

"Sir, we can help. What's your emergency?"

"My boyfriend is unconscious. I found him lying in his own vomit in the cold, and he's not breathing." The words spill out of him higher and faster than he intended.

"What's your address, sir?"

"I... I don't know. I'm at the marina. On a houseboat. Please, send someone. Send someone quick. I think he's dead," he cries, his voice not his own. "Please. I can't hear his heart beating."

"Paramedics are on their way. Is your boyfriend breathing?"

"I don't know. I don't think so."

"Is his airway clear?"

Chris forces Eli's mouth open, sliding his fingers in to check for obstructions. "I think so."

"Do you know CPR?"

"I've seen it on TV. I don't know."

"Okay, what's your name?"

"Chris."

"Okay, Chris. Do you know what happened to your boyfriend?"

"I don't. I think he was drunk and wandered out here at some point last night and passed out with no heat."

"Okay. Do you know how to find a pulse?"

"I'll try." Chris presses his fingers to Eli's neck. The skin under his beard is warmer than his face. Chris presses where there should be a pulse and says a silent prayer. Desperation screams through him as he feels nothing.

"Fuck," he shouts and tries again. Eli's face is pale; his gray lips hang open. "I think he's dead. Please. Please send someone now."

"Chris, the paramedics are on their way. I need you to stay calm so you can help. Will they have access to the boat?"

"I don't know. Can't they drive right up to the dock? I need them here. I need them here now. I think he's dead. I think Eli's dead."

"Chris, did you find a pulse?"

"No. No, I didn't. I can't. I think he's dead."

"I need you to try again."

Chris pushes two fingers harder onto Eli's neck and feels the slightest of pulses. "I feel something. I feel something. It's weak, but it's there," he shouts, a tendril of hope growing in his chest.

"Good. That's good news, Chris. I need you to start doing chest compressions."

"Okay. Just like in the movies?"

"Not quite. I need you to push hard and fast on his chest. Give thirty pushes, then two breaths, then start the compressions again. I need you to do that until the paramedics get there."

"Okay."

Chris starts in right away, pushing hard and fast. The rhythm of Eli's heartbeat is ingrained in his memory from the hours he spent resting his head on Eli's chest.

He knows the beat of Eli's heart better than his own. He pushes with each count, imagining Eli's heart full of blood and life and joy.

He says a prayer to whichever god will listen to bring Eli back. Then, pressing his lips to Eli's cold, open mouth, he breathes two breaths and starts his compressions again. Each push is an appeal to the universe to bring his lover back.

Every compression comes with a memory of Eli's smile, his warm embrace, his playful words. Chris's pleas are answered by the blaring of sirens. "They're here. Should I keep going?" he asks the dispatcher.

"Will they be able to find you where you are?"

"We're the only houseboat in the marina," Chris says before lowering to breathe into Eli's mouth again.

He hears the heavy thuds of boots on the dock. Within moments the tiny houseboat is a flurry of activity. Paramedics and firefighters move quickly to secure Eli to a stretcher and move him off the boat to the ambulance.

Chris stands to the side, answering questions as best he can. They assure him Eli is alive but needs immediate care. They tell him he'll have to follow them to the hospital. In a matter of moments, he's left standing alone in the silent bedroom.

Gray light slips through the thin curtains of the tiny window. He crumples to the floor and sobs, fear wracking his body, coupled with relief and anger. *How could he do this? Why would he put himself in this kind of danger? How could I send him away like that? God, I hope he's okay. Olive needs to know.*

She answers after one ring. "Find him already?" He can hear the smile in her voice.

"Yeah." His voice cracks, followed by more sobs.

"Is he okay? What happened?" Her tone changes dramatically.

"He was here on the boat. Unconscious and half-frozen. I had to do CPR. The ambulance just took him away." His words spill out again in a rush. His heart pounds in his chest. His throat constricts. "Olive, I thought he was dead, but he's breathing. They said he needs immediate care and took him away. I need to get there. I need to follow him."

"Can you drive?" she asks. He hears shuffling and Vic's voice in the background.

"Yeah."

"Okay, I'll meet you there."

***

Time moves differently in the ICU. It's somehow slower and faster in the same instant. Days bleed together in a monotonous blur. So many have passed since Eli laid his keys on the table and walked out of the Speakeasy toward his almost certain death.

Chris wishes for a miracle as he watches several numbers blinking, unchanged on a small monitor. The beeps and whirs of many machines and Eli's slow steady breaths have become a sort of hymnal to Chris's vigil.

Paired with the stream of regret and self-loathing, all he can think is: *This is all my fault. I know how sensitive he is. I should've followed him. Told him I was angrier with myself than anything. I never should've let him leave.*

A nurse slips into the room, offering a comforting smile as she checks Eli's vitals. He stirs: his eyes flutter open, stare at the ceiling, and close again. It's happened a number of times over the last two days.

The first time, Chris's heart soared. He jumped from his seat and rushed to Eli's side, pressing the nurse call button several times. But before she entered the room, Eli was back to his previous state, sleeping soundly while the world went on without him.

Olive comes and goes as often as she can, bringing Chris food he barely eats.

Every day at eight o'clock, the night nurse comes in and shoos him out. The doctors are kind but give Chris only a little information.

Considering Olive is Eli's only family, Chris has to wait for her visits to get the full update.

"Things are going as well as can be expected."

"All he needs is time."

"He's in the best place he can be for now."

"Lucky to be unconscious for this part."

The last comment came from a rather blunt young doctor during the height of Eli's withdrawal.

Eli had been sweating. His heart rate was erratic, spiking up and down, and up again. He stirred fitfully and even groaned in his unconscious state.

When he shook uncontrollably, they would bury him under warmed blankets until he was sweating again.

It went on like that for two days.

Once the worst passed, Eli lay unmoving, aside from the occasional twitching fingers or fluttering lashes.

Chris has stayed by his side all day, every day, longing to see his smile, to hear his laugh, to wrap him in his arms and hold him.

The tubes running from Eli's nose and arms keep Chris from giving a true embrace.

All he can do is hold Eli's hand, stroke his arm, and occasionally place a lingering kiss on his forehead, paired with silent prayers to bring him back.

***

*Eli*

*Light.* Light filters through the trees, doing a playful dance at his bare feet resting in thick, lush grass. A melody floats on the fresh spring air, gentle, yet full of joy. Eli follows the sound of fiddle and bow, up the hill and across the yard. His dad is there, seated on the porch steps, fiddle to his chin. He's playing with his eyes closed and humming along. Eli's heart swells with joy, longing to stroke his father's beard. To feel the strength and warmth of his embrace. Dad looks up from his song and smiles, green eyes sparkling.

Eli opens his mouth to speak. Dad shakes his head and stands. He lowers his fiddle and opens his arms. Eli runs into them, sobbing with relief to know safety and peace once more.

The melody continues to play as he curls into the embrace, into himself, while seeming to shrink. He's a boy again, naïve and full of bliss. The screen door swings open, and Olive runs past on bruised and skinny legs, her long dark hair swinging, and she's full of laughter.

As she runs down the hill toward the woods, she becomes a doe, leaping and twitching her fluffy white tail.

The door swings open again. His mom is standing on the porch, smiling after Olive, watching her bound out of sight. Mom's dreamy smile widens as her gaze drops to Eli. He can all but smell her as she comes down the stairs and wraps both him and his dad in her arms. She's as soft and warm as he remembers.

But there's a sadness in her eyes. Guilt.

Eli holds them both with his juvenile arms. He clings to them as if holding more tightly might keep them here. Might keep him here.

He wants to stay, to be with them, and never leave. To have the life he was meant to. He attempts to speak, to tell them he's here to stay. To let them know Olive is happy and well and that she'll meet them later.

He wants to stay.

They smile down at him and shake their heads, blinking away their tears.

Then he's on the boat, still a child, handing books one at a time to his father as he places each one with care on the shelves they built. He's talking, but Eli can't hear the words, only the rocking of the boat on the water and the songs of birds and bugs and frogs.

His dad stops and holds up the last book Eli handed to him, saying something that seems important. He shows Eli the cover, and though the words don't penetrate Eli's mind, a feeling of desperation and confusion builds. He's being pulled away, spinning and reeling.

Chris is there in the cold and dark. Grinning above him, then dancing into the light, into another place, through trees and stage lights, laughter and joy. He dances among the stars and beckons to Eli. He follows Chris into the inky blackness sprinkled with twinkling lights. He follows on his heels, just out of reach.

What he wouldn't give to crush Chris to his chest, to kiss his smiling lips and run his hands over Chris's taut and smooth body. There's nothing again. Chris is gone. Darkness surrounds him.

A subtle gray light creeps over the edge of his mind's horizon.

Then he's warm, buried under a pile of sterile, starchy blankets.

Pillows crinkle beneath his head.

The distinct, antiseptic smell of a hospital introduces itself.

His mouth is dry.

He tries to roll over and finds himself tangled in tubes and wires.

There's a murmur of voices in the distance and incessant beeping near his head.

His eyes flutter open.

The assault of stark fluorescent light blinds him.

"Olive." Chris's voice raises above the muddle of sounds. "He's awake."

Chris's face hovers above him. Chris's cheeks are tear-stained, and he's wearing a sappy grin while gripping Eli's hand in both of his.

"Hey," Chris says, blinking away more tears. "How are you feeling?"

"I'm thirsty," Eli croaks, his throat bone dry, his lips cracking with movement.

"Let me call someone." Chris pushes the button on the side of the bed. A muffled female voice comes over the speaker. "Eli's awake. He's awake, and he's thirsty," Chris tells her. He sounds almost giddy.

"Hey, you." Olive appears above him, wearing a similar mask of tears and joy. "You scared the hell out of us."

Eli pushes through cobwebs of thoughts and dreams and memories. New Year's Eve, making out with Chris backstage, cocaine, attempts at lovemaking, Chris's hangover, the diner. The memories crowd around until they don't. He was packed up and ready to leave town. Then he was drinking and drawing and smoking.

"What happened?" His words scratch in his dry throat.

"You almost killed yourself," a booming voice answers as a stranger in black scrubs approaches the bed. "You're damn lucky Chris found you when he did. I'd wager you were minutes from death. You owe this man your life."

Eli's mind swirls. Flashes of walking through the cold, of falling into bed. Then, nothing. "I don't understand. How did I get here?" He looks from Olive to Chris, then to the doctor. The doc doesn't share the concern and love of his lover and sister.

"The levels of drugs and alcohol in your system were enough to kill you. Factor in exposure, and you shouldn't be here. I don't know how many lives you have, but I'd say you're down two."

"Wait. I'm sorry. I don't understand. What's even going on right now?" Eli's foggy mind tries to process the information, grasping for even the tiniest thread of reality. "This isn't real."

"I'm afraid it's very real, Eli," the doctor says, his expression grim. "Do you know what day it is?"

"The second. January second," Eli says with complete confidence.

"Try again." The doctor looks from Eli to Chris, exasperated.

"It's the tenth, Eli," Chris offers, stroking the back of Eli's hand while blinking away tears.

"What?" Eli sits up, tugging at the tubes and cords attaching him to various machines. "No, that's not right. It's the second."

"It was the second when you arrived in the ER half-frozen with more drugs in your system than our entire pharmacy. I don't know if you were attempting to end it all, but you were almost successful. You've been unconscious for over a week. These two have barely left your side." The doctor nods at Olive and Chris, who are standing side by side opposite the doctor.

Olive and Chris share pained looks, then force their smiles.

"I'm gonna go call Vic and Bunny," Olive says, patting Eli's knee.

"I'll go call Mom. She's been worried about you." Chris leans in and kisses Eli's forehead before looking to the doctor. "I'll be just outside." He gives Eli's hand one more squeeze before disappearing through the door.

Once alone, the doctor begins checking Eli's vitals with a brisk indifference. "I meant what I said. You owe that man your life." He continues with his examination. "How are you feeling?"

"Honestly?" Eli says, leaning back against the pillows while the doctor shines light in his eyes. "I'm fine. I feel great. Well rested even." He shrugs and looks past the doctor to Chris and Olive standing outside his room. The doctor follows his gaze.

"Without him, you wouldn't be here, and I don't know what miracle saved you after that. But there you are. Alive and well, fit as a fiddle."

The doctor's words bring his dream back. The pleasant melody that streamed from his dad's favorite instrument, even after he stopped playing it. He recalls the pure joy and serenity he felt there with them.

And how he hadn't wanted to leave, until he saw Chris.

Not only did Chris literally save his life, but he's also given Eli something to live for.

In that moment Eli stops listening to the doctor berate him about his drug and alcohol abuse.

Eli pays no attention as the doctor pokes and prods at him and mumbles about his miraculous recovery and the dangers of hypothermia.

All he can do is watch Chris as he paces in front of the window to Eli's room, talking on his phone. His hair is clean but messy. He's in sweats and looks like he's barely slept in days. But he's not the washed-out, hungover soul that Eli left in the Speakeasy over a week ago.

He's vibrant and beautiful and waiting for Eli.

"I'll tell you what, Doc. You can rehabilitate me later. Right now, I want to see my man."

The doctor pauses mid-sentence, his mouth set in a grim frown. He raises a brow and clucks his tongue against his teeth. "Well, despite your best efforts, you seem to be pretty healthy for a guy who was two ticks away from death." He shakes his head. "You'll have to eat some solid food before we can let you go. I'll have the nurse come in to remove your catheter." He tucks his tiny flashlight in his breast pocket and leaves as abruptly as he came.

Eli sinks into the crackly pillows as he watches as Chris and Olive talk with the doctor, and only then does he feel the weight of guilt settle in his chest.

# CHAPTER TWENTY-THREE
*Chris*

"I've been staying with Olive," Chris says as he and Eli enter the houseboat for the first time since that terrible night. Eli looks down at the bed where Chris found him so close to death. He looks back to Chris, and the pain of regret is plain on Eli's face.

"I'm so sorry I put you through that," Eli says, his tone a bit desperate. Maybe it's sobriety, maybe the near-death experience, but his voice is different. Not so erratic. Calmer, more controlled.

"I'd go through it again and again if it meant I got you back. Having you here, now..." Chris looks around the recently cleaned houseboat. He came over that morning to get it ready while they waited for Eli's discharge. It's warm and cozy with freshly washed blankets and new pillows on the bed. All signs of Eli's near death and the following rescue have been wiped clean and swept away.

Chris removed every trace of drugs or alcohol he found. Eli is clean and well, and Chris is determined to do whatever he can to keep him that way.

"I don't deserve you." Eli steps toward Chris with a shy smile and reaches for him. Chris takes Eli's hand and steps closer, pulling Eli into his embrace. Tears well up in his eyes, and a lump forms in his throat as he thinks about the loneliness he felt without Eli.

How terrible life would be without him. How close he'd come to living that life.

He sobs into Eli's neck, squeezing him tightly.

"Don't say that," Chris admonishes, breathing in the smell of Eli's skin. "If I learned anything at all from all of this, it's that I don't want to live in a world without you. In such a short time, you became my everything, and I'm okay with it." He squeezes Eli's waist. "Maybe we were on a dangerous and unhealthy path toward self-destruction. But we were on it together, and I'd do it again in a heartbeat."

All the words he said to himself over and over in the hospital come spilling out between kisses on Eli's neck and cheeks.

"I never want to know another day without your smile." Chris pulls back and holds Eli's bearded face in his hands. Eli looks back at him with glistening eyes. He blinks, and his smile doesn't reach his eyes. "What's wrong?"

Eli sighs. He places his hands over Chris's as they hold his face. "I'm scared."

"Of what?"

Eli runs his hands down Chris's arms to rest them in the crook of his elbows, then pats them both before turning away. "I'm scared I'm going to fail. That I'm going to fail you and Olive. I don't know how to be sober. But here I am, given this second chance. This bizarre blessing of almost dying from my own stupidity, and all I can think about is where I put my weed. I wanna get high and kiss you all over. I want to drink wine and snuggle under the covers until spring."

Eli turns back to Chris, his eyes wild with desperation, and lets out another heavy sigh.

"How about we skip the getting high and go straight to the kissing-me-all-over part? We'll take the best parts of everything you want to do and leave the rest." Chris offers a playful smile, stepping close enough to wrap Eli in his arms again. "We'll take one step at a time, and we'll do it together. It's not going to be easy, and it won't always be fun, but we can do it. You can do it. I know you can." Chris pulls back to place a kiss on Eli's waiting lips.

"But what about burlesque? What about your job? How the hell am I going to resist a drink at a bar? How can I make it through a show night without one? I know myself. I won't be able to resist." Eli moves away again and paces in their small space.

"Again, we take it one step at a time. There isn't another show for two months, and Bunny is pregnant, remember. She can be your sober buddy. *I* will be your sober buddy. You will *not* be alone."

"I can't ask you to make those sacrifices for me."

"What sacrifice? Until I met you, I drank wine with my girlfriends and smoked the occasional joint offered to me by a handsome stranger at the bar."

"This is exactly what I'm saying. Look what I was doing to you. How could I have been so selfish?"

"You didn't do anything to me. I did it all myself as a full-grown adult person. Stop beating yourself up. We're here now. We're clean. It's warm and cozy, and I haven't properly held you in my arms for far too long."

He takes Eli's hands in his own.

"Can I kiss you now? Can I hold you and be thankful for this moment? Can we leave the future where it is and be here in the now?" Chris runs his hands up Eli's arms to his shoulders and back to his hands.

Eli looks at him with sullen eyes. His full, soft bottom lip is slightly pouted. Chris takes the opportunity to kiss him fully. To suck gently at that soft bottom lip. He runs his tongue over it softly then lingers there, his lips slightly parted, hovering over the offered kiss.

Eli answers by taking Chris's face in both hands and kissing him back hungrily. He sucks and pulls, his tongue darting fiercely between lips. Chris's cock springs to attention, the tingling shooting right to his taint.

The moment is beautiful and excruciating as he reminds himself to take his own advice. *Don't think about what might have been or what's to come. Be here now.*

Eli's hands roam his body with unexpected zeal. He thought they'd take it slow. That they'd while away the hours with playful kisses and caresses until Eli had his strength back.

Chris was wrong.

As Eli tugs at his clothes, Chris is more than aware of his own insatiable needs.

Within moments, they're tangled on the bed, Eli's warm, fuzzy skin against Chris.

They roll under the blankets, one cock bouncing off the other, pressing their lengths together, grinding and writhing. Their hands, lips, and tongues are everywhere. They're feasting as if starved for decades, lapping and savoring every inch in a passionate blur.

Chris's insides tremble and shake with every touch, every kiss. The desire to have and be had is mounting to delirium.

Eli's body is smaller from the weight he lost, but he's just as sexy.

Through eyes at half-mast, Chris watches their tumbling bliss. Words are lost in the air; they communicate with breath and body parts. The throbbing ache in Chris's groin is answered by Eli's fingers wrapping around his cock and pumping him furiously. Then suddenly, Eli's lips are there, sucking and pulling Chris's cock into the depths of his warm, wet mouth.

Eli works the length of Chris's cock with his hands while sucking the tip as though the very essence of life and all the answers of the universe are hidden there.

Chris lets his head fall back as pleasure runs through him, first rolling and gentle, then coursing with the heated rush of climax.

Eli works every drop out of him before rising up to wrap him in his arms again, leaving kisses all along the way.

Chris is raw with sated desire. He pulls Eli close and nuzzles his chest.

"My turn."

He smiles and kisses his way down the soft fuzz of Eli's chest and stomach.

***

*Eli*

*This is my life now,* Eli thinks as he watches the morning sun grow brighter on the bookshelves built into the wall. Chris snores softly beside him. They'd been making love nonstop for what seems like hours.

Every time he wanted to smoke or drink, Chris was there, seducing him away from one addiction to another. Chris's skin, his lips, his cock—every bit of him fulfilling Eli's needs, his desires.

When he started to lick his lips and think of whiskey, Chris was there to kiss away those thoughts. When he longed for a hit or a pill, for the buzz that would follow, Chris offered his body any way he could.

They'd barely left their little hovel on the houseboat in days. Sleep, eat, fuck, repeat. It's not a bad existence. But something's got to give. He can't live off Chris forever. Eli will eventually have to get a job. *Maybe Pam will take me back. I'd be surprised if they were able to replace me already. I bet they'd love to have me back. Plus, I could tell her I'm clean now.*

Chris stirs beside him, blinking away his sleep and looking positively delicious.

*Maybe I'll call tomorrow.*

"'Morning," Chris says sleepily.

"'Morning," Eli responds, opening his arms to offer him the spot on his chest where Chris fits so perfectly. "I was just going to make coffee."

"You stay. I'll get the coffee. You've been doing everything for me since we got home from the hospital. I thought I was supposed to be taking care of you." Chris pops up from the bed and walks across the room, his bare ass swaying delectably.

"Gotta earn my keep one way or another."

"Shit, you keep fucking me like you have been, and I'll keep you as long as I can," Chris calls from the kitchen, then appears in the doorway, his bare, creamy skin and fully erect cock a delightful sight.

"How does it feel to be my new and only addiction?" Eli asks with a grin, his own cock growing in response to the sight before him.

"I'm sure there are doctors and psychologists everywhere who would frown at the idea of replacing one addiction with another, but I can't see a single thing wrong with it."

Chris crosses the room and practically leaps back into bed.

Eli folds him in his arms and begins showering him with kisses, paying extra attention to his neck and ears.

"That tickles," Chris purrs.

Responding to the sound of appreciation in Chris's voice, Eli tickles more aggressively, getting his fingers involved, finding all of Chris's most sensitive places.

Chris's purring becomes outright laughter as he tries to pull away from Eli's prodding fingers. He wiggles, writhes, and jerks away quickly with more force than intended, hitting the wall with a loud thump. Several books fall to the bed beside them.

"Oh god. I'm sorry. Are you okay?" Eli asks quickly, regretting his playful aggressions.

"I'm fine." Chris laughs and pulls at his arm. "Now stop playing games and come over here."

Eli does as he's told and brushes the books onto the floor, then makes his way to Chris's side of the bed. His cock seems harder than he can ever remember. Sobriety seems to have its perks, and his cock aches as he tastes Chris's skin, kissing his neck more gently now. He nuzzles Chris's ear and drags his lips over Chris's smooth jawline. Then he kisses Chris's lips, slow and searching. Every time their lips meet, he's overwhelmed with love and admiration for Chris, paired with an appreciation for everything he's done for Eli—for how he's changed Eli's life in a matter of months.

No one has shown him this much true and pure love since he was a child. He fights back tears as his tongue travels the lovely, sculpted hills and valleys of Chris's body.

Eli's mouth waters as he comes upon the rosy pink tip of Chris's cock. He draws it into his mouth, rolling his tongue over the slit at the top. Still stroking Chris's length with one hand, he drops lower to pull Chris's balls into his mouth. One, then the other. He drops lower still, lapping at Chris's taint, sucking at the juicy flesh.

His tongue dips lower to the cleft where Chris's ass meets his taint. Chris cries out with pleasure as Eli slips his tongue further between his cheeks. He laps at the tight little hole, his own arousal building with every wiggle from Chris's hips and every sigh from his lips.

Eli lies on his stomach, grinding his own cock into the bed as he holds Chris's legs apart to expose his taut scrotum and ass. He works Chris over, erotic anticipation coursing through him every time he thinks of sliding his rock-hard cock into Chris's ass.

"Fuck me, Eli. Do it now," Chris pleads.

Quickly, Eli snatches the lube from the table beside the bed and works it over his cock. He smooths lube onto Chris's hole with loving attention, then settles his cock's head on the resistant opening.

Slowly, he eases himself into the tightness, inch by blissful inch, until they become one.

The blush rises to Chris's cheeks, practically the same color as his stiff and glistening cock. Eli strokes him slowly, matching the pace of his own gentle thrusts until Chris begins to grind his hips.

Chris pumps his ass up and down on Eli's cock while his shaft moves quickly in Eli's grip. As he builds to jackhammering speeds, Eli can't contain himself.

Chris cries out and spurts his warm cum onto Eli's hand and over his own stomach.

As Eli watches Chris's face contort with pleasure, he erupts himself. Carnal bliss courses through him, a high like no other.

He collapses onto Chris and kisses his face and chest.

Chris's words fall out like breath, unintelligible but full of love and contentment.

The smell of coffee fills the small cabin.

*So, this **is** my life now.*

It's the happiest thought he can ever remember having.

# CHAPTER TWENTY-FOUR
*Chris*

"Are you sure you're all right with me leaving?" Chris asks from the doorway. He's bundled up for the cold in his sleek black coat and Eli's stocking cap. "It's open mic night, so it won't be too busy. Nothing that Olive can't handle." He pulls his gloves on as he speaks.

Eli smiles from his seat at the table. Chris is anxious about leaving him alone for the first time since his release from the hospital, but he's been going mad with boredom.

"Go. I'll be fine," Eli says as he stands to clear the dishes from the dinner he prepared for them. "Nothing special," he'd said, "a simple pasta with red sauce." Though simple, Chris had practically licked his plate clean. "I'm going to clean this up and start my job search. Shouldn't be too hard. Kitchens are always hiring."

"Take your time and find the right place. You don't want to go back to work for Pam. She seems awful."

"She wasn't so bad, really. Merely racist, sexist, classist, and intolerant of anyone who doesn't share her very tiny world view."

Chris cocks his head and scoffs, "Well, when you put it that way, I can't imagine why you would ever want to leave." Eli chuckles. The sound of his easy laughter pulls at Chris's heart. He imagines a world without Eli's laugh, without his smile, and a lump forms in his throat.

Chris crosses the small kitchen to kiss Eli lightly. He holds Eli's face in his gloved hands. "Call me if you need anything. I'll be home in a heartbeat." He slides his hand from Eli's face and lets it rest on Eli's chest. Tears wet Chris's eyes as he remembers pumping Eli's barely beating heart back to life.

"What?" Eli rests his hand over Chris's and gives it a gentle squeeze.

"It's..." Chris smiles wistfully. "I'm so happy you're still here. Sometimes, I think about how close I came to losing you, and I can't stop the tears from falling. It's usually when you're sleeping, though, so you don't see it. I love you so much, Eli. I never want to lose you."

A sob escapes his chest as Eli pulls him close, squeezing him tightly.

They stand, wrapped in one another's arms, Chris willing all his love and devotion into their embrace. The moment transcends words as their hearts communicate all that can't be said.

Eli breaks the silence. "I'm not going anywhere," he says, his voice barely above a whisper.

"Promise?" Chris asks, reluctantly slipping from Eli's arms to look into his two-toned eyes. They crinkle at the corners as Eli offers an indulgent smile.

"There's nowhere I'd rather be. Now, go to work so I can do mine."

***

*Eli*

Chris comes back for three more kisses before he finally leaves. Eli knows his man is nervous about leaving. He can't blame him for it. He can only imagine what he would've felt if he found Chris's body limp and nearly dead on the bed they had shared for so many nights.

Eli wonders if he would've known what to do. Would he have been sober enough, or would he have lain down and passed out beside him, welcoming his own death?

"Get out of your head," he says to the empty room.

*No sense in wondering about things that never were. That never will be.*

He focuses on the water running in a trickle from the faucet and washes each dish with more care than necessary. He runs his finger along the flowers painted on the edge of each plate. Plates his mother had lovingly washed and placed in the cabinets after many family meals shared around the small table or on the deck of the boat. He always loved their trips down the river, never wondering about the contingency plan his father joked about. Never wondering what a contingency plan even was.

As the last dish is placed in the cabinet, he wonders what his parents would think of Chris. Eli's sure they would love Chris as much as he does. *How could anyone not?* He pictures them older, grayer, fatter, and happy. They sit around a weathered picnic table in their yard, just as they left it, with flowers and weeds growing together in wild harmony. He and Olive are there, along with Chris and Vic. *What would they think of Vic? Mom would like him for sure.* Eli laughs at the thought of his dad doing his best to hide how he really felt about Vic from Olive and their mom. He'd come around though.

Darkness creeps in where the sunny warmth had been growing. The images of a big, happy family passing dishes around a picnic table, smiling and laughing like a Hallmark movie, disappear and are replaced by the reality of a broken, empty house, overgrown in a way his parents would've never allowed. The picnic table missing its bench on one side. Nothing but ghosts there. He and Olive were on their own and would've like to make their own happy Hallmark ending. Eli slumps on the bed, noticing the books that fell the night before.

A small pile of old pulp fiction, the covers faded, the pages curled. Mostly detective novels with drawings of scantily clad women hiding guns behind their backs or peeking from behind shades that'd been pulled aside. The sharp angles of their lips and tits are laughable.

Among the pile is a copy of *The Poseidon Adventure*, the one he remembers handing to his father so many years ago. He picks it up with a vague sort of reverence and runs his finger over the title before thumbing through the yellowed pages dyed red on the edges. The unmistakable smell of old books wafts to his nostrils, bringing back another slew of memories of his dad reading, either quietly to himself on a winter afternoon or settled next to Eli's bed with something from Jules Verne or H. Rider Haggard.

Eli remembers fondly how he would hang on every word that fell from his father's lips, and how animated he was in his delivery. As his heart begins to break yet again, a slip of paper falls from the book. It's been torn from a tiny spiral notebook and adorned with his dad's tidy, slanted script.

*When down is up, and up is down, that's the time to look around. We're still floating, we're not dead, and we've got a lifeboat under our heads.*

*When did it begin to roll like a pig?*

"What the fuck?" Eli flips the paper over. There's nothing on the back. "What the fuck?" A curious excitement bubbles as he turns the book and shakes it out, hoping for more. Anything that might make sense of the strange little note on a faded scrap of paper. He remembers his father leaving trails of clues to lead them to different surprises. He sent them on many adventures, searching for clues leading to different treasures.

Eli considers calling Olive and remembers she's at work with Chris, and Eli doesn't want to trouble her or worry Chris. Besides, he can figure it out on his own. He grabs a can of La Croix and settles onto the rumpled bed, *The Poseidon Adventure* in hand, and begins reading.

The answer to his father's question is right there in the first paragraph of the first chapter. Seven o'clock in the morning on the 26th day of December. *But what does it mean?* Eli asks himself as he reads on. The story introduces each character, flawed in the most realistic ways, as they navigate their hangovers on the reeling boat.

Eli recalls Chris on New Year's Day, the way he retched and shook. He imagines what it would've been like if their little houseboat had been truly rocking. He searches the pages for any clues they might hold, looking for something reminiscent of his father's written words.

The story carries on with more introductions, people eating, drinking, and attempting to stay upright as the waves swell and the boat rocks. He laughs at the fact that he's reading a book about a boat on a boat, but he grows weary of the story. There's nothing there. Nothing that makes itself known.

*Maybe I should call Olive*, he thinks as he skims the paragraphs.

He knows the story. He watched the film adaptation some years ago in the foster home where they gave him more freedom than guidance. The one where he spent too many late nights watching whatever he wanted on TV.

This is a story about the tipping and eventual sinking of a luxury cruise ship and its passengers' harrowing journey from the ceiling of the ballroom to the hull at the bottom and their eventual escape. *But were there lifeboats? Did they make them from something?* He can't remember all the details. It's been years since he saw the movie, and he only watched it the one time.

*Lifeboats under our heads...* He continues to skim the pages, more interested in his father's cryptic note than the story itself. What did he care about a bunch of spoiled, rich white folks saving their imaginary lives? The words run together; the pages become a blur. He's never enjoyed reading.

He examines his dad's note again, looking for anything new. For something that might jump out at him that didn't before. *Under our heads?* He uses the note as a bookmark and sets the book aside, then stands, surveying the room. "Lifeboat under our heads." He's struck with an idea and begins stripping the blankets and pillows from the bed. He pulls up the mattress and examines the wooden base.

There's nothing there. He thumps his knuckles along the board, listening for a sound that might give something away. It's hollow.

"Under our heads…" He goes to the kitchen and digs a hammer out from under the sink. He returns to the bed and swings the hammer without a second thought, bringing it down and splintering the wood at the head of the bed frame. A cloud of dust swirls around him. Bits of wood bounce off his glasses, and he sputters and spits out the bits he nearly swallows.

Using his phone as a flashlight, he shines it into the newly made hole, his heart racing over what he might find. He peers in and finds nothing but years-old sawdust and decades of cobwebs. The smell is somehow fresh and stale all at once. His heart sinks for a moment, then he stands and opens the book again to thumb through the pages, barely skimming the words, searching to no avail for any sort of clue and coming back to the note. *When down is up, and up is down…*

"If up is down, then under is over," he mutters to himself, holding the book and hammer in one hand, the scrap of paper in the other. He scans the bookshelves that line the ceiling around the small cabin space and begins knocking books from them with the claw side of the hammer. They tumble around him, clunking to the ground, filling the air with dust and the smell of home. He climbs on the bed frame and peers up and down the newly emptied shelves. Nothing. Tapping lightly along the now exposed wall, he listens for variation in the thumps. Nothing.

"Maybe the kitchen."

He's opening cabinets and drawers like a maniac. *I've officially lost it*, he thinks as he pulls dinnerware and groceries with a bit more grace than he had the books. He slides a chair up and shines his flashlight along the newly emptied top shelves of the cabinet. More cobwebs and dust bunnies. On the second shelf, tucked back in the furthest corner, lies the battleship from an old boardgame. Eli's heart races. He taps the hammer along the back wall. One hollow thud follows another until he hears a heavy thunk on the shorter side wall.

Jamming the claw under the wooden frame, he pries it away. More splintered wood and dust fills the air.

Hitting the wall, he sends more wood raining down until he's met with the distinctive clang of metal on metal. He drops the hammer and begins pulling broken pieces of wood paneling away from the wall with his fingers, exposing the cold gray metal of a safe.

It's much larger than the space covered by the cabinet wall.

With the hammer, he breaks and pries away more wood, revealing a two-by-three-foot door with an old-school combination dial. Eli stares at the lock in silence, his pulse racing with the exertion of tearing down a literal wall.

He catches the breath he hadn't realized escaped him.

*Now to find the combination.*

He tries his parents' anniversary, his and Olive's birthdays, and any other significant date he can think of.

Nothing works.

He dials all even numbers, all odds, and random combinations that really could never possibly work.

Leaning in close and holding his ear to the metal door, he listens for clicks that so many movies have told him would alert him of tumblers sliding into place.

Nothing.

As the initial excitement of the discovery begins to ebb, he wonders if he should call Olive before he goes any further. Then, as if summoned by the very thought of her, he hears Olive's voice directly behind him. "Eli, what the fuck?"

He turns to find Olive and Chris standing in the small kitchen, surrounded by his debris, looking shocked and a bit frightened.

***

*Chris*

"I knew I should've stayed home tonight." Chris frets as he and Olive walk shoulder to shoulder toward the dock. Every window on the boat is shining brightly as if lit for a party, and the boat is rocking and bobbing in the otherwise still water. "God, what if he went out and got something to drink, or worse?"

"Was he going to walk? Besides, he doesn't have any money," Olive offers, though her voice holds little conviction.

"Well, what the fuck is going on in there?" Chris asks, gesturing to the boat. "And why wasn't he answering either of our calls?" The rocking of the boat stops, and Chris imagines the worst. He and Olive share a worried glance, then run the rest of the way.

Olive is the first through the door. Chris hurries behind her. "What are you doing?" he asks as Eli turns from the broken wall, a wild look in his eyes.

"I found something," Eli says with a grin.

Chris looks from Eli to Olive with concern. *Has he lost it?* he asks with his expression.

Olive shakes her head in response, wide-eyed and worried.

"Look," Eli all but shouts and gestures to the hole in the wall, revealing a relatively large safe. "Wait." He holds up a finger and hurries into the living room, which looks like it's where he began his search. He comes back, brandishing a book: *The Poseidon Adventure.* "I found this."

Olive takes the book and flips through the pages with a wistful grin. Chris looks on with confusion. She holds up a small piece of paper.

"This is Dad's," she says, drawing her brows together. "I don't understand. How did this"—she holds up the note—"lead to this?" She gestures to the destruction and safe in the wall.

"I don't really know," Eli answers. "Call it a hunch. You know how he used to leave little clues for us to find our birthday presents and stuff? When the note fell out of the book, I tried to find another clue in the pages but couldn't. You know I'm not a reader."

"So, you tore the whole place apart?"

"Well, yeah. Sort of. I guess." Eli looks down at the floor and back to Chris and then to Olive. "I know it sounds crazy. But I dreamed about that specific book when I was in the hospital. I was a little kid handing it to Dad from a moving box. If I hadn't, I never would've given it a second glance. Then the note fell out, and I knew it had to be something. But the question isn't even why or how I found the safe. It's what's in it and how do we get in?"

"Did you try their anniversary?" Olive asks.

"Yes, and all of our birthdays."

"Nothing?" Olive asks.

"Obviously, nothing," Eli responds with an exasperated laugh.

"What about the note?" Chris asks, reaching for the slip of paper in Olive's hand.

"When did it begin to roll like a pig?" Chris wrinkles his nose and looks from brother to sister, shocked for a moment by their resemblance. Though he's noticed it before, in this moment, as they stare at him like eager children, they look more alike than he previously thought. "What does that even mean?"

"It's in the first paragraph of the... Wait," Eli shouts and snatches the book from Olive. He turns to the wall and quickly spins the dial on the safe. "Seven... Twelve... Twenty-six." With a barely audible click, the door swings open. Stacks and stacks of crisp, clean hundred-dollar bills sit inside, neatly stacked, filling the safe. The color drains from Eli and Olive's faces. They stare wordlessly at the money.

"They did have a plan. They had a plan all along." Olive steps back and leans against the door. "The *S.S. Contingency*." Olive laughs.

"Looks like I don't have to go back to work after all," Eli says with a grin, stepping in close to pull Chris and Olive into a hug. "I don't think any of us do." He laughs.

# EPILOGUE

"But we don't talk about the money laundering," Chris jokes as he passes a bowl of fresh cut fruit and berries to Mike.

"No. We don't talk about that," Mike says with steely indifference. He takes a spoonful of the offered fruit. His gaze is set a few yards away on his daughter, Mona, as she toddles through the soft, lush grass. Though his mouth is set in grim determination to avoid the subject, his eyes sparkle with joy only his daughter could bring. Bunny watches him watching their girl and smiles.

"You can't marry a wild animal like me and not expect to break a few laws," she purrs and leans in to kiss his cheek. "Besides, what's a little laundering among friends? And look at the payout." She places the fruit bowl in the center of the table and spreads her arms wide, looking up to the bright blue sky.

"You're right," he agrees, offering Bunny an indulgent half smile. "But I'm not sure what you're talking about." He laughs and stands to retrieve Mona, who's toddled too far for his liking.

"I don't understand why we didn't think of something like this sooner." Bridgette looks up from the jar of olives she's been nibbling at and over to her lover, Henri. "I mean you," she dips her head toward Henri, "could've taken care of the finances, no problem. What's two and a half million from one of your accounts? I imagine buying a farm is a hell of a lot easier than buying a theater or two." She laughs, Bunny giggles, and even Mike joins in. Both Bunny and Mike have had firsthand experience with what happens when Henri is too generous for Bridgette's liking.

Henri looks down at the empty plate in front of him. A smile plays at the corner of his lips. "Well, *ma chère*, if I'd known there was a rescue needed, I'd have surely come to it." He lays his smooth New Orleans' charm on thicker than necessary. Bridgette rolls her eyes, but the color in her cheeks gives her away.

"I for one am overjoyed by all of it. The lawbreaking and the outcome," Vic says loudly and plucks a large ripe strawberry from the bowl before popping it in his mouth. "Tomorrow, this place will be teaming with people, all here for one hell of a time." He looks to the once old and weather-beaten porch and grins widely.

Olive pushes through the freshly painted screen door. She holds it open, wearing her light-colored sundress, the floral pattern a perfect complement to the large pots and flower boxes overflowing with bright blossoms in various shades of pink, purple, and white. With two baguettes wrapped in a kitchen towel under one arm, she holds the door with her other. Susan comes through with an enormous glass bowl of salad. Eli follows close behind with an even bigger platter of the most delicious-smelling pasta.

Their joyful words are lost in the warm summer evening air as they approach the table and lay down their offerings, then take their seats. Bottles of red and white wine, dark green frosty mineral waters, and a huge pitcher of fresh-squeezed lemonade welcome them.

Eli pours himself a glass of sparkling water and watches as hungry, appreciative guests fill their plates. His eyes grow misty, and he presses his lips tightly together to hold in the emotions welling up.

Chris lays a hand on Eli's shoulder and squeezes gently. When Eli's gaze finally meets Chris's, he blinks back tears and smiles serenely.

"I never thought I would have this again. Three years ago, I would've given anything for a moment like this. I still don't fully believe it's happening."

"Oh, baby, it's happening, and *you* made it happen." Chris smiles. "It was your idea to buy this place and bring it back to its former glory. And after that, it was your idea to turn it into an artist retreat, featuring A La Mode's Burlesque Summer Camp." He raises his voice with the last bit and fans his fingers in the air.

The people at the table cheer, hoot, and whistle in response to Chris's shameless plug. "I don't know how you came up with it. But it's brilliant."

"You had to make a lot of tough decisions to be here with me. It seemed like the best way to bring it all together."

"It was never a tough decision. I knew exactly what I wanted, and it was this. It was this moment, and a million more just like it."

# ABOUT THE AUTHOR

Kitty Bardot juggles a life full of excitement and love. By day, she's a chef with her own catering company, by night she puts ten years of burlesque experience to use in various venues in the Quad Cities. She writes from her country home not far from the Mississippi River, enjoying every moment with her husband and their three children.

## Connect with Kitty:

website: kittybardot.net

instagram: @ktbardot
tiktok:@kitty_bardot
twitter: @KittyBardot
fb: /Kitty-Bardot-312641412082507

## www.BOROUGHSPUBLISHINGGROUP.com

If you enjoyed this book, please write a review. Our authors appreciate the feedback, and it helps future readers find books they love. We welcome your comments and invite you to send them to info@boroughspublishinggroup.com.

Follow us on Instagram and TikTok, and be sure to sign up for our newsletter for surprises and new releases from your favorite authors.

Are you an aspiring writer? Check out:
www.boroughspublishinggroup.com/submit and see if we can help you make your dreams come true.

Love podcasts? Enjoy ours at
https://boroughspublishinggroup.com/podcast